Cover design by Dragonfly Press Design
www.dragonflypressdesign.com
Book design by Sandy James
Published by James Gang Publishing

This book is a work of fiction. Names, characters, places, and incidents either are products of the author's imagination or are used fictitiously. Any resemblance to actual persons—living or dead—events, or locales is entirely coincidental.

Sandy James
sandyjames.com

Printed in the United States of America
Second Printing: June 2013
ISBN: 978-1-940295-07-7

DEDICATION

To Jeff—I promised you no mushy dedication, so let me just say one
thing.
After all these years, I'm still happy to be stuck with you.

Prologue

A birthday lament...

What exactly is middle age?

It seems to me that my mother has been middle-aged just about forever. She covers her gray hair with gobs of Miss Clairol, rubs gallons of moisturizer onto her face and hands, and has been retired for a few years. Oh yeah, and she's been through menopause. Of course, my father and I used to joke that she'd been going through menopause for at least the last thirty years. Funny, but Mom never thought we were very amusing.

Now I realize middle age has come and gone in my mother's life. She saw its hand waving goodbye in her rearview mirror years ago. Unfortunately, that can only mean one thing.

It's my turn.

I get to be the woman who is constantly checking the part in her hair to see if a gray hair or two or twenty have sneaked into the mixture. I get to be the one who wonders if the little lines that are forming around the eyes should be called "laugh lines" or "wrinkles." I get to be the lady who wonders if she is too old to wear the t-shirts with the cute, naughty sayings on them or if that skimpy little skirt shows too many spider veins or cellulite.

You know, birthdays used to be so much fun. Remember when you'd look forward to presents and cards that had checks and ten-dollar bills tucked in them? Well, those days are all over once you hit twenty. Then on your twenty-first birthday, you get to drink legally, and another mile marker passes by on the highway of life.

The rest of your life you use birthdays to gauge exactly how close you're getting to the magical and tragic age of forty. When a person passes that milestone, birthdays just cause a fight or flight response. You watch the pages of the calendar drop from the wall like some old corny movie showing a rapid advance in time. Your days, weeks, and years are skiing down a slippery slope as you struggle to keep pace.

I turned thirty-twelve today. I'll just give you a second to catch on. It always takes my high school students a beat or two to do the math. Some even whip out a calculator.

So the question I have to ask myself is... *Am I middle-aged?*

And, since I obviously know the answer to that one, I ask myself, what exactly is middle age? Now that one is a toughie!

Is it a chronological phenomenon?

I doubt it. I mean if that's the case, I *am* middle-aged. Women born the same year as I was should live to be almost eighty. Divide eighty by two. That would seriously suck. I choose to push that definition of middle age aside and deal with it like any normal human female. I'll simply wallow in denial.

Is middle age a psychological occurrence?

This is much more likely. If it's a state of mind, I can fight it. Don't they always say you're only as old as you feel? If it holds true and I try to act young, then I can miraculously be young. Maybe I'll get some body art, a tattoo. Or how about a new piercing? That'll make me young again. Not! I just wish my boobs believed that tripe about feeling young making you young. Those twin sisters are most definitely middle-aged and falling faster than the thermometer in a Minnesota winter.

Is middle age a sociological event?

Ding, ding, ding! We have a winner!

Of course it's entirely sociological. People become middle-aged because other people tell them that they're officially middle-aged. It's a product of watching the girls in advertisements become thinner and thinner and younger and younger. It's from watching men trying to feel younger than they are by having an arm around some twenty-something waif with perky boobs and no stretch marks. It's because women over forty are, in many ways, disposable.

Look at it this way—men turn forty and go on the prowl for a red sports car or a trophy wife. Women turn forty and start hunting for the cheapest Botox clinic and over-the-counter hormone products. That hardly seems fair.

Who exactly made these ridiculous rules? I know that I was not invited to that particular convention. In fact, I would venture a huge leap out on a brittle limb that not too many females were involved in the assigning of "middle age" as the last stop on a woman's journey through having a fascinating and important life. Everything after that is stereotypically supposed to be wretched. First divorce, then menopause, then death. Seriously depressing.

I have decided that middle-aged women shouldn't be deemed unwanted. We still matter. Even if we're over forty, we still matter. I still matter, and I intend to prove it.

So, on my thirty-twelfth birthday, I, Jacqueline Marie Delgado, swear on my cake bearing a tombstone reading "Over the Hill" that my sons bought to help "celebrate" the occasion, that I will not be a clichéd middle-aged woman. I promise to continue celebrating being me regardless of what chronology is telling me to do. I vow to make this a year of self-discovery and productivity.

And I promise to never again drink as much white zinfandel as I did tonight.

Welcome to my year.

CHAPTER ONE

"Put it in the closet," Nate ordered as Patrick carried another box into the dorm room.

"What closet?" Patrick asked, dropping the box on the ground in the middle of the ten-by-ten cinderblock cell. "You mean that tiny hole in the far wall? My hamster had a bigger cage. Why won't you even think about the frat?"

"Because I'm not fraternity material. I have functioning brain tissue," Nate responded. "Where's Mom?"

I'd been standing just outside the door, listening to them, and feeling a bit melancholy. With a sigh, I dragged the too heavy box full of stuff Nate probably didn't really need into the tiny room my youngest son would call "home" for the next nine months.

"I'm here, I'm here. Geesh. What are you two fighting about now?"

"Do you want me to help with that?" Patrick asked.

"Typical guy," I commented. "You ask to help after the job's done."

Patrick just laughed at me. The brat.

Nate zipped around the room going from box to box like a bee trying to pick the most succulent flower. "I need to get the bed on stilts or I'll never have enough room."

"It's a dormitory," Patrick countered. "You shouldn't expect to have any room."

"Well, at least I don't have to share it with some drunken preppy who probably slips girls roofies," Nate replied.

I couldn't help but laugh at them. They were twenty-one and eighteen and still fighting as though they were both in grade school. My sons hadn't changed a bit. Still as blond as any California surfer, their faces bore that I'm-not-all-grown-up look, dimples and all. But they really weren't children any longer. They had changed in so many ways.

That thought instantly brought tears to my eyes. My babies were all grown up. I was going to have to leave Nate behind and drive back to my big empty house all by myself.

Patrick had always been the independent and stubborn one. It didn't frighten me to let him go. School was almost too easy for him, so I knew his grades would be good. He was active in pretty much any organization he could join, and I knew he'd network and meet new people. And I was right—Patrick thrived at college.

But my Nate? My baby?

Who would be there to take care of him?

"Uh oh," Patrick said as he took the two steps necessary to cross the entire room and stare down at me from his six-three world. "Waterworks."

"Ah, Mom." Nate groaned. "Please don't cry."

I sniffled. "Who says I'm crying?"

Yeah, like that tack was going to work. It wasn't a highly effective message when a tear slid down my cheek. I wiped it away with the back of my sleeve.

Patrick put his arm around my shoulder. "Mom's got empty nest syndrome. We learned all about it in psychology class. Women hate it when the last chick flies the coop." He tucked his thumbs in his armpits, flapped his wings, and clucked like a chicken.

My son was a smart-ass.

"I don't have empty nest syndrome," I insisted, while secretly wanting to have a long talk with Patrick's psychology professor. The man really needed to learn to mind his own damn business.

Nate rolled his eyes. "Mom, I can take care of myself."

"I don't have empty nest. The room's just... dusty." I had no idea how I was going to leave my little boy behind. I supposed the fact that my "little boy" stood six-two and out-muscled half of maledom should have impacted my opinion of his ability to be independent. But the mother in me only remembered the little boy who would cry when his older brother wouldn't play with him.

How could such a fragile little creature possibly survive the cold, cruel world? Maybe he should stay home with me for another year or two. He didn't need to be in college. I could home school.

My "fragile little creature" came over and gave me a hug that almost knocked me off my feet. "I'll be fine, Mom."

I sniffled a little more and started to unpack the closest box. It didn't take us long to get Nate set up in his dorm room. Of course, my ex-husband didn't show up until after almost everything was unpacked. It just showed that the apples didn't fall too awfully far from the paternal tree.

"Jackie," David said as he walked in the room and deigned to acknowledge my presence in the universe with a curt nod. "You good?"

I gave him the visual once over, noting how impeccably he was dressed. Not a salt and pepper hair was out of place, and he had that scruffy I'm-too-cool-to-shave look that reminded me of several bad eighties television shows. "I'm fine. And you?"

"Fine."

Eighteen years of marriage, and the only word we ever seemed to exchange regularly was "fine." I figured that was at least a better choice of vocabulary than when we were still together. The only word that popped up then was another word that began with "f." We'd used it as a noun, a verb, an adjective, and an adverb. You name any part of speech; we would have found a way to throw the f-word into the mix.

At least now we could have a civil conversation—as long as we didn't talk about anything other than the boys. I really believed I was lucky. At least my former husband paid the kids' bills and didn't drag the trophy bimbo with him everywhere he went. I only had to see Ashley occasionally, which was a really good thing. I would've hated to scratch her pretty little blue eyes out in front of too many witnesses.

"You all settled in, Nate?" his father asked.

"Yeah, but thanks for coming Dad. Hey, do you want to go get some lunch with us?" my entirely too generous and totally naïve youngest son asked.

"I can't stay that long," my ex replied much to my relief. "Ashley and I are taking Duncan to see his grandparents."

Good God, was it hard not to make a snide remark about David's age making him a more likely candidate to be his new son's grandfather instead of his father. But I was the well-behaved ex-wife who bit her tongue and made nice for her boys.

"That's a shame," I said.

David shot me one of his patented, incredulous glares, and I gave him one of my fake, patronizing smiles. I hoped he realized that I was tremendously grateful that Duncan and Ashley were probably waiting in his Hummer, so he couldn't join us for a happy family lunch.

My heart clenched when I glanced over and saw how disappointed Nate looked.

Damn it all anyway.

I had to constantly remind myself that David might have been a pathetic excuse for a husband, but he would always be the father of my boys.

I quickly sucked up my own misgivings. "David, why don't you and Ashley bring Duncan along for lunch? I'm sure it would mean a lot to Nate."

He cocked his head and stared at me as if I had just spoken to him in Mandarin Chinese. "What's gotten into you?"

I shrugged. "Nothing. I just thought it'd be nice for you to spend some time with the boys."

"Really?"

Didn't this man have a single solitary clue how hard I was grinding my teeth together, so I wouldn't make one of my typical smart-ass comments? "Really."

"That's nice, Jackie, but Ash's parents are expecting us."

I added yet another demerit to David's perpetual misconduct column since he'd hurt Nate.

Turning back to my son, I said, "Then it's your choice, Nathaniel. Sky's the limit."

He gave me a weak smile that made me want to smack his father, and then Nate went back to unpacking the last of his boxes.

David crossed the room to slap him on the back and say some macho fatherly things that I was sure they didn't want me to overhear. When the word "condom" floated in the air, I excused myself to go see if there were any more boxes to carry up from my mini-van. The notion of my baby needing condoms didn't sit well on my already emotionally overwrought brain.

There are simply some things mothers are better off not knowing about their sons.

I wasn't surprised in the least that David's big black phallic-mobile was idling in a handicapped parking spot. Ashley sat in the passenger seat admiring herself in the visor's mirror. Not a long, blond hair was out of place, but she adjusted it anyway. Her face was perfection. The woman really could have been a model. Of course, her figure had instantly returned to its pre-pregnancy state the minute Duncan was born. I was still trying to lose those last few "baby pounds" from giving birth to Nate eighteen years ago. And my hair had always been mousy brown and way too short and baby fine to do anything except just... lie there.

She flipped the visor closed and caught me staring at her.

I actually gave her one of those goofy half-waves. God, I could be so damned lame sometimes.

I often wondered exactly what flew through Ashley's mind whenever she saw me. Did she feel any kind of guilt for the nights she stayed late to help David "organize his files" when what she had actually been doing was unzipping his fly? Or did her mind justify her actions in some way? Did she wish I would fade away so she didn't have to acknowledge that she was wife number two and that wife number three was parked in some junior high school just waiting to finish growing up enough to have her turn at bat?

I'd desperately tried not to hate her. I really had. It was poison for me to carry that kind of loathing around. I was entirely aware of this because the marriage counselor had told me so. He even told me that I should've thanked

Ashley for showing me that David and I weren't really all that compatible. By luring my husband away, she'd only revealed the fundamentally unstable foundation upon which my marriage had been based. And he charged us a hundred and fifty freaking dollars an hour for this super-duper advice. So I had really tried not to hate her.

But, damn it all, I wanted to hate her anyway.

I didn't see David waltzing up behind me until he started to talk to me. I jumped a good foot, which was pretty phenomenal considering the weight I carry in my caboose.

"Jackie? You okay?"

I nodded.

"I'm sorry we couldn't take you up on the lunch invite. We'll have to do it some other time."

I just nodded again.

"Well, I need to get going."

The asshole actually hugged me. I awkwardly patted his back and then turned him loose. It crossed my mind that it was one of the first times I had stopped hugging before he did. Back in the day, I always squeezed a little bit harder and clung a little bit longer.

Ashley glared down at us from her perch in the huge SUV. I saw the flash of insecurity, and I was petty enough to let myself enjoy it.

***

The house was like a tomb.

I went over to let my cockatiel out of his cage, and he didn't even whistle at me. The boys had taught the little gray bird to wolf-whistle, and Jellybean seemed to condition himself to make that particular sound whenever I walked in the door. It was the closest thing to a compliment on my looks I'd received from any species of male in years.

But he didn't whistle at me tonight.

I wondered if Jellybean felt the same type of gloom that had settled over me the minute I drove away from the dorm. I decided that I'd have to leave the TV on for him to listen to when I went to school the next day. I'd hate to have a depressed bird on my hands. My own case of the empty nest blues was hard enough to handle.

How odd—an empty nest that still held a bird.

Logic told me that Patrick and Nate were only an hour away, just forty, teeny miles. Yet the house was still like a tomb.

I dropped my purse and keys on the table and let my eyes wander for a minute. The bottom floor of my Cape Cod was mostly one big open area. The kitchen and the great room were joined, and during the time my boys were growing up, the joint was jumping. Between raising Patrick and Nate and the litany of friends that drifted in and out of my home, there had been very few quiet moments.

As my gaze flitted about the room, I noticed that the place was spotless. The afghan was folded neatly and draped over the chair. The only pairs of shoes piled by the door belonged to me. The size thirteen and fourteen Nikes had all been packed away as they followed their owners to Indiana University. No *Sports Illustrated* swimsuit issues were strewn on the floor. The discarded food wrappers that couldn't seem to find their way to the trash—unless a female took the initiative to move them—were absent. There was no blaring stereo, television, or iPod, just a home that was too neat and too silent.

Tears welled up in my eyes again.

I remembered some days wishing for a just few moments of peace and quiet so I could gather my own thoughts and catch my breath. All I really wanted was a short respite from the bustling world of raising two boisterous boys—three if you counted David.

A hard lesson, but I was learning to be careful what I wished for.

CHAPTER TWO

The first day of the new school year has always been a teacher work-day for our school district. Of course, it's not as if the teachers actually get any real work done during those eight hours. Most of us start popping in the building during the last few weeks of summer vacation to get lesson plans ready, to make copies before the copier breaks down and stays broken for an entire semester, or just to hang some new posters on our bulletin boards. As a result, most staff members spend the teacher "work-day" attending faculty meetings and catching up on all the juicy gossip we missed over the break.

As I pulled into my usual parking space, a wave of *déjà vu* washed over me. It didn't seem like I'd even been away from Harrison High School for more than a day or two. The familiarity was akin to that feeling when dragging the artificial Christmas tree up from the basement the day after Thanksgiving and setting it up. Doesn't it always seem as though the silly thing got put away a couple of days ago? That's what it's like for teachers on the first day back from summer break.

With an exaggerated, resigned sigh, I forced myself out of the car and into the school. My sons were gone, but I took comfort in the notion that at least I could mother my new students.

My friends were waiting in the cafeteria as the arriving teachers congregated around the donuts provided by the administrators. I grabbed a couple of warm Krispy Kremes and vowed to walk a few extra miles after school to make up for them. After fetching a cup of coffee, I took a seat at one of the long tables our students used for lunch.

"I can't believe it's August already," I complained.

The two women I considered to be my best friends dropped down on the benches attached to the table.

"I'll be fine until I see my class lists," Julie chimed in. "If I've got Trevor Taylor in world history for the third time, I'll scream."

Abby laughed. "There ought to be a rule about having a kid more than twice. Can't we put some of the kids on waivers or something? Trade 'em like athletes?"

"That would be nice," I added, "but what happens to the ones no one wants? It's not like we can just release them from their contracts."

"Bummer," Julie replied.

When Keith Sloan came into the cafeteria, we all smiled. Sauntering over like a conquering gladiator, he had one hand on his hip, the other cradling a donut. With his chest spread wide, highlighting that nice middle age spare tire he carried around, he marched up to our table. "If it isn't the prettiest women in the entire school corporation."

The man was a shameless flirt and very politically incorrect, but we loved him anyway. He always made everyone laugh by passing along the dirtiest jokes and funniest comics. The fact that he'd been married to the same woman for thirty-five years only made him more appealing.

"What do you see when the Pillsbury doughboy bends over?" he asked with his usual twinkle in his eye.

We all waited for the punch line.

"Doughnuts." He took a big bite out of his cruller, chuckled, and walked away.

Our laughter followed in his wake.

"Well..." I wadded my napkin. "Time for our meeting."

My friends groaned. It was hard to work up any momentum to move, knowing we were in for a good two hours of sheer boredom when we'd learn all about the ridiculous new paperwork we'd need to fill out this year.

Things would go much smoother if the powers-that-be would simply put all of the useless information from our meeting into an email. The faculty would probably be more cooperative if they had set up several pitchers of margaritas instead of coffee.

***

As usual, our table at lunch was loud.

About a dozen of the veterans pushed several tables together at T.G.I.Friday's and sat around to talk about our summer accomplishments while we toasted the end of our vacation with iced tea.

Unfortunately, the teas were not the "Long Island" variety.

Julie and Abby started in on me immediately. After allowing me a year to "get over" my divorce, they believed it should be their mission in life to get me back into a relationship.

The last two years of tolerating their meddling had been both endearing and exhausting. The fact that I had absolutely no desire to be tied down to another man was entirely beside the point. I just could *not* seem to convince either of them that I was happy on my own.

Who needed a man when Sharper Image makes several perfectly good vibrators?

Not that I would have known anything about that.

Julie was still happily married after thirty-some years, which drove her to actively seek a mate for me as loyal and wonderful as her Larry. That fact allowed me to forgive her interference in my lack of a love life.

Of course, if I still looked as great as Julie did, David might not have noticed Ashley's many...assets. Julie didn't have a gray hair anywhere in her warm brown hair. She still wore a bikini on the cruise Larry insisted they take every year. The Indiana Legislature actually passed a law last session that made it a felony for me to wear any type of swimsuit in public.

Abby was "Miss Fix-it" with everyone. She always knew someone who knew someone who would be "perfect" for whomever she was trying to wrangle into a blind date. Even though she'd never created a long-lasting relationship between any of the poor souls for whom she'd played matchmaker, she never gave up hope. I couldn't help but admire the fact that she was the eternal optimist and believed that love would always find a way.

She probably still believed in Santa Claus, the Tooth Fairy, and the Easter Bunny.

"Seriously, Jackie," Abby continued on her current tirade, "You've got to meet this guy. Suzanne told me he was a great date."

I gave her a skeptical squint. "If the guy's so great, why isn't Suzanne going out with him again?"

All Abby did was shrug in response.

The chap in question had to be another winner. Translate "winner" as a dud. I had a quick flash to a mama's boy still living at home at forty-five. I wasn't about to take her up on her offer. I'd done that once—the month after the divorce was final—and I still had nasty flashbacks to that date from hell.

"Suzanne thought this guy—"

"Give it up, Abs," I insisted.

"He's a cop and has two daughters. His wife died a couple of years back. Breast cancer, if I remember right. I really think you two would be good together," my redheaded friend insisted.

Julie gave me a sympathetic look, but I knew she probably agreed with Abby.

I shot back a stern glare, but it didn't faze either of them. They were like well-meaning mothers trying to get a child to eat more when she was already full.

Knowing they would never give it up, I groaned in resignation. "Go ahead and give him my number."

Abby started clapping like a little girl at her first circus.

Amazing.

It wasn't like the guy was going to call me anyway. Who wants to date a forty-something woman suffering from an advanced case of empty nest syndrome?

***

A teacher's favorite place is always the closest and cheapest office supply store. After finishing the gossip sessions that often make up the teacher workday, I headed to OfficeMax to round up the items on the list I'd made as I checked through my desk that afternoon. I needed all the things that kids "forgot" most days—pens, pencils, paper, highlighters. Having that stuff handy saved me writing passes to send students to the already chaotic locker bank.

Knowing I needed more than my arms could possibly carry, I grabbed a cart and prowled the aisles like a lion stalking a gazelle. My personality made shopping predatory. I always had to find the best bargain before some other underpaid teacher cleaned out the display.

As I shopped, I came across two girls with dark curly hair who were looking at day planners. I didn't mean to eavesdrop, but it seemed the older girl was trying to impress upon her pony-tailed sister the need to keep better track of her assignments.

When they mentioned Harrison High School, I couldn't resist poking my nose where it probably didn't belong—one of the personality traits that kept me from getting a really good husband.

"All of the Harrison kids will get a school planner tomorrow," I offered, hoping not to appear too pushy.

The older girl flipped her long, loose hair over her shoulder and smiled. "See? *Everyone* should have a planner."

The younger girl grumbled, twisted her ponytail around her fingers, and threw the planner she held back into the wire basket of the display.

Figuring it might be nice to make conversation instead of being bossy, I asked, "Are you both going to Harrison? I teach there."

The older girl shook her head. She was very pretty with warm brown hair and big, dark eyes set in a heart-shaped face. "I'm going to Indiana University. I moved into the dorms over the weekend. I just came back to help get my sister ready for school."

The younger girl didn't bother to answer. She kept rolling her brown eyes and twisting her brunette ponytail into knots, showing her obvious impatience with having any type of conversation with an adult.

I smiled at her anyway as I asked the older girl, "Which dorm?"

The girl had a wonderful smile. "McNutt."

"My son's in Briscoe."

"Oh. Party dorm."

"Exactly what I wanted to hear." I didn't recognize her from school, but we had over three thousand students on campus. I couldn't possibly have known every kid who went to Harrison High School. "Are you a Harrison grad?"

She shook her head. "We just moved to our new house a couple of months ago. I graduated from Evansville South."

Having run out of polite conversation, I was just about to shuffle off when a man appearing to be in his forties came up to the three of us.

The first thing that crossed my mind was one word.

Yummy.

This had to be the girls' father because I could see exactly where their dark good looks had originated. The guy had a face that looked like it was chiseled in the finest marble. Every plane, every angle, every line was perfect. Good God, those full lips were the sexiest things I'd ever seen. His hair was a warm chestnut and had an ever so subtle waviness to it, with just a peppering of gray at the temples. And he was tall. I always liked tall guys, especially those with brown eyes. Being five-nine, I appreciated someone I could look up to, and Adonis here was probably six-two or more.

I was in love.

Well, I was at least in lust.

"Daaaad!" the youngest girl squealed in that freshman girl voice that always found a teacher's spine and worked its way up inch by agonizing inch. "Kathy was going to make me buy a stupid planner, but this lady says I don't have to. Tell Kathy to leave me alone."

He turned to me and smiled, flashing the most perfect set of white teeth I'd ever seen.

Oh, yes. I was definitely in lust.

"She doesn't need a planner?" he asked.

I stood there drooling like one of Pavlov's puppies. Even his voice was perfect. The good Lord just didn't make them any yummier than this one.

When I finally located some of the few wits I had remaining, I smiled back. "No. If she's starting at Harrison tomorrow, we'll pass them out to the students. I'm Jackie Delgado. I teach science there." I extended my hand, hoping he'd ask for it permanently.

The guy had one of those strong but not too strong grips. I instantly melted like a stick of butter in a hot pan. "Mark Brennan. Nice to meet you." He inclined his head toward the youngest girl. "That's Carly. "

The older girl quickly chimed in. "I'm Kathy."

How does one politely ask a guy she just met if he wanted to go into the nearest closet, get naked, and play doctor? Especially when his daughters were standing right there... "Nice to meet you."

"What science do you teach?" Mark asked.

The unusual thing was that he asked as if he really wanted to know. It didn't seem like one of those questions asked politely when conversing with someone he had absolutely no interest in getting to know.

"Biology. Three Bio One classes for freshmen. Three Bio Two classes for seniors."

"Maybe Carly will be in one of your classes. I think she's taking biology." His voice was rich and soothing.

He could sell water to a drowning woman.

"Maybe. They didn't have class lists printed before I left."

God, I hope she's one of mine. I'll put an hour or two aside for parent-teacher conferences. We can plan the wedding.

To keep my hands occupied so they didn't reach out to touch his well-developed bicep, I grabbed one of the planners and threw it in my cart. "I guess I'll be seeing you around school. Nice to meet you, Kathy, Carly, Mr. Brennan."

"Mark. Please."

"Mark. Please call me Jackie." I turned to Carly. "Ms. Delgado at school." Then I winked at her. She actually smiled at me. "Well, I better get going."

I turned my cart and moved toward the next aisle, hoping I wasn't drooling too awfully much. I couldn't tell if it was just my imagination, but I think he actually watched my butt as I walked away.

CHAPTER THREE

Carly Brennan showed up at my classroom door the very first period of the next day. She seemed pleased to already know one of her new teachers, and I was thrilled to realize I had at least one normal teenager.

I went through my well-rehearsed spiel over the school rules, my classroom rules, and what I expected as far as student behavior. Judging from their looks, my hard-earned reputation of being strict had subdued my new kids.

Well, at least *some* of them. The young man sitting front and center smiling at me obviously wasn't afraid.

He'd braided his hair into small twists that popped out all over his head like tiny branches growing from a tree trunk. He'd also taken an obviously lengthy amount of time to dye the braids several different colors—green, blue, red, yellow.

He reminded me so much of an odd man who used to show up at every sporting event in the 1970s in a rainbow wig that I smiled despite myself.

He smiled back.

I sure hope God loves teenagers. They need him.

As class ended, Carly stopped to talk to me. I had to resist the urge to ask about Mr. Yummy. He was the girl's father, after all.

I wasn't honestly any better than the hormonal kids I taught. The man had plagued my thoughts—had even slipped into my dreams—since I met him the day before.

What the hell?

What happened to my cool self-control? Where had my casual aloofness where men were concerned gone? What happened to my independent streak that didn't want another guy hanging around?

Must be perimenopause. Oprah said it made women a little loopy and sometimes horny.

I held tightly to that excuse to explain away my silly thoughts.

"My dad says, 'Hi.' He told me to make sure and tell you." Carly gave me an enormous smile.

Was she serious? Mr. Yummy actually asked her to talk to me?

I had a quick thought about writing him a note and having her slip it to him.

That's what I get for hanging around hormone-drenched adolescents all the time.

I finally decided to avoid the subject of Mark Brennan and focus on Carly. "Are you finding your way around okay?"

She nodded. "I think I'm going to like this class. I love science."

"Nice to hear. I love it too."

She scooted away with some students who passed my door.

Maybe Abby and Julie were right—I needed to get out more often. Here I was drooling over a student's father. I couldn't remember feeling as uncomfortable as I was at that moment in a very long time. It just didn't seem right.

The day went smoothly for the first school day after a long break. Before I knew it, we were herding the little buggers out of the door and onto the busses or into their cars. The faculty always breathed a huge sigh of relief when the building finally emptied each day. And—if we were lucky—maybe a couple of the students actually learned something.

Abby came striding up the hallway, holding a small piece of paper. I assumed it was the name she had threatened to give me earlier.

I was correct.

"You're gonna love this guy, Jackie. He's something special." She pressed the paper into my hand.

I unfolded it. All that was written on the slip of paper was a phone number.

"What's his name?"

"Mike, I think," she replied.

"You don't even know his name? And you're telling me he's the best thing since sliced bread? What are you doing to me here, Abs?"

"No, I don't know his name. Suzanne's the one who said I should hook you two up. He goes to her church. She really liked the guy, but she said they just didn't...click. She thinks he needs someone like you. Someone..."

I arched an eyebrow, waiting for the adjective she would choose to describe me. I'd heard them all before—loud, boisterous, obnoxious, and forceful.

Not a pretty picture.

"Vivacious," Abby finally finished the thought.

I laughed in relief. "At least English teachers use nicer words when they insult you."

She stared back at me, looking a bit perplexed. "What do you mean?"

"Vivacious. It's a lot nicer than noisy."

"But you are vivacious, Jackie. You have a *joie de vivre*."

I laughed again, thanking God for friends who made me feel better about myself—even if they were just being polite.

My nickname as a child had been "Gabby." I knew I had a problem keeping my thoughts to myself. At least my friends saw it as an endearing trait instead of an annoying one.

Abby went on with her hard sell. "He's supposed to call you and arrange a date. Let me know when he does."

"I will. I promise." I pushed the paper into my pocket and promptly forgot all about it.

***

Jellybean wolf-whistled at me as I walked in from the garage.

"Why, thanks, Pal." I opened the cage door to let him out to play. "It's nice to be appreciated."

He went to a small mirror I keep on the top of the cage and began to whistle the theme song from the old *Andy Griffith Show* and ignore me.

I dropped my purse and briefcase on the table and kicked off my shoes. Rubbing the sole of one sore foot and planning a massage for the other, I glanced around my empty home.

I still hadn't gotten used to the quiet. I missed my boys.

The answering machine flashed two messages. I punched the button to listen to them.

Nate's voice was first. It warmed me just to hear him. "Hi, Mom. I wanted to tell you how great my classes are. I love it here. I met a neat girl in my econ class. I think I might ask her out. Gotta go. Love you."

"Good for you," I said aloud to no one.

I started to wonder if I was talking to myself to banish the quiet or because I was losing my mind.

Jellybean was still butchering the Andy Griffith theme, but he'd added a few notes of "Pop Goes the Weasel."

I sure as hell didn't want that medley stuck in my head for the rest of the night.

The second message wasn't as much fun. "Jackie, it's David. I need you to sign some insurance papers. Since the boys are both over eighteen, I'm dropping you as beneficiary and adding them, Ashley, and Duncan. I'll bring the papers over. Call me and let me know when you're home."

Yeah, I'll get right on that one, loverboy.

"End of new messages," the machine said in that annoying feminine, mechanical voice.

I wished the electronics companies would get some guy with a deep, seductive voice to record the prompts for answering machines. I figured it would make life a little more pleasant for old ladies like me. Plus, I had someone perfect to recommend.

The phone rang, and I jumped in surprise. Picking up the handset, I was a bit shocked to see "Brennan, Mark" in the caller-ID window.

Mr. Yummy!

I punched the answer button. "Hello?"

"Um, hi. Is this...Jackie?" He sounded incredibly nervous. I think his voice actually cracked like one of my student's might.

I nodded before I stupidly realized Mr. Yummy couldn't see me. "Yes, this is Jackie."

"Hi. This is Mark. Mark Brennan. I'm a friend of Suzanne Roberts. We go to the same church. She thought... She figured that we might... I don't know. She said we might want to go on a blind date."

My heart started pounding so hard I could hear the rhythm roaring in my ears. Mr. Yummy was the guy that Suzanne and Abs had been trying to force on me.

God, love them!

I sure did!

Although my head was spinning, I had enough sense remaining to realize that he didn't recognize my name. Knowing Suzanne and Abs, they had probably just written down my first name and phone number.

"You still there?" Mark asked.

"Sorry. Yeah, I'm still here. I was just thinking that I should probably tell you that I know who you are, and that you might not want to take me out when you find out who I am."

"Why? Are you a serial killer or something?" He chuckled.

Mr. Yummy has a sense of humor.

"My last name's Delgado. We met at the OfficeMax. Remember?"

"I thought the name sounded familiar. You're Carly's biology teacher, aren't you?"

I nodded again. Boy, could I be lame sometimes. "Yeah. I understand if you don't want to go out now."

"Why?"

"I'm your daughter's teacher."

"Is there some rule against parents going out with teachers?" He sounded confused.

"Well, no. But..."

"Look, I wasn't really thrilled about this whole idea—"

"Fine!" I interrupted. My insecurity was already thrumming through me like the beat of a big bass drum at the notion of a man as gorgeous as Mark Brennan wanting to spend time with me. Now that he knew who I was, he was balking. "Don't bother."

"Will you let me finish?" he asked with a note of irritation.

Mr. Yummy has a temper.

"Fine. I'm sorry."

"What I was saying was that I wasn't thrilled about the idea until you told me who you are. Now, I'd really like to take you out."

"Why?"

I let the word slip out before I could censor myself. I had never been very good at using that protective filter most people have between their brains and their mouths. Mine failed me on a regular basis.

"Excuse me?" he asked.

"Never mind," I mumbled.

"I want to go out with you because you seemed nice. Funny. Real."

"Real?"

"Yeah. You don't seem to be the type of woman who plays games. Carly likes you too. How about Friday?"

Mark seemed to be gaining some confidence. It dawned on me that he probably hadn't asked out many women. This was obviously something he wasn't horribly comfortable doing.

"Friday," I repeated.

"Is that a yes?"

"Yes," I echoed in my delirious trance as I nodded my head.

I'm going out with Mr. Yummy!

Oh, my God! I'm going out with Mr. Yummy!

***

Suzanne sat down at the lunch table where Abby, Julie, and I had already set up shop.

The smell of the school cafeteria was usually nauseating, but I was in such a strange frame of mind that I didn't notice the scent for once. Besides, I never ate anything except salad—for whatever good that was doing me.

"So?" she asked with an anxious note in her voice. "Did he call?"

"Who?" Abby asked. "Do you mean Mike?"

"Mark," Suzanne corrected.

"Who's Mark?" Abby asked.

"Mike," Julie corrected.

I shook my head and laughed. "You guys sound like a really bad Abbott and Costello routine. It's Mark. And, yes, he called." I shifted some food around on my plate, savoring their wide-eyed stares. I waited another second or two to raise the tension, then I took mercy on them. "We're going to have dinner on Friday."

Abby clapped her hands in that way she always does whenever she's excited.

"So?" Suzanne asked again.

"So *what?*" I asked.

She let out an exasperated groan. "What did you think of Mark?"

"Mike," Abby insisted.

"Mark," Julie corrected.

Abby looked puzzled, but she had a habit of getting that way rapidly and often.

"I think that I already knew the guy."

Three faces of confusion immediately turned and focused on me.

"I met him at OfficeMax on Teacher Work Day. I have his daughter first period in biology," I explained, knowing they wouldn't leave me alone unless I did.

Abby clapped her hands again. "What does he look like? Is he cute? Still have his hair?"

Suzanne took the burden from my shoulders and my mouth. "He's about as dreamy as anyone I've ever met." She actually sighed as she recollected the guy I was going out with on Friday.

I almost felt...jealous. A weird reaction on my part.

"Nice eyes," Suzanne continued. "Thick hair. I'm just sorry we didn't hook up."

I wasn't sorry about it in the least, but I kept that juicy tidbit to myself.

Julie, the voice of reason, chimed in. "Why isn't he taken? If he's so wonderful, why's he on the market?" She shook her head. "There's got to be something wrong with him."

"Julie, I'd hate to buy a car with you," Abby responded. "You think everyone's got an angle. You could get it for wholesale and you'd question the salesman's motives."

"Just askin'," she said in her own defense as she picked at her salad. "Great guy like that? Still free as a bird? I don't know..."

They all stared at me as if I had all the answers to the questions of the universe.

I kept my silence for once and shrugged.

"He's just now starting to date again. He's a widower," Suzanne explained. "He lost his wife to breast cancer a while back. Two years ago, I think."

My heart went out to Mr. Yummy.

After David and I separated, and even more so after the divorce, I used to sit around feeling sorry for myself and wondering if things might've been better if David had died rather than left me. I had to admit to harboring a macabre fantasy of his demise when I found out he was screwing around with Ashley and when he filed for divorce.

I dreamt of the respect and reverence I would have received at his funeral. Of course, I would have been twenty pounds thinner, wearing a tailored black Halston dress, and sporting perfect hair and nails. My friends and relatives would have patted my manicured hands in sympathy while David was lying in the coffin and looking pristine. There would have been no answering ridiculous but well-meaning questions about why he'd left. Instead, I would've said, "These things happen." We'd have thrown handfuls of roses and dirt on his grave, and my sons and I would have moved on to face the world with stoic bravery.

And I wouldn't be a discard anymore.

"Jackie?" Abby asked, bringing me back from my own little world.

"Sorry. What did you say?"

"Where are you two going to eat?"

"He said it would be a surprise."

I gathered together the food I couldn't stomach eating. My friends had worked my guts into nervous knots again with their speculation. I stood up and grabbed my tray, feeling the need to run like a scared rabbit. Before I could make my legs move, I glanced down at my friends and let my fear show.

I dropped back down onto the bench. "What if he doesn't like me?"

"Oh, Jackie, honey." Julie wrapped a reassuring arm around my shoulder. "Everyone likes you."

"Yeah. You make us laugh," Abby added.

I shook my head. "Guys don't like smart-asses. What if I can't keep my mouth shut?"

"He'll love you," Suzanne said. "We just didn't click because... Well, just because. No chemistry."

"No chemistry?" I asked.

She nodded and gave me a naughty smile. "You know—no funny feeling in my stomach. I mean, he's handsome and all, but I have to feel... *chemistry*."

"Yeah, we know," Abby said. "You've felt chemistry three times already. And those are just the ones you married."

Suzanne didn't even appear offended at the jab. "*C'est la vie.* I have to have passion. What can I say?"

Abby shook her head and glanced back at me. "Maybe you'll have chemistry with Mike."

"Mark," Julie corrected. "Are you all right, Jackie? You look a little...shaky."

I shook my head. "I haven't been on a date since Washington was president." Then I remembered the date from hell. "Except for Stanley."

Abby caught the inference. "Hey! He wasn't *that* bad!"

"Neither was Norman Bates," Julie said with a chuckle.

"I don't know what was worse," I added. "The pager and cell phone he carried so his mother could stay in touch or the really bad toupee." I snorted a laugh. "I swear it looked like a small animal crawled on his head and died."

"Maybe Mark will be different." Julie patted my hand.

"Yeah. Maybe Mike will be different," Abby chimed in.

Shit. For almost a full minute, I'd forgotten.

I was going out with Mr. Yummy. I tried to control the panic that suddenly threatened to drown me. "I'm not sure I remember *how* to date. Wh–what do I wear? What do I do? How will I ever be able to keep my mouth shut?"

"You've already asked that," Suzanne said. "You don't have to keep your mouth shut. You're funny, Jackie."

Yeah, right. I'm hysterical.

That's not what guys want in a woman.

***

Carly Brennan found me in my classroom a few minutes after the final bell rang on Friday. "Ms. Delgado?"

I turned to see her standing in the doorway, staring intently at her shoes and nibbling on her bottom lip. "Hi, Carly. What's up?" I asked as I finished lining the desks back into neat rows. They had a tendency to drift across the floor as the classes went on, and I was too anal retentive not to straighten them back up at the end of every day.

"Dad asked me to give you a message."

I gave my head a small shake, knowing how uncomfortable she must be passing information between Mark and me. "Carly, your father shouldn't use you as a messenger. It's not fair to you."

"What'd you mean?"

"I'm your teacher. He shouldn't be telling you to give me messages."

"Why not?" Her face bore the same incredulous meaning as her question.

It dawned on me that she didn't feel awkward about her father going out with her biology teacher. The sticky situation just wasn't "sticky" to her.

I was perpetually amazed at the adaptability of teenagers.

I didn't have an answer to her question. "Fine. What's the message?"

"Wear comfortable pants and bring a jacket."

"It's August. Why would I need a jacket?"

She smiled showing me her braces. "It's a surprise. I'm supposed to ask if you're allergic to anything."

"Just bee stings," I replied. "Why?"

"I told you. It's a surprise."

CHAPTER FOUR

I had been standing by the door in my shoes and jacket for almost thirty minutes before the doorbell rang.

It wasn't that Mark was late. In fact, he was a couple minutes early. The problem was me.

I'd managed to work myself up into such a collection of nerves that my hands literally hurt from wringing them. Jacket on, jacket off. Jacket on, jacket off. I let out a small squeal when I heard the doorbell.

Jellybean started to whistle the theme from *The Addams Family*.

When I opened the door for Mark, I tried to appear casual and aloof at the idea of going out on a real date in who knows how long. My demeanor probably came across as utterly terrified.

Mark looked great. He had on a pair of tan khakis and a dark blue polo shirt.

Casual sophistication.

He gave me a quick glance from head to toe and smiled.

I wasn't sure exactly what to think about that. Self-esteem issues always make me wonder if people smile at my appearances because I'm peculiar or because I'm acceptable. I voted for acceptable this time when he said, "You look great, Jackie."

I smoothed my hands over my navy blue Dockers and felt the heat of a blush. "Thanks. So where are we heading?"

He smiled, showing those incredible white teeth. "Someplace you've probably never been before."

Mark grabbed my jacket I'd draped over my arm, and then the guy actually took my hand in his. I think I blushed some more because my cheeks still felt hot.

Perimenopause.

But, God, I liked the feeling of that warm hand encasing mine. His touch radiated security, which was a notion I hadn't entertained in several years.

Mark didn't drop my hand until we were at his car. He opened the passenger door to the blue Honda Accord, and I slid inside. The interior was immaculate. The sedan still had that wonderful new car smell. I envied him for a moment.

The last new car I had purchased was the Chrysler mini-van I still drove. The model year was sometime in the latter part of the twentieth century. The damn thing had more miles on it than the tracks of the Transcontinental Railroad. I had some abnormal attachment to the big red monster, even though it tended to break down on a regular basis at very inopportune moments. In the recesses of my demented mind, that van signified the last remnants of what had once upon a time been my family.

I should trade the silly thing in for something new in the spring.

Mark eased into the driver's seat and buckled his seatbelt. He glanced over at me. "Got to wear a seatbelt, Jackie."

"Why?"

"Because it's the law." He reached across me to grab the belt from the door and pull it across my shoulder and waist. The man actually buckled me into his car!

The temperature in the Accord instantly rose by a good ten degrees when his fingers brushed my hip. My stomach did a quick somersault.

Chemistry.

I must have looked like I was sporting a wicked sunburn, judging from how warm my face felt.

"Carly seems to be okay with...*this?*" I asked, trying to recover my scattered thoughts.

He nodded as he started the engine. "She's encouraging it. She really likes you. Likes your class, too."

"Thanks. That's nice to hear. She's a great kid."

"What made you choose to be a teacher?"

Let the fishing expedition commence.

The problem with a first date was trying to get enough information to see if a second date was warranted while not appearing to be conducting a criminal investigation for the FBI. Blood samples at this point would be a simple courtesy, but highly expensive and a tad messy. So a person works with what's available and asks a ton of questions.

Let's be honest, no one wants to date a loser.

The truth about a person and her baggage had to come out somehow. On a date, those nice little "small talk" questions were a hell of a lot more than simple chatter.

"What made you choose to be a teacher?" translated in my insecure mind as, "Why did your husband divorce you if you are such a great person?" I didn't want to get my guard up, but it snapped right into place before I even had a chance to prevent it.

"Look, I don't know what Suzanne told you, but I'm divorced." My voice sounded strained.

He appeared a bit perplexed at the statement, even cocked his head at me while also trying to drive. "What does that have to do with why you wanted to be a teacher?"

"I know Suzanne tends to build up people she wants to fix up to be more interesting than they are. I'm probably not exactly what you expected and—"

He was shaking his head and interrupting before I could even get my pathetic thought to finish tumbling from my mouth. "Suzanne didn't tell me anything. I don't like to play twenty questions with other people about someone I'd rather get to know on my own."

"You want to get to know me?" That stupid and entirely undependable filter between my brain and my mouth had obviously decided to stay at home.

Mark pulled the car over and threw it into park. Then he turned to me with a perturbed look in those gorgeous brown eyes. "Okay, Jackie. You can let the firewall down now."

I knit my eyebrows and stared at him. The fact that he seemed to be able to read my mind was slowly freaking me out. I wondered if he knew I called him Mr. Yummy.

God, I hoped not. "What firewall?"

He stared at me intently for a moment. "I'm not sure what some idiot did to make you so insecure, but you need to stop it."

I waved my hand to dismiss the thought, but I knew deep down that he was entirely correct.

It happened before I even knew what he intended. With a quick reach, he wrapped his warm, slightly calloused fingers around the back of my neck and gently pulled me toward him. When those heavenly lips touched mine, my toes actually curled. The kiss was sweet. Soft. Warm. It lasted long enough to make me blush—but not long enough to satisfy me.

He tasted so good.

"Now that I've got your attention," he said as he slowly withdrew his hand, "let's start over. Hi. I'm Mark Brennan. I met you at OfficeMax. I thought you were a fascinating person, and if I'd have had any type of courage at the time, I would have asked you out on the spot." Mark chuckled. "What can I say? I'm a chicken-shit, but I lucked out. You fell into my lap anyway."

Don't I wish!

The sincerity in his eyes made my heart pinch. The guy was being honest. He really wanted to go out with me.

I held out my hand. "Hi, Mark. I'm Jackie Delgado. I'm just going to dump my enormous bundle of insecurity out the window here, and we can go on a real date."

He laughed as he shook my hand, then he threw the car into gear and eased back into the flow of traffic. "So why did you decide to be a teacher?"

"I love kids. Well, not *all* kids. I could never teach elementary. Little rugrats would drive me nuts. But teenagers are great. They're funny and so full of life."

"Sounds like my girls."

"They're really sweet. I adore Carly. What do you do for a living, Mark Brennan? I don't know anything about you, either."

He steered the car into a small parking lot. "I'm a cop."

You could have blown me over with a single puff of air. I'd forgotten that Suzanne said he was a cop.

I wasn't sure if the notion made me excited or frightened. "A cop. Wow. How long have you been a cop?"

"Too long." Mark's handsome smile seeped into my heart.

He got out of the car and actually came around to open my door.

As I hoisted myself out of the vehicle, he continued his story. "I've actually been on the job for fifteen years. I was in the Army for a while. I made detective ten years ago."

He pulled a small leather wallet out of his back pocket and flashed me a gold shield.

I was impressed.

"Army, huh? My dad was Army. He retired several years back." I should have known from the way Mark carried himself. Proud. Ramrod-straight spine. No-nonsense stride.

"You're an Army brat. Awesome."

I hadn't really taken notice of our location. He was holding the door open for me, and I slipped through.

The interior of the restaurant was a surprise—it was nothing more than a fancy picnic ground. Wooden tables with benches were scattered all around and covered with plastic red and white checkered tablecloths. Loud country-western music thrummed through the joint. Most of the people were eating enormous piles of crab legs as they cracked the shells with tongs and threw the discarded shells into small silver buckets that sat in the middle of each table. The place radiated home-style warmth from every angle.

Mark walked us over to one of the smaller picnic tables.

I took the opposite side so we could talk more easily. That and I wasn't entirely sure I could keep my hands off him if I sat next to him. If our thighs brushed, I wouldn't know how to handle it.

Damn, it had been a long, long time since I felt that elation of a simple touch or that quickening of a heartbeat. I enjoyed the heady mixture of anticipation and knowledge of what could be. I wanted him.

And that scared the hell out of me.

Almost immediately, a teenage server came over with menus. The poor kid hadn't quite grown into those big hands and feet.

Mark waved the menus away. "All-you-can-eat crab legs for both of us." The teenager nodded. "What do you want to drink, Jackie?"

"Iced tea, please."

"Long Island? I'm driving."

I shook my head. I wasn't entirely sure alcohol and Mr. Yummy would be a good combination if I wanted to hold off any type of embarrassing and wanton display at the end of the evening. Hell, I was already fantasizing about kissing him at my doorstep.

"Just iced tea, please. With lemon."

"I'll have the same," he told the waiter before the kid disappeared into the kitchen through some swinging doors. "I take it you've never been here before."

"Never." I stared at Mark, ignoring the restaurant entirely. "What's it called?"

"The Wharf. I've known the guy who owns it since high school."

"You're from around here?"

He nodded before taking the glasses of iced tea and a basket of hot rolls from the waiter and setting them between us. He pulled one of the rolls from the basket and handed it to me.

I broke it in half, took a bite, and sighed. Light as air with a touch of cinnamon. Bad carbs, but who cared tonight?

"I grew up in Evansville." Mark contently munched on his roll then asked, "Where are you from?"

"Me? Just about everywhere. We moved around a lot when I was little. I call Chicago my hometown, because I lived there for three straight years once. Westmont, actually. I miss it sometimes. There was always something to do, someplace to go. Indiana is a bit..."

"Antiquated?" he offered.

I smiled. "Good word choice. I seriously think the state is two decades behind the rest of the country."

"There's a lot to be said for that when you're raising kids, though. I like that my girls aren't running around trying to look like some of the kids I see on MTV."

I laughed aloud before I could stop myself. "You watch MTV?"

Mark laughed back. "Kathy and Carly make me. They love the reality show about the rich girls planning their sweet sixteen parties."

"Yuck. You must really *love* that."

"Believe it or not, I do. Watching those spoiled brats spend hundreds of thousands of dollars on one damn party makes me appreciate my girls."

He ate another roll and seemed to contemplate me for a moment. I could feel the heat spreading over my cheeks again. Even my ears felt warm.

Good God, what am I? Sixteen?

The notion that Mark's stare was turning my insides into nothing more than a mixture of warm soup was totally unnerving. I didn't like the idea that any man had that kind of power over me. I could feel all of my defenses rising to the surface again.

Being vulnerable only got a person hurt. I'd already been hurt enough. Letting someone new into my life would only lead to more wounds. What I suddenly realized was truly upsetting me was recognizing that Mark Brennan could hurt me.

I wasn't about to allow him inside enough that he would leave mortal wounds when he finally discarded me.

Like David had.

His brown eyes twinkled for a moment. "You're thinking too hard, Jackie."

I tried to act surprised.

"Someone hurt you. Bad."

"Are all cops so nosey?" I asked in that defensive tone I tended to use when I was...well, *defensive*.

"Oh, yeah." Mark chuckled. "Especially detectives. So how old are you, Ms. Delgado?"

"I turned thirty-twelve a couple of weeks ago." I smirked at my own answer.

"Thirty-twelve?" His question held the hint of laughter. "That's...*old*." He winked. "I take it that magic word 'forty' is hard for you to say."

"Actually, it's just a joke between my friends and me. Guys can be forty and still be...I don't know...*wanted*. Attractive."

He regarded me with curiosity, so I decided to regale him with my middle age sermon. "Alan Rickman is still sexy. He still plays the hero. Diane Keaton isn't. She gets to play the mother—or the grandmother. And they were born in the same stupid year. When a woman hits forty, it's all downhill. So my friends and I always say something like we're celebrating our thirtieth birthday the tenth time."

I stopped talking. I probably sounded a little bitter which wasn't an attractive trait on a first date, especially when I wanted a second one—and probably a third. "Just how old are you, Detective Brennan?"

"Forty—" An easy smile spread over his face. "*Thirty-eighteen* on my last birthday."

"Glad to see you're getting with the program."

Our brilliant conversation was interrupted by the waiter. At least when the enormous piles of steamed crab legs were put on the table, we had something to occupy our mouths.

I pushed the little bowl of melted butter toward Mark so I wouldn't be tempted to soak my crab in it and increase the size of my waistline.

He pushed it right back at me.

I decided to avoid being rude and enjoy some of it.

I'd never seen so many crab legs. I sure as hell hadn't ever eaten so many. About the time I was entirely convinced that I'd need to unbutton the waistband of my pants, Mark wiped his hands on his napkin and threw it on his plate. "Man. I'm full. Good though, wasn't it?"

I nodded. "I love seafood. I wish I'd have known about this place. My boys would eat them out of business."

"Your boys?"

I hadn't been horribly forthcoming with any really revealing facts all evening. "I have two sons. Patrick and Nathaniel. They're both away at college."

"College? You must've been in junior high when you had them."

Will you marry me? You're tremendously good for my ego.

We spent the next fifteen minutes talking about my favorite subjects as he paid the bill and dropped a tip on the table.

Once we were back in the car, Mark steered us toward our next destination. Unfortunately, he hadn't shared the location with me. When we pulled up in front of an ice skating rink a few minutes later, I almost couldn't believe my eyes.

"We're going ice skating?"

Do I even remember how?

He nodded, grabbed our jackets, and got out of the car. After he opened the door and I crawled out, he put his hand on the small of my back and guided me in the front door. I liked the way that telling gesture made me feel. That foreign security was floating through my mind again.

I was practically sleepwalking as I told him my shoe size, watched him rent some skates for us, and lead me to a long bench where we both started taking off our shoes.

"Mark, I don't skate very well," I finally confessed as I laced up the rented white skates that he'd handed to me.

"That's okay. I'll help you." I liked the smugness in his voice.

"I take it you skate well." I finished tying the double knots in the laces.

We both slipped on our jackets, and then I tried to stand up. My ankles immediately rebelled. I was way too out of shape to even be *attempting* this. But Mark's enthusiasm was contagious, and I let him lead me toward the rink, hoping I didn't look as stupid as I feared I did.

"Used to play hockey." He pulled me out onto the ice. He smiled broadly and pointed to one of his front teeth. "See the chip? Busted my face on the ice."

I didn't see a chip. I saw a perfect smile that made me warm all over.

The place was almost deserted. Since it was summer, I wasn't surprised. One girl who appeared to be ten or so was working in the center of the rink with a clearly frustrated coach. There were two boys who blew by us a couple of times as they played "tag" around the rink. I was having a hard time not yelling at them.

You can take the teacher out of the school, but you can't take the school out of the teacher.

Mark helped me get my feet straight enough so he could stand behind and push me. Even with his help, I was a little pigeon-toed. He put his hands on my hips and skated behind me as I tried not to let my knees buckle from the sensations this guy sent ripping through me as he pushed me around the rink. I tried desperately to keep my frightened squeaks to a minimum.

I couldn't remember any man smelling as good as he did when he leaned over me and rested his chin on my shoulder. He was wearing my favorite men's cologne. The combination of Mark and Polo Black was warm, strong, and almost as intoxicating as alcohol.

I'd been living like a nun in a cloister for far too long if I was reacting to this guy like a cat in heat. I liked the way his hands didn't grip my hips, but instead they moved around, almost like simple caresses.

The guy was making me hot. Damn hot. And he wasn't even trying.

He distracted me so much I wasn't paying attention to what I was doing. I suddenly tripped over my own skates. I fell to the ice and sprawled out face down in the most unladylike pose one could imagine. My dignity fell with me.

I braced myself and waited a split-second for the impact of Mark falling on top of me. He caught himself over me as if he had been doing a pushup. His groin was pressed hard into my backside.

I was mortified at my clumsiness.

He was laughing as though he'd heard a particularly witty comedy monologue.

Mark pushed himself to his feet as I rolled over to stare up at him. He smiled and reached down to offer me a hand. I grasped his and was thoroughly amazed how easily he pulled me back onto my feet, skates and all. Had to admire that kind of strength. He used the opportunity to pull me a little closer until our chests touched. I looked up into his big brown eyes and wanted to drown in them. I was sure he was going to kiss me again, and this time I planned to be ready when he did.

Then his stupid cell phone rang.

The silly thing played the theme from *Dragnet*. At least I was pleased to notice that he didn't appear very happy about the interruption, either.

He popped the phone off of his belt clip and glanced at the caller-ID. "Sorry. Gotta take this one."

Trying not to eavesdrop, I groped for the wall of the rink so I wouldn't fall again.

After what seemed like a short, intense conversation, he clipped the phone back to his belt and skated next to me. "I've gotta go. I need to get you home first. I'm really sorry to cut things short."

I nodded and tried not to look too disappointed, even though I was. It wasn't as if I was entirely stupid. I knew the phone call had to have come from his "rescuer"—the person who was scheduled to call at a certain time. This way he had an "out," a way to get the hell away from the person he was stuck with as a blind date. Mark had engaged his safety net.

Then it dawned on me that I had wanted to go out with him so badly I hadn't even made the same contingency plan. I suddenly wanted to cry because I knew I had been right all along. Men who looked like Mark really didn't want to go out with women like me. Suzanne had probably twisted the poor guy's arm. I promised myself I wouldn't cry in front of him, but damn it was tough. I knew I'd be weeping like a willow when I was safely home.

I wanted to die of embarrassment when I realized it might have been Carly who bailed Mark out of the date. How was I ever going to face her again?

That's what I have coming for dating a student's parent.

Hands were suddenly waving in front of my face. "You did it again," Mark said with a chuckle. "You're thinking too hard again."

"I can get a cab."

"Where the hell did that come from?" he asked, looking a bit confused.

"You need to go, remember? Just trying to expedite matters for you." I tried not to sound too hurt, but I was.

Shit. I'd already let the guy in.

"I need to go to a crime scene, but I can drop you off first," he insisted.

"Fine. Whatever." I flippantly dismissed him with a wave of my hand.

I tried to be nonchalant as we took off our skates and put our shoes back on. My ankles ached enough I'd be sucking down Tylenol the instant I got home. Since it was Friday and my pride was aching from the smacking it just received, I'd be drowning it in a wine cooler or two.

Mark didn't say anything, but he acted a little angry. I seriously heard him growl.

We dropped our skates off and walked back out to the parking lot. When we got to his car, he reached to open the door, but suddenly seemed to change his mind. He grabbed his cell phone and punched the screen. Then he held it up to me and showed me the list of incoming calls.

The last one read, "Police HQ."

Detectives are too damned smart for their own good.

I had no idea what to say to him, so I chose to babble incoherently instead. "Mark, I'm sorry... I didn't... It's been so long..."

He actually laughed. "It's all right. I'd have been suspicious too."

By the time we got back to my house, I'd blown the chance to get to know Mr. Yummy any better. After all, who wanted to date an obviously neurotic forty-something?

Mark walked me to the door. When I retrieved my keys from my purse, he gripped my arm and turned me to face him. He leaned over me and put his hand on the door behind me. I felt as though I couldn't breathe as his face hovered close to mine.

"I'm sorry I have to go, Jackie," he whispered, his lips inches from mine. "Would you like to go out tomorrow?"

I couldn't have been more surprised if someone had told me I was going to be a mother again. "You want to go out with me again?" slipped out of my mouth before I could stop the question.

He leaned in a little closer and ran a warm finger down my cheek to my chin. "Of course."

My body started to tremble.

As he pressed his lips to mine, every bit of tension fled my muscles. I leaned in as he wrapped his arms around me and pulled me against him.

It was one of those movie kisses that seem to go on forever, and you know it will make you sigh when it ends. The man did magic with his lips. When his tongue slid into my mouth, I feared my knees were going to give. It had been years since I felt the kind of warmth Mark's kiss sent racing through me.

Hell, I didn't think David *ever* kissed me like that.

Mark didn't seem to want to pull away. His face lingered in front of mine for a moment. "I'm sorry I have to go," he said again as he brushed his knuckles across my cheek.

I nodded, not trusting myself to say anything.

"I'll call you tomorrow."

I nodded again.

He quickly brushed his lips against mine one last time before he turned and jogged back to his car.

As he drove away I stood on the front porch and waved.

Good God, I could be so damned lame sometimes.

CHAPTER FIVE

"Mom? You okay?" Patrick asked.

I shifted the cordless telephone to my other ear. "I'm fine. Why do you keep asking me that?"

"You seem kinda...distracted for so early in the morning. So are you coming?"

"Yeah. I appreciate you calling to let me know. I know Nate probably won't. Then again, it's not until October. I'll give him the benefit of the doubt and assume he'll call before then."

It was almost Parents' Day. Even though I had gone to the event when Patrick was a freshman, I'd forgotten all about it. It dawned on me that if Patrick hadn't bothered to call, Nate would've hidden the occasion. He wanted his independence as badly as I wanted to hold onto him. Realizing how Freudian the whole situation seemed, I wondered if Nate would be angry if I went down to visit uninvited.

I'd have to think about that one.

Shit. I'd have to call David to see if he was aware there was a Parents' Day and if he and the "little woman" were going.

Call-waiting sounded, so I said my farewells to my oldest. Knowing it had to be Julie checking in to get the scoop on my date, I sarcastically greeted the new caller. "You've reached The Sex Emporium. Dominatrix Mistress Jackie speaking. How may I punish you?"

"Um. Okay. I'll bite. Sex-slave Mark here. I prefer black leather and a light spanking."

I slapped my forehead with the heel of my hand. Why hadn't I even bothered to check the caller-ID?

Now what, Ms. Sarcastic? Get yourself out of this one gracefully.

"Can we please forget that I just said that?"

Mark chuckled, warm and kind despite my *faux pas*. "A greeting like that? I seriously doubt it. Did you mean it last night when you said you wanted to go out tonight?"

Why did I always feel the need to nod when no one was around to see me? "Yeah. I meant it. But if you've made other—"

"Stop thinking, Jackie."

I had to laugh at that. "All right. And just where are we heading tonight? We could always play nine holes. How about a good game of 'horse'? Maybe toss a football around?"

"I was thinking something a little more...relaxed."

"Relaxed?"

He chuckled again. "Yeah, relaxed. Do you like movies?"

Quit nodding, moron. "I love movies." I went almost every weekend. The paper was already open to the entertainment section when I'd answered Patrick's call. "What do you want to see?"

"Doesn't matter. The girls have collected just about every DVD known to mankind."

"You mean you want to stay in?"

Why was I in such a panic over the idea of an intimate evening alone with Mr. Yummy?

Probably because I'd have a hard time keeping my hands off him.

"Sure. We can pop some popcorn, grab some Twizzlers, and watch a good show or two. I know. We'll get pizza."

"Um... All right, I guess. My place or yours?"

"Maybe we better come here." He laughed, the rumbling sound so deep and so obviously sincere it was heaven to my ears. "I'm not sure I'm up to the Sex Emporium."

"Coward."

"Do you mind if Carly sticks around? I miss Kathy, and I think Carly does to—although she'd never admit it. I think she'd like the company."

"I'd love to spend time with Carly. She's a nice kid." *And I think she's on my side.*

"Thanks. Give me your email address and I'll send some directions."

***

"What was I thinking?" I asked Julie for the hundredth time. "I can't go to his house. Carly will be there. What if he kisses me again or...or...something?" I threw more dirty clothes into the washing machine and poured in some detergent.

"Jackie, you're being silly."

"Gee, thanks. That helps a whole heap," I replied before realizing how snotty I probably sounded. "I like this guy, Julie. I really do."

She sighed. "Then quit acting like you're terrified of him."

I slammed the lid on the extraordinarily small load of clothing. With the boys gone and very little laundry of my own, I was going through some kind of withdrawal. I used to spend most of every Saturday in the laundry room, buried under piles of sweaty socks, gym shorts, t-shirts, and jeans. "But I *am* terrified. I don't want to like him. I don't need this. I have a great life. He'll just be...I don't know. A...complication."

I could tell Julie was quickly getting exasperated with me. The sound of her fingers drumming on some surface was easy to hear. I couldn't really blame her for being irritated. I'd probably talked to her ten times already, and it was only two o'clock. I was supposed to be at Mark's around six. Julie could probably anticipate at least a dozen more calls including the one from my cell phone when I finally drove over there.

"What are you going to wear?" she asked.

"Nice diversionary tactic."

"Thank you. Look, I'm sorry, Jackie, but I've got to go. Are you going to be okay?"

"Yeah. I'm just nervous. Tell me again."

"You're doing the right thing."

"Thanks, sweetie. Love you."

"Love you too." The sound as she hung up echoed through my brain like the chiming of a gong.

I was alone again.

I walked out of the laundry room and peered around for something to do. The emptying of my nest had thrust so many changes into my orderly world. Saturday had always been the day when I spent quite a bit of time making my house look like something other than a landfill. I'd yell at the boys to pick up their stuff as I used an old pair of ratty underwear to dust the furniture. Then we'd move on to the "who's-going-to-have-to-vacuum" dance. Of course, I usually ended up leading.

No matter which room I checked, the house was clean. It didn't really appear any different than when I'd cleaned it the day after Nate left.

Funny. This was what I'd always wanted. Now my pristine house made me sad.

I decided that I needed to get another pet—like a puppy or a kitten. Maybe then I'd have someone to clean up after.

***

I couldn't believe I'd found his house so easily. Mark gave really good directions. And really nice kisses.

Grow up, Jacqueline.

I grabbed the cell phone I'd propped up in the cup holder and slipped it in my pocket. With a deep, steadying breath, I left my minivan and walked to the front door. It opened before I could even reach my finger up to push the doorbell.

"Ms. Delgado!" Carly squealed. "Come in! Daddy's been pacing around waiting for you. And he's been running around picking stuff up all day. And he even shaved. On a Saturday!"

I smiled. The fact that she was so glad to see me warmed my heart. When Mark walked up behind her and put his hands on her shoulders, I warmed up a little more.

"Brat," he said as he squeezed her arms. "You're tattling on me."

She grinned at him over her shoulder. "Can we order pizza now? Please?" She turned back to me and gave me a smile that showed all of her silver braces with tiny purple rubber bands. "What do you like on your pizza, Ms. Delgado?"

"Pepperoni."

"Me too!" She turned back to her father. "That's your favorite too, isn't it, Daddy?" Her attention flipped back to me. "Daddy likes the same stuff you do. Pepperoni pizza." She stopped, laying her index finger against her cheek as if in deep thought. "Oh! And he likes biology, too."

It suddenly occurred to me that Carly was matchmaking. She was a budding Yenta straight out of *Fiddler on the Roof*. God love her, she wanted me to like her father. That wasn't something she needed to worry about. I already did.

He reached up and ruffled her hair.

She threw him a disgruntled glare and tried to comb her bangs back into place with her fingers.

"I'll go call Domino's," she announced. She started to run out of the foyer, but quickly whirled back around. "Breadsticks, too? And some cinnamon sticks?"

Mark nodded.

Carly was practically skipping when she left.

"Sorry." He took my hand and started to pull me out of the foyer.

"Why? She's wonderful."

He chuckled. "And a little too enthusiastic. She likes you. A lot. And she... Well, she misses her mother."

I'd forgotten all about his late wife. Didn't Suzanne say she passed away because of breast cancer?

A wave of sadness washed over me. I had a habit of absorbing other people's emotions, and I could tell exactly how much the subject was still haunting Mark.

"I'm so sorry about her mother." Tears stung my eyes.

"I still…" He swiped his hand over his face. "I miss her sometimes."

His long sigh sounded mournful to me. He must have loved his late wife a great deal. I wanted to pull him into my arms, stroke his hair, and tell him I would make it all better.

But I couldn't do that—wouldn't do that—because I wasn't capable of making this better for him. Life could be so cruel sometimes. I gave his hand a reassuring squeeze and fought my own tears.

It was the best I could manage.

Mark shook off his melancholy and he favored me with a weak smile. "Let's go see what kind of junk food she's ordered. Maybe we can pick a flick before she chooses something lame."

The house was beautiful. He led me through a dining room, a den, and a formal gathering room that looked like a damned museum. The carpet still bore the marks the vacuum left in its wake.

I was about to make some smart-aleck remark concerning whether he suffered from obsessive-compulsive disorder when it dawned on me that with Patrick and Nate gone there were probably several rooms in my house that I never set foot inside anymore. They were probably exactly like this room. I bit my tongue and enjoyed the rest of the tour.

We settled in the kitchen. Mark pulled out a long-legged wooden barstool that was sitting next to a large island of cabinets. I took a seat while he poured soft drinks for the three of us. Carly scooted onto the barstool next to me, leaned her elbows on the counter, and stared at her father.

He raised an eyebrow at her, held up his wrist, and pointed to his watch. She smiled and nodded.

I realized I'd missed something. These two communicated well without words.

Carly bounced off the stool and held out her hand. Mark pulled out his wallet, set a twenty-dollar bill on her palm, and shoved the wallet back into his pocket. She frowned, narrowed her eyes at him, and began to tap her toes on the tiled floor. He let out an exaggerated sigh before he fished his wallet back out of his pants. He pulled another twenty out and held it out to Carly. She snatched the bill from his fingers, kissed his cheek, and headed back toward the front of the house.

The doorbell rang only a moment or two later.

Mark smiled at my confused star. "She gets to keep the change."

"Ah. Now I know why she was so happy."

"Yeah, but she has to give the delivery kid a tip. She can be pretty stingy."

Carly brought back the pizza boxes, set them on the counter, and grabbed some plates from one of the cabinets.

Mark handed me a plate and then piled his own with a several slices of pepperoni pizza, a couple of breadsticks, and a container of cheese dipping sauce. He disappeared into the family room.

I took a slice of pizza and followed Carly as she headed the same direction.

She nodded toward the large sofa, so I sat down. She left her plate on the glass coffee table and ran back to the kitchen. When she returned, she set our glasses of soda down on the table, picked her plate back up, and plopped down in a recliner.

Mark was fiddling with a DVD player connected to a large-screen television. "I took the liberty of choosing a movie. Let me know if you don't like it, Jackie."

"I'm sure it's fine." I picked up my pizza and took a bite. I almost choked when *Jackass* came on the screen. With some embarrassment, I quickly chewed and swallowed the pizza. "Your favorite show?"

He laughed. "Nah. Just wanted to see your reaction."

"Cops are weird. He's always trying to find out about people by watching them," Carly added from her perch on the recliner.

He winked at her before he asked, "What do we watch, Ms. Delgado? I vote for one of the *Lethal Weapon* shows."

Carly wrinkled her nose. "If I have to watch one of those again, I'll... I'll..."

"Leave us alone?" her father asked with a raised eyebrow.

"You said I could stay for a while!"

Fearing a family fight over the presence of a teenage chaperone, I intervened. "I don't like cop shows. Too much...macho. All that testosterone and all."

In actuality, I hated violence in any form—especially guns. They made me queasy and nervous. For me, watching an action flick would've been akin to having a nasty root canal without any anesthetic. The only thing I would have hated worse was a slasher flick. My theory was those kinds of movies would eventually lead to the downfall of mankind.

Mark appeared to be properly outraged.

I retaliated with a smile. "And Carly, you can stay. I enjoy your company."

He looked properly pleased. After plucking a DVD from the shelf, he shoved it in the player and then flopped down next to me on the couch hard enough I bounced.

Happy Feet came on the screen. I hadn't seen it, so I was thrilled. At least I was thrilled until I realized how many references to sex would be included in what was supposed to be a children's cartoon. Jesus, the temperature went up rapidly. Mark and Carly didn't seem to mind.

Maybe the problem was my own dirty mind.

Sometime during the show, she brought in the cinnamon sticks, and I ate a couple despite the fact it would be faster to apply them directly to my thighs and bypass the stomach entirely. They were going to wind up there eventually anyway.

As I held one up to take a bite, some of the icing began to drip, and I quickly caught it with the fingers of my other hand.

Carly jumped up and ran to the kitchen—probably to get me a napkin.

Mark glanced over his shoulder toward the kitchen, then he reached for my sticky fingers and licked off the icing with one long, caressing lick of that heavenly tongue.

My face must have flushed the same red as the old Soviet Union flag. My heart was pounding a frantic rhythm as I realized just how much this man affected me.

He gave me an entirely wicked smile and dropped my hand just as Carly came back into the room and gave me a paper towel.

I pretended to wipe off the icing that was no longer on my fingers. I hoped she didn't see what her father had done to cause my blush. I looked back at Mark to try and give him a chastising glare, but he wiggled his eyebrows at me. The temperature instantly shot even higher.

I tried to settle down and watch the cartoon. Carly flipped the footrest up on her recliner and relaxed. Mark draped his arm on the back of the sofa.

I felt like a teenager again, waiting, anticipating, longing. He subtly dropped his arm to my shoulder, caressing me with those clever fingers. Fire raced through my gut—that giddy warm feeling that you get when something excites you and reaches you on a visceral level.

After the movie, I asked for directions to a bathroom. As I walked away, I saw Mark talking quietly to Carly. She was nodding her head in response to his whispered words.

When I returned to the family room, she'd disappeared.

Mark stared at me with that little boy I-did-something-naughty twinkle in his eyes. He finally answered my unasked question. "Carly wanted to go...um...surf the net for a while."

I wasn't going to let him think I didn't know what he was doing, even if I did find it both flattering and exciting. "Oh. I see. And she wanted to do this because?"

"I asked her to let us have some alone time."

Got to love a man who's honest.

I walked back to the coffee table and began to pick up the plates and glasses. He came over to help me. We carried everything into the kitchen. It felt downright domestic to stand side-by-side and wash and dry the dishes together. It was so comfortable. So like a real couple. So...

Stop it, Jackie. Just because your family is gone doesn't mean you can adopt this one.

"Want to watch another flick?" Mark asked as I finished wiping the counter with the damp cloth.

"I should probably go. We lost our chaperone after all. People will talk."

He grabbed my arm and turned me to face him. He reached out and caressed my cheek. "Stay. We can...talk."

I turned my face toward his warm palm. The man was a magnet and I was metal. "Talk?"

"I barely know anything about you. Let me play detective." He took the dishrag out of my hand and tossed it next to the sink before he wrapped his hand around mine and led me back to the sofa.

As we settled in, we turned to face each other. He casually rested his bent knee against mine. It was so relaxed and entirely too comfortable. I knew it. I'd let him in already.

Damn it all anyway.

"Tell me about you." Mark laid his hand over mine where it rested on the back of the couch.

I shrugged. "I'm a teacher. I've got two boys away at college."

He shook his head as he stroked my hand and wrist with his warm fingertips. The touch was so gentle it sent shivers running up my arm. "Tell me about *you*."

I had to take a minute to think about that. For most of my life, I'd been either a child or caregiver. I'd been my parents' daughter, then I was suddenly David's wife. We'd married so stinking early in life, barely out of our adolescence. It still embarrassed me that I'd had to get married. And then I became Patrick and Nate's mother. The hardest transition for me had been changing my name back to Delgado when David and I divorced because I'd been "Mrs. Ryan" for so long to all my students.

Hell, I'd been that identity so long to *me*.

So exactly who is *Jacqueline Marie Delgado?*

Mark loudly cleared his throat.

I came back from my reverie, blushing all the way. "Sorry," I offered. "Thinking too hard again?"

He tossed me a nod. "Since telling me about you seems to be a difficult topic, let's just start with the simple stuff. Where were you born?"

"Georgia. Fort Benning. My dad was assigned to dishing out basic training."

"Army brat. I remember." He began to stroke my hand again.

We started to play a chase with our fingers.

I let him win.

"I suppose Suzanne told you I'm divorced."

A slant of his head and a raised eyebrow told me he was confused. "That's quite a leap. Born in Georgia, then divorced. Child bride?"

The guy made me laugh at myself. Aloud. That was a gift from God if I ever knew of one. "Not that young, but young enough. Nineteen."

A low whistle spilled from his lips. "That's only a year older than Kathy. Way too young. How old were you when your oldest came along. Patrick, is it?"

"Yeah, Patrick." I was flattered he'd remembered but not thrilled with confessing my youthful indiscretion. "Let's just say he was a big baby for being six weeks premature. I was only twenty. Nate was a few years later. Then we learned about this miraculous invention called 'birth control.'"

He chuckled. Then his face turned serious. "Elaine and I were high school sweethearts."

My heart clenched in empathy. He was sharing stories with me about his late wife, and it was an important sign, a tell. He felt comfortable with me— just like I was comfortable around him.

I suddenly felt pulled in two directions. I wanted to know about her, but I didn't. It wasn't as if I couldn't recognize that her ghost was sitting between us, I just didn't want to know her well enough to mourn her passing. But I quickly realized I already did. I mourned what Mark and his daughters had lost.

"It took us some time to have the girls. Not horribly long, but Elaine was getting...nervous. It's not like the Army has a lot of fertility benefits."

We talked for some time about our lives, our families. Mark kept touching me. Sweet little caressing touches on my hand, my wrist, my knee. They were simple pats, almost absentminded. I'd forgotten how much I loved that type of contact and realized just how desperately I'd missed it.

After the first couple of years, David hadn't been very demonstrative. Toward the end of our marriage, sex had become more a biological function than a loving expression of affection. I drank each of Mark's caresses in like good, smooth whiskey, and he made me feel just as drunk.

We never did get around to watching another movie. By the time I recovered from my "Mark bender," I looked up at the clock and gasped.

Midnight.

"Oh, my stars. How did it get to be midnight?" I asked.

"Good company and pleasant conversation. Are you afraid your car will turn back into a pumpkin?" He chuckled and gave me one of those incredible smiles.

"It's already a pumpkin." I stood up and stretched. "I really should be heading home. I've abused your hospitality long enough."

Mark jumped to his feet, grabbed my hand, and tugged me into his arms. Damn, it was like some romantic movie as he stood there staring into my eyes. He was kissing me a second later.

Only four guys had kissed me in my entire life. At least it was four if you didn't count my father and my weird cousin Henry who kissed every woman he could get his hands on. But even with my limited experience, I knew this man was something special—this kiss was something special.

My heart pounded a rough, fast cadence. My blood ran so hot, I felt like I was sixteen again. His lips were soft, his tongue skilled. I stretched my arms up around his neck and let him hold me even closer.

It was similar to leaning against a solid brick wall. The guy had to lift some heavy-duty weights to have a body like that. I could feel how hard my breasts were being flattened against his concrete chest. I don't think I'd ever felt as aware of being a woman as I did when Mark was kissing me, when he was holding me.

Of course, as much as I wanted to turn my mind off and simply revel in his kiss, the stupid bells started chiming in my head.

He's a parent. You have to see his daughter first period every morning.

Ding, ding, ding, the bells continued to ring.

He still misses his wife. He's too good looking for you.

Ding, ding, ding.

I reluctantly eased away before things got too steamy. With the way my body was reacting to Mark, I could very easily fall into casual sex for the first time in my life. I'd never even been tempted before. All this man had to do was take a couple of steps toward a bedroom and crook his finger. I'd run after him like a bloodhound following a fresh, strong scent, tongue hanging out all the way.

He sighed and his warm breath was a caress against my cheek. "Sweet Jackie," he whispered. "Where do we go from here?"

How about your room? "I don't know, Mark. I really don't know."

He ran his hands down my arms and then laced his fingers through mine. "I know it's probably weird to be kissing one of your student's parents—"

I interrupted with a chuckle. "To say the least."

"But I'd really like to us to get to know each other better."

His face shifted into a mask of deep thought.

I waited patiently as he sorted through whatever it was that was tumbling through his brain. I wondered for a moment if this was how I looked when I disappeared in my own thoughts.

He turned his attention back to me as he gave my hands a reassuring squeeze. "I didn't think... After Elaine died... I miss her so much. I never thought there would be someone else—that I'd replace her." He took a ragged breath.

I brushed the back of my knuckles across his cheek, enjoying the sensation of his light whisker stubble rubbing against my skin. "I'd like to see you again."

Mark grabbed my hand and then he pressed a kiss to my fingers. "I'll walk you to your car."

"Van."

"Whatever," he said with a chuckle.

At the door to my ancient minivan, I had a hard time letting him go back to his house. My ego didn't suffer because he seemed to be having just as much difficulty in leaving. There was nothing hurried about him or his attention.

I felt the need to warn him. This could all come back to bite us both in the ass. "You know, people will talk. Carly might...hear gossip."

The grapevine in this small town rivaled the Internet in speed of transmitting information. Unfortunately, the "facts" it passed along tended to be as distorted and inaccurate as the World Wide Web could be. I could almost feel the eyes peeking through their drapes as Mark leaned against my van and tugged me back into his embrace.

Mind your own damned business! I wanted to scream at them.

"Sweet Jackie. What are we doing here? I barely know you, but I feel like I've known you forever. And you're right. I know people will talk, but I just don't give a damn," he said in that wonderful deep voice.

I touched my forehead to his. "I don't know what we're doing either,

Mark. But I'm willing to take some time to figure it out."

"Okay then."

"Okay."

"I'm heading back inside now." He still held his forehead to mine.

"I can see that," I said with a laugh. "I really should go."

He kissed me again. Not a simple peck, a slow, toe-curling, promise of making slow, passionate love to you at some later date kiss. Just like some silly romance novel.

Shit!

I'd let him in, all the way in.

CHAPTER SIX

"He *still* hasn't called?" Julie asked as we sat down to our pathetic rabbit food lunches.

I shook my head and fought back the threatening tears, knowing I would be putting very little of the carrot sticks, celery, and lettuce in my stomach. I had absolutely no appetite and even less inclination to talk, especially about Mark Brennan.

I never cried in front of other people. Patrick and Nate might have seen a tear or two. But David? *Never.*

If I cried in front of my mother, she would always tell me to suck it up and develop a spine. I learned at an early age to hide what I was feeling. Let's just say I spent a lot of my adolescence hiding in my walk-in closet with a pillow to my face just so she wouldn't hear me. I still used that tactic when I was married, preferring to conceal my hurt than display it.

I had only wept at school once. A parent called me all sorts of foul names because I refused to pass her child who'd turned in zero assignments for an entire grading period. The woman caught me right outside my classroom door a few minutes before first bell, so there was no escape. After her tirade, she was escorted from the grounds by one of my bosses, but I still had to face my first period class. I couldn't stop the tears. The students had gaped at me as if I'd lost my mind.

Kids must believe their teachers are some kind of reverse vampires. Evidently, they think we retreat to some sort of coffin during the evening and rest until the next dawn when we emerge to torture them. Running into a student at the mall always resulted in the students flashing me one of those deer-in-the-headlights looks and stammering out a greeting. At least when they waved at me in a public place, they tended to use all their fingers. They also think educators are not entirely human. Losing your temper, crying, or any other expression of real emotion leaves students confused.

I kept my emotions to myself when I was at school. Hell, I kept my emotions to myself everywhere. Yet today, I sat in the teacher's cafeteria with tears brimming my eyes.

I'd trusted a man again, and I'd been hurt. Despite what Mark had said about how he felt about me, he hadn't called in six damn weeks.

Carly seemed a little less happy every day in class, but I resisted the urge to go and talk to her. We exchanged cordial words, and we functioned fine as teacher and student. But I couldn't ask her about Mark. It would be too embarrassing, and it didn't seem fair to drag her into the middle of things.

His ignoring me—discarding me—hurt. It hurt like hell. I hadn't wanted to let it. I didn't want to face the fact that I'd let him get to me despite all my promises that I wouldn't put my heart on the line again. I'd let him in anyway. I was humiliated at how quickly I'd allowed the attachment to form.

I could have loved Mark Brennan. Then I was honest enough to admit to myself that I probably already did. And how was I rewarded for being open and honest with another man and handing him my heart on a silver platter? It was the same old shit. Mark was no better than David. They were two of a kind.

Julie looked at me with that compassionate smile she must have floated my way a hundred times during my divorce.

I knew she meant well, but I didn't want to talk about Mark, didn't want to think about Mark. I knew I'd cry.

I don't cry in front of people.

"No," I finally said in reply to her question. "He didn't call. Drop it, Julie. Please. I don't want to talk about it."

"But—"

"I don't want to talk about it!"

I shoved some salad into my mouth to give it something to do except talk about Mark Brennan and the fact that he'd gotten the better of me. The lettuce tasted like cardboard as the tears formed again.

Damn him.

"Have you tried to call him?"

If I hadn't just finished chewing my lettuce, I would have spewed it across the table at the ridiculous question. "Are you freakin' kidding me? Call him? Call *him*?"

I was practically screeching at the notion of doing something as foolish as announcing to him that he'd gotten to me. The group of male teachers who were eating at another table in the faculty lounge gaped at me. Then they elbowed each other and chuckled.

Go coach football or some other macho sport and mind your own fucking business.

"No, I'm not kidding. You're a grown-up, not some kid in junior high school. Call him. Find out what he's thinking," Julie replied before she sipped some of her diet soda.

"I know what he's thinking." I pushed the remaining salad around the plate with my plastic fork. "He's thinking some neurotic, under-sexed, middle-aged woman came on too strong and way too fast. You know, his silence speaks...*volumes*."

Julie shook her head. "You don't know what's going on in his head, Jackie. He could be...I don't know...thinking about his daughter. Maybe he was uncomfortable dating one of her teachers."

I snorted a small, sardonic laugh that made Julie glare at me. God love her, she was trying to make me feel better. I didn't have the heart to tell her nothing would make me feel better, once a discard, always a discard.

"Maybe he and I didn't click. No chemistry."

"That's not what you told me the other—"

"Well, maybe I was wrong." I was snapping at my best friend when she had done nothing to deserve it. I reined in my temper. "Maybe he didn't feel the way about me that I did about him. Please drop it. Please."

I don't want to cry in front of you.

***

The phone was ringing when I walked in the door. I got to it before the answering machine took command, not even having time to check the caller-ID. "Hello?"

"Hi, Mom."

Hearing my youngest son's voice brought me some familiar comfort and reminded me I wasn't all alone in the world. "Hi, Nate. How's school?"

I dropped my purse and briefcase on the kitchen table and kicked off my shoes.

"Fine. I hate my econ prof, but I love the rest of my classes. Patrick said he told you about Parents' Day a while back. Are you coming on Saturday?"

"Despite the fact you didn't invite me?" Mothers have a real problem not exercising their right to create guilt in their offspring. Nate had left a perfect opportunity dangling there like a ripe tomato on the vine. "Yeah, I'm coming."

Walking over to let Jellybean out of his cage, I was rewarded with a wolf whistle. I responded by ruffling the feathers on his neck the way he always enjoyed.

"Ah, Mom. I'm sorry. I'm just so busy, it slipped my mind."

"It's okay, Nate." *I've slipped a lot of men's minds lately.* "What time do you want me to be there?"

"Most of the stuff for parents doesn't start until one. But...um... Would you...maybe...come for lunch. I–I want to introduce you to my girlfriend."

I don't think I'd ever heard so much naked fear in my son's voice. Nate was in love with this girl, no doubt about it. And he was terrified I wouldn't like her.

I felt old at that moment, and if not old, at least middle-aged.

"I'd *love* to meet her," I said, hearing his breath rush out in a nervous gasp that made me smile. "What time? And which restaurant?"

"Eleven-thirty. How about The Chuckwagon? Do you remember where it is?"

I could hear the relief in his voice, and I hoped this girl was worthy of my tenderhearted son. "I remember. Is Patrick coming too?"

"Yeah. And Kat invited her dad and her sister. You don't mind, do you?"

"Kat?"

"My girlfriend. Kat."

"Ah," I replied, ridiculously nodding like a Bobble-head.

"You don't mind if her dad comes, do you?"

I shook my head, and then realized I was doing so. *Old habits die hard.* "No. No problem. Do you need anything, Nate? Money?" *Condoms?*

Having watched Nate grow up mimicking almost all of my own mannerisms, I smiled when I realized he was probably shaking his head too. "Nope. I'm good. See you Saturday, Mom. Love you."

"Love you too."

***

The Chuckwagon hadn't changed in twenty years. It was still the rundown converted warehouse just a few blocks from campus that served home cooking. The place had all the ambiance of a grocery store, but if tradition held, the servings would be huge, cheap, and delicious. I decided to skip the diet for the day.

Since neither Nate nor Patrick was outside waiting, I got out of the bright light to spare my skin a few more sun-damaged wrinkles. As I opened the door and stepped inside, I whipped off my sunglasses and came face to face with Mark and Carly Brennan.

Son of a bitch.

"Jackie? Wh–what are you doing in Bloomington?" He appeared as surprised as he sounded.

Carly just looked confused.

About a million sarcastic replies crossed my mind, and about a million more rude ones gave the sarcasm some heavy competition. They ended up canceling each other out. "I'm here to see my sons. It's Parents' Day." I shoved my sunglasses in my purse, desperately wishing life had a rewind button that could take me back several minutes so I wouldn't have to face him.

"I know. I'm here to see my oldest girl."

Shocked at the entirely crazy turn of events, I'd forgotten that his daughter had told me she was attending Indiana University. What was her name? Candy? Katie?

"Kathy!" Mark practically shouted as the young woman I recognized from OfficeMax walked in the door.

My heart almost stopped beating when my Nate followed her inside—especially when they were holding hands.

You've got to be freaking kidding me! Is Candid Camera here? Or is it America's Funniest Home Videos?

Mark's daughter and my son were a couple.

Nate dropped Kathy's hand and came over and gave me a hug. I was so shocked, I'm not even sure I hugged back. From the corner of my eye, I saw Kathy hugging Mark and then Carly before she went quickly back to Nate's side. My son took her hand and dragged her to me. For a quick and very bizarre moment, it reminded me of a cat dragging a dead mouse home for its owner's approval.

My mind raced in about a thousand different directions, none of which I could control. I was furious with Mark. I was happy for Nate while simultaneously being angry with him for picking the only girl on the enormous campus who could make me face Mark Brennan. If these two were dating, there was a distinct possibility I'd have to see him again and again.

It took every ounce of strength I had not to run out the door, jump in my car, and get the hell out of there. I was on the verge of a panic attack as my heart pounded and my stomach clenched.

Breathe, Jackie. Breathe.

I kept telling myself that I could not throw up now—not in front of Mark.

"Mom," Nate said, sounding tentative, "this is Kat Brennan."

"We've met," I replied.

My son stared at me with wide eyes.

"That's right." Kathy snapped her fingers and a smiled. "Jackie, right?"

I nodded.

Kathy glanced over at her father. "Daddy, this is Nate Ryan."

"Ah. *Ryan*, not *Delgado*. Different name," Mark said. "That's why I didn't catch the connection."

I rolled my eyes. "Way to go, Sherlock. No wonder you're a detective. I'm can't believe you even remembered my name." I muttered it sarcastically, hoping no one heard me. My stupid brain-before-mouth filter was obviously on the fritz again.

Things were already entirely too surreal when Patrick stirred up the mix by walking into the restaurant, whistling a tune. He punched his brother's upper arm as he passed, and then he hugged me. It must have felt like embracing a stiff board.

I was still ready to bolt.

Or vomit.

I hadn't decided.

"Mom? What's wrong?" Patrick pulled away, knit his brows, and stared down at me with concern clearly etched on his face. I must have looked as bad as I felt.

I tried to swallow my escalating anxiety so everyone in The Chuckwagon didn't suddenly figure out I was a damned basket case. "I–I'm fine." My mouth was full of cotton, and my hands were shaking as if I'd just guzzled my third espresso.

"Mom? Don't you feel well?" It was evidently Nate's turn to ask.

"I'm...fine. Look, Nate. I really... I mean I'd like to..."

Shit!

If I asked him whether I could just leave, Mark would know he'd won— that he'd gotten to me. If I stayed, I'd have to talk to him. Either way, I lost.

God damn it anyway.

"I really need to go back. I–I forgot to...lock the door at home. And I think I left Jellybean out of his cage."

You're a coward, Jackie Delgado.

"You're leaving?" Nate's voice held so much disappointment that it made my heart clench and my stomach roil some more. "You're really leaving?"

I nodded and tried to hold back the angry tears as I started edging a few hesitant steps toward the door.

Carly stopped me with a simple hug. Of all the surprises in the world, I don't think I could ever have been prepared for that girl throwing herself in my path and wrapping her arms around me.

"Don't leave, Ms. Delgado. Please."

I was so flabbergasted that I couldn't move, couldn't even put my arms around her and hug her back.

"I hate my dad," she said. "He's so effing stupid."

"Carly, I—"

Before I could even spit out the words, Mark gently tugged Carly's arms away from me, grabbed my elbow, and walked me right out the door. Our children all stood frozen like mannequins, watching us with dropped jaws.

Several yards away from the restaurant, Mark stopped and dropped my elbow. He opened his mouth to say something, but I beat him to the punch. "What could you possibly have to say to me that you can't say in front of our kids?"

He put his hand behind my head, pulled me to him, and settled his mouth on mine before I even had the chance to protest. For a few very long, wonderful moments I surrendered to that incredible chemistry that we seemed to have in bushel barrels. Then my badly injured pride kicked back in, keeping me from drowning in that kiss. I pushed against his chest to get away. He tried to hold on for a moment or two, but then he let go.

"Why did you do that? You...you...horse's ass! You have no right..."

"I know. I'm really sorry I didn't call, Jackie. I am."

I shook my head. "I don't want your stupid apology. Just stay the hell away from me." I started to stomp toward my car, but he clutched my upper arm.

"Don't go. Please. We need to talk."

"Screw you." I tried to jerk my arm away, but Mark wouldn't surrender it. I leveled a stare at his restraining hand. "Let me go."

He shook his obstinate head. "Not until we talk."

Patrick and Nate came charging out of the restaurant with Kathy and Carly close on their heels.

Judging from the heat shooting from his eyes like laser beams, my oldest was angry. "I don't know what in the hell is going on here," he said, "but you better let her go. Now."

Great. Just what I needed, an audience to witness my humiliation at the hands of Mark Brennan.

Damn it!

Why couldn't I have been aloof? Why couldn't I pretend for just a short time that he hadn't hurt me? Why couldn't I feign indifference to the fact that Mark had discarded me? And now, not only were my children seeing me in the role of an immature, abandoned woman, but so were his.

Damn it all anyway.

Mark stubbornly shook his head again. "Not until she hears what I have to say."

Patrick clenched his hands into fists and made a threatening move toward Mark.

"No!" I squealed as I quickly put my body between them. I might want to give Mark a sound slap upside the head, but it was clear Patrick had less subtle tactics in mind. "No, Pat. No." I turned back to Mark, desperately fighting the urge to kick him in the shins. "Fine. I'm listening. What exactly did you want to tell me about a couple of silly dates we had a couple of months ago?"

Yeah, that sounded aloof. Not.

"I'm sorry, Jackie. I really am. I... I..." He turned back to the kids who were all gaping at us like they were watching a grisly car accident.

Patrick still had his fists clenched at his sides and steam pouring out of his ears. Carly had tears in her eyes and a quivering lower lip. Kathy was clinging to Nate as if he was Leonardo DiCaprio and she was aboard the sinking Titanic. Poor Nate just looked confused.

Mark turned to stare holes in all of them. "Can we have a little privacy? Please?"

"No," Patrick replied with a very authoritarian tone in his voice. I suddenly saw my ex-husband standing there in the form of my oldest son. "*No,* you can't."

"Fine." Mark turned back to me. He seemed to take a few extraordinarily long moments to consider his words. "I needed some time, Jackie. Just some time." Looking over his shoulder at the kids, he sighed heavily. "I really wanted to tell her this in private."

"Tough shit," Patrick replied, drawing a chastising glare from me. "You can say it to Mom—you can say it to us. I'm not sure exactly what's going on here, but one thing's crystal clear. You hurt her. And I'm not stupid enough to let you hurt her again, asshole."

"Patrick David Ryan," I scolded before Mark interrupted.

"You're right, Patrick." Mark narrowed his eyes at my oldest son. "I hurt her. But that doesn't give you the right to talk to me that way." Patrick just snorted, and I started to see the cop side of Mark's personality assert itself. "Son, you're treading on dangerous ground."

I had to shake myself out of the stupor I had been in since running out of the restaurant. "Let it go, Pat. Please," I begged. Then I pointed at the restaurant. "Why don't you all go back inside? Get a table or something. We—we'll join you in a minute." I had no intention of staying. Pat opened his mouth, but I cut him off. "Go. Please, Pat. Just go."

Pat gave me a curt nod and took a couple of steps back to talk to his brother. After a short conversation, the kids retreated a safe distance to the restaurant's entrance.

"Thank you." Mark reached for my hand.

I crossed my arms over my chest to try and discourage him from touching me. I couldn't possibly talk to him if he touched me.

How had I let my feelings get so deep so quickly? Two dates shouldn't have equaled the utter devastation I felt. "I didn't do that for *you*, I did that for *my son*. I don't need you waving that badge around and getting him in trouble just because he has the balls to stand up for me when I'm too chicken-shit to stand up for myself."

I hated to hear the shrew in my voice, but despite my best efforts, I couldn't stop it. Mark would never realize how much he had hurt me—how much I had let him hurt me.

"I really am sorry, Jackie. I had, I don't know, an attack of guilt. I kept thinking about Elaine. The more I realized what I was feeling for you was so, so...strong, the more I felt like I was abandoning her. Like I was choosing you over her." His voice had fallen away to a whisper

I closed my eyes.

No. No. No.

My mind screamed at me, trying desperately to protect me.

Raise the defenses, you idiot. Don't you dare let him back in. Tell him to leave you alone.

I held my tongue.

"Yesterday, I did something I hadn't done since the funeral," he continued to explain. "I went to visit Elaine's grave. And I–I had a long talk with her."

For the love of God, don't tell me this. Please don't tell me this. You'll make me care again.

But I realized I had never *stopped* caring. Even after six weeks of silence, of hurt, of rejection, I still wanted this man. My insides were tied in enormous knots I didn't think I'd ever be able to work out.

I finally opened my eyes—in more ways than one—and looked up at Mark. The man had tears in his eyes. *Tears.* I took a long, ragged breath to hold off all I was thinking, all I was feeling. It sounded perilously like a sob.

"I–I finally let her go, Jackie. I let her go. I love Elaine. I always will." The catch in his voice made my heart hurt and made my own eyes tear up even more. "But I'm still alive. She wouldn't want..." He raked his fingers through his hair. "She wouldn't want me to mourn her for the rest of my life."

Stop Mark. Oh, please stop.

"I want to be with you, Jackie. Please, please forgive me." He put his hand over his eyes in that wonderfully masculine way men wipe tears away by pinching the bridge of their nose with their index finger and thumb. After a couple of deep and what I assumed were calming sighs, Mark said, "I was going to call you tonight. I swear to God, I was going to call you tonight."

This time, when he reached for my hand as it lay against my chest, I let him have it.

What in the hell are you thinking, Jackie?

Why couldn't I be cool, calm, and collected? He shouldn't be touching me—my shredded ego shouldn't allow it. But as he drew my hand toward him and wrapped that big strong hand of his around my fingers, I started to cry.

I don't cry in front of people!

I tried to turn my head away. He took a step to the side to follow and plant himself in my line of vision.

"I'm so sorry, Jackie. I'll make it up to you. I don't want to lose you." He kissed the back of my hand before I jerked it away and tried to wipe away my tears. I couldn't even talk because my throat was closed up. "Are you all right?" Mark asked as he cupped my cheek in his palm.

I sniffled and nodded, but I really wasn't all right. I wasn't sure I'd *ever* be all right. It was way too much high drama for one day.

Now, we had four young people staring at us, and I had not a clue as to what I should say to them. It's impossible to explain something to other people when you don't really understand it yourself. "Wh–what do we tell the kids?"

"I'll handle it. Why don't we go inside, have something to eat, and we'll just...talk to them." His hand fell away from my face. "Come on." Mark took my hand and led me toward the firing squad.

"I made an ass out of myself," I mumbled as we neared the door, my hand still in his.

"No, I made an ass out of myself. This is all *my* fault."

***

Mark and I sat opposite each other. The guy actually played footsie with me under the table. I figured it was only polite to respond. After all, I didn't want him to think I was rude. I had to remind myself several times that he had hurt me.

Funny, I was having trouble remembering that I was mad at him at all every time the toe of his shoe rubbed lightly against my shin.

Stupid perimenopause.

It had been obvious to each and every person at our Chuckwagon table that the battle lines had already been drawn.

I saw Patrick's gaze settle on Mark several times during the meal, and knowing my oldest as well as I do, he'd already decided Mark wasn't worthy of me. Those blue eyes of Pat's regarded Mark with the same smoldering, controlled anger that I saw every time David was around me. My oldest had assigned himself the role of my champion. And now he viewed Mark as a challenger who wasn't worthy, just like he viewed David as fallen from Grace.

Carly was easy to read. She had already bonded to me, even sat beside me at lunch trying to "sell" me her father by listing his assets like a salesperson trying to get me to buy a really good used car.

One owner. Low mileage. Dependable. Nice chassis.

Nate and Kathy were a little more guarded. Probably because the only thing they seemed focused on was each other. Their hands touched often, with fleeting, loving glances passing between them.

Nate talked to Mark, but Mark usually just grunted or answered him in one or two words. That was a little unnerving. Mark had always seemed chatty and friendly.

Then I suddenly understood. Mark thought Nate should quit touching his daughter. The grunts and throaty growls seemed to coincide with Nate's hand brushing Kathy's skin.

Amazing.

I imagine my father would have looked at Mark the exact same way when I was Kathy's age. Pop had stared David down a time or two. When I got pregnant with Pat, my father threatened to geld David on the spot. And I think he meant it literally. Mark was Kathy's father—it was a role he obviously decided included protecting his daughter from male attention.

Sigmund Freud would have had a field day with all of us.

Being around teens on a daily basis allowed me to come to an educated conclusion. Recognition hit me like a blow to the gut. The way Kathy and Nate acted, each tender little caress screamed the fact. They were already intimate. And they were definitely in love.

I thought back to the conversation between David and Nate that day we moved Nate into the dorm, and I hoped in earnest that Nate had heeded his father's warning and was using protection. It was the only good advice I think David ever dished out. Not that he had practiced what he preached. Patrick was conceived slightly before our wedding, and Ashley walked down the aisle bearing her wedding gift to David in her womb. I only hoped that Nate, and Patrick for that matter, had learned from their father's mistakes.

Kathy was such a pretty girl, who would obviously make a beautiful woman. I could see why Nate fell for her. Her dark eyes and gorgeous hair were the same things that had attracted me to her father. But she clearly had some reservations about her father being with me because her main topic of conversation was Elaine Brennan. Kathy talked about her mother as if the woman was sitting right next to us. I suppose, in a way, she was. Mark might have let Elaine go, but Kat obviously hadn't.

It appeared that if Mark and I were going to work this out, we'd only face a few hundred hurdles placed in our path by our offspring. Pat would be the tallest and most imposing of the obstacles. Kathy would be a close second.

Nate and Kat insisted on taking us on a walking tour of Indiana University after our somewhat tense lunch. The campus was gorgeous. Leaves of yellow, orange, and red twisted in the cool breeze. Students played Frisbee, studied in the autumn sunlight, or picnicked on the grassy hills.

Patrick and Carly led the way. He seemed to want to set a pace like an Army drill sergeant trying to work his squad into a good sweat. Carly looked at everything Pat pointed out, taking in his words like he was a tour guide. He turned around from time to time, shooting a glare at Mark as if he thought he was getting too close to me.

Kathy and Nate still held hands as they matched Pat and Carly's cadence without complaint. The two of them were so lost in each other, they might as well have been alone. They were oblivious to the beauty of the Indiana autumn and the family dynamics bursting like fireworks all around.

Mark and I followed close behind our children. His gaze met mine often, causing me to blush, shyly smile then look away. My tongue was still. It was one of the first times in my life I didn't chatter away out of nervousness. I just didn't know what to say. My heart ached for Mark to reach out and take my hand, to soothe my hurt feelings. Instead, he walked with his own hands clasped behind his back like a child trying to resist temptation. When he wasn't looking at me, his eyes drilled holes through my youngest son's back.

What an odd little group we made.

The drama before lunch and the walking tour consumed the time of the university's planned parent activities. I was greatly relieved, too drained to deal with well-meaning guidance counselors. Mark seemed just as happy to head back to our cars.

With heartfelt hugs, we bid Nate and Kathy farewell before they hiked back toward the library.

Patrick embraced me—a little longer than his usual hug—and then shook hands with Mark. The two of them eyed each other warily, the handshake taking on the appearance of the clasp wrestlers offer each other before one throws the other onto the mat.

"Call me if you need anything, even if you just want to talk," Pat said with a strange parental tone in his voice.

I simply nodded in response.

"Dad, can I...um...go get a soda for the trip?" Carly pointed to a soft drink machine standing right outside the small convenience store that bordered our parking lot.

I realized she was trying to give Mark and me a moment alone, something we both desperately needed.

Thank you, Carly.

He fished his wallet from his pocket and pulled out a couple of dollar bills. "Please get me a Coke," he said as she took the bills and headed away from us at a leisurely pace.

Crossing his arms over his broad chest, he leaned against the front fender of my red monster of a minivan. Not knowing what to do with my anxious hands, I followed suit, kneading my upper arms with my fingers.

"I'm really sorry, Jackie. I hope you believe that."

"I believe you, Mark." How could I not? No man could ever come up with such a heart-wrenching story just to placate the feelings of some woman he forgot to call or didn't really want to see again. "But I just don't know where we go from—"

He didn't even give me a chance to finish the sentence. In a cat-like motion, he whipped around to press his body against mine before he settled those heavenly lips against my mouth. I was too shocked at first to even kiss him back.

Then that chemistry kicked in—that chemistry that, no matter what he had or hadn't done, found me molding myself to him. When he kissed me, there was nothing between us. There was no late wife, no disapproving children, no hesitation. Just heat—pure white heat.

As I looped my arms around his neck, he let a little growl rumble in the back of his throat. The sound instantly sent desire racing through me. His tongue rubbing against mine felt wonderful. His whiskers teasing my face felt like heaven. His embrace felt like home.

Somewhere in the back of the scramble he was making of my wits, I sensed people staring at us as they passed. Knowing we were making a spectacle of ourselves was enough to cool the blaze, at least a little of the blaze.

Mark must have felt my reticence. He eased back and stared into my eyes.

"How about I come over to your place later? We can...watch a movie or–

or just talk." His eyes searched mine. When I didn't immediately reply, he frowned. "Jackie? Will you let me come over later?"

So, now what?

Are you going to let him come over, Jackie?

Are you going to let him back in?

Are you going to let yourself get hurt again?

"Yes." *To all of the above.*

CHAPTER SEVEN

I puttered around the house, straightening up things I had already straightened at least four times. Not that the house had even needed it. No boys, no mess. An empty nest was a clean nest.

Mark Brennan was coming to my house.

A new man was going to be in *my* house.

He'd called after he was back from Bloomington to ask how I was. The fact he was being so solicitous soothed some of my lingering hurt, and I knew when he asked if he could come over to talk there was an enormous danger that we wouldn't be *talking* much.

Was I ready for that kind of step?

Just hours ago I loathed the man.

Well, not loathed exactly. But I had been mighty pissed.

There's a thin line between love and hate after all.

What I needed was to talk to him, to really talk to him about important things—things people spend their lives avoiding discussing. I needed to make him understand. Mark might have come to terms with losing his wife, but I wasn't sure *I* had. The lunch we'd shared with our kids had opened my eyes to many things. One of those realizations was that I was insanely jealous of a dead woman.

Mark, Kathy, and Carly all talked about Elaine as if she'd been a saint. She'd been the perfect wife, the perfect mother, and the perfect person. A good person dead before her time.

The first week after our dates—when Mark's silence had been deafening—I let my rampant curiosity drown me. I had called a friend from college who teaches at Kathy's old high school to see if she knew anything about Elaine. It was immature, but not knowing anything about her, the de facto competition, gnawed at me.

My friend had an awful lot to say. Elaine had volunteered at a local hospital. She'd been the president of the Parent Teacher Association. She'd taken in retired greyhounds to foster before they were given to a permanent home. She'd taught Sunday school, even when she'd lost all her hair because of chemotherapy.

The woman taught freakin' Sunday school!

And what about me? How did I compare to Saint Elaine Brennan?

My husband had left me because I wasn't pretty enough, or thin enough, or young enough. He'd knocked up his secretary for pity's sake.

I stayed in my jammies until noon almost every Sunday instead of going to church. Catholics tend to frown on divorce, and although I hadn't been the one at fault, I still felt the weight of the stares whenever I was brave enough to take communion. I had slowly become a Christmas-Easter church-goer.

I gagged whenever I went into hospitals because I couldn't stand the disinfectant smell. It goes back to my childhood when I had my tonsils out. The smell made me think of pain. I didn't even stay a full twenty-four hours after either of my boys' births because I had to get the hell out of there.

The only pet I owned loved his mirror more than he loved me, judging from the amount of time Jellybean spent rubbing up against it.

Doesn't help that I'm allergic to most dog dander.

In other words, I was absolutely nothing like Elaine Brennan.

What in the hell could Mark possibly see in someone like me? He'd probably view me as a step down in the world. The insecurity was racing through my every thought, pushing aside any self-esteem I might have mustered in the last few years.

Tears threatened, but I sniffed them back. I grabbed a pillow off the couch, fluffed it a little too roughly to release some tension, and then threw it back at the sofa.

Somehow, we had made it through that agonizing lunch, but everyone had spent an inordinate amount of time staring at me.

Why? It was because I was quiet. I was never quiet. But as Mark and his girls talked about nothing in general, Elaine came up too often to make me comfortable, especially when Kathy had something to say. All I got out of the conversation was an inferiority complex.

I'd let my stupid mind wander, and it had begun to form the idea that I was just a replacement for Saint Elaine, a poor man's substitute.

Damn it.

Why had I agreed to let Mark come over? Was it to humiliate myself a little more?

The doorbell set Jellybean to screeching and flying around the room. I really needed to clip his wings.

"Coming!" I chased the silly cockatiel to the draperies.

After he landed on the curtain rod, I stood on my tiptoes, shoved my finger to his chest, and got him to perch on my hand. I carried him to his cage, let him hop inside, and shut the door.

The doorbell rang again. Jellybean screeched a little more, but at least I didn't have to chase him again. "I'm coming!"

I was a bit breathless when I opened the door, and not simply because I had to catch my wayward bird. It had to be Mark ringing my doorbell, and my heart was pounding just knowing I was going to see him again.

I smoothed my hand over my wild hair, resigned myself to the notion that I probably looked terrible, and answered the door.

David stood there with his finger ready to press the doorbell again.

Son of a bitch.

"Well? Are you going to let me in?" he asked in that old husbandly tone he used whenever he was annoyed with me.

I'd heard it way too often when I was married to him. I sure didn't think I should have to listen to it now that I wasn't. "Why?"

"I need to talk to you." He pushed his way inside.

"Gee. Come right in," I mumbled to his back.

He headed from the foyer to the kitchen.

I stuck my head outside, gave a quick glance around to see if Mark's car was on the street, and then I shut the door. "What do you want?" I joined David where he leaned against the counter with his arms folded sternly over his chest.

"Patrick called me. What's going on, Jackie?"

"Pat called you? Why on earth would he call *you?*"

"He said some guy was taking advantage of you. Damn it, Jackie. Why would you bring some bozo you dated down there to meet the boys?"

What in the hell was my oldest thinking? That his father would "rescue" me from the evil clutches on Mark Brennan? Knowing the animosity Pat nurtured for his father, he must have really hated Mark to think David was a better choice.

How could Pat possibly believe my ex-husband needed to hear about any of this?

"First, I don't see how anything I do is any business of yours, and—"

"Damn it, Jackie," David interrupted using his favorite phrase.

"Don't interrupt me!" I had grown heartily tired of the fact the man had never listened to a single thing I had ever said in the twenty-odd years I'd known him. Well, he was damn well going to listen now! "Second, I didn't take him to meet the boys. He was there when I got there. But if I had, it *still* wouldn't be any of your business."

He narrowed his eyes, getting ready to scold me.

Screw that. "You can leave now," I insisted. "I'm expecting company."

His eyes shot fire, and that surprised the crap out of me. "*Another* guy? Jesus, Jackie. Are you that desperate? *Two* guys in one day?"

"Yeah, two guys in one day. *Three* if you count the sadomasochist I have coming over at midnight. I need to find my leather corset and my barbed whip, so you can go *now*." I took a couple of steps toward the foyer.

David grabbed my arm. "I'm sorry. I didn't really mean that. I'm just... Pat sounded concerned. He said this guy hurt you. If you didn't take him to meet the boys, why was he in Bloomington?"

It took me a moment to decide just how much of the sad little tale I needed to share with him. "His daughter's dating Nate, and he wanted me to meet her. I guess she wanted Nate to meet her dad."

"Then how did you hook up with him?"

"His other daughter is one of my freshmen." I immediately wished I'd have censored that bit of information when I saw his condescending frown.

"You went out with a student's father? That's pretty stupid. Is the guy married? Damn it, Jackie. You could lose your job carrying on like that. Didn't you even think about that?"

"You've obviously mistaken me for Ashley. You know, your *current* wife—the one who slept with you while you were still married to me." I wanted to slap him. Instead I just fisted my hands at my side. "Not every man screws around on his spouse."

His nostrils flared at that statement.

Good. *Hope I hit a nerve, loverboy.*

"He's a widower. Not that you really need to know any of this. Is the Spanish Inquisition over now? I told you, I've got comp—" The doorbell interrupted me.

Shit.

Now what did I do?

I wanted to give David the bum's rush out the back, but he went charging to the foyer and to the front door. He *ran* to get there first.

Flinging it open, he gaped at Mark who glared right back. I felt like a boxing referee before a match and thought about telling them to go back to their corners and then come out swinging.

"And you are?" David asked with such a rude, snide tone I seriously considered kicking him in the shin.

Mark gave David a quick head to toe appraisal and obviously figured out who he was. He was a detective, after all.

He held out his hand.

David ignored it, refusing to even offer a polite handshake.

"I'm Mark Brennan. Judging from that gray hair, you must be Jackie's father. Nice to meet you, sir."

I snorted a loud laugh, and David turned to glare at me. I had to put my fingers to my lips to keep from laughing again. After a long moment to regain my composure, I decided to intervene. "David, this is Mark Brennan. Mark, this is my ex—"

"I'm her husband. Name's David Ryan." He still didn't shake Mark's hand.

Mark withdrew his as he folded his arms over his chest. Those handsome brown eyes grew stormy.

"Ex. My *ex*-husband," I snapped, hoping Mark wasn't reading more into the situation than there really was. It wasn't like I'd invited David over.

Boy, was I going to have a word or two with Pat later for getting me in the middle of this nonsense.

"Jackie, are you ready? I thought we'd go out," Mark said without taking his eyes off David. "Especially since your house is so...crowded."

"Jackie, you're going out with this clown?" David jerked his thumb at Mark.

"Jackie, did you invite—" Mark started to say.

"Damn it, Jackie," David interrupted.

"Enough!" I yelled, feeling like I was some bizarre prize in a macho tug-of-war. "I know my own name, so you can both stop shouting it at me." I tried to salvage what little dignity I had left. "David, I appreciate your concern, but it's time for you to go home. You know, back to your wife and son."

I ignored his threatening expression as he stared at me for a moment then stomped out the front door, shoving past Mark, and getting in his Hummer to drive away.

"You were married to...*that?*" Mark shook his head. "Nice car, though. Big. Makes up for his tiny little—"

"Mark!" I tried not to giggle too much.

He stepped into the house, and I shut the door behind him.

The awkward quiet ate at me. Whenever I'm this nervous, I tend to ramble. And right now I was in danger of making a total ass of myself if I said even a single word because a million others would spill out in a flood after it.

"How about we have a seat? Maybe on the couch?" Mark smiled at me with those gorgeous lips. "You do sit, don't you?"

I smiled back. "Yeah, I sit. Come on in. Want something to drink?"

"I need a scotch, but I'll settle for some tea. If it's not too much trouble." He made himself comfortable on my sofa.

"No trouble. Just give me a minute."

He sprang to his feet. "I'll give you a hand." He followed me into the kitchen.

I could have talked to him quite fine if he had stayed on the couch. Now, I was in danger again. He was too close. I could smell him, that wonderful mixture of Mark and Polo Black that made me light-headed. I tried to concentrate on mixing a pitcher of iced tea.

"What can I do?" he asked as I bent over to grab a glass carafe instead of my dollar-store plastic pitcher. I wanted to at least look semi-classy.

The stupid thing was wedged behind the iron that I never used. The moment my hand grasped it, I felt a caress on my back. I popped up, hitting my head on the cabinet. "Ow," I groaned, putting the carafe on the counter and rubbing the top of my head.

"Sorry." Mark had that naughty boy twinkle in his eye. "Didn't mean to startle you."

I opened one of the upper cupboards and found the instant tea.

His hand was on me again, rubbing circles from my shoulder blades to the small of my back. He was making it impossible to do something as simple as measure a couple of tablespoons of powder into the carafe. Because of Mark's touch, I was turning into a dimwit.

I hadn't felt this rattled since the junior high school dance when Pete McKinnon had slipped his hand under my arm to brush my boob.

When Mark's hand slid up to my neck, I spilled the spoonful of instant mix on the counter. "Shit."

I tried to reach past Mark to get the wet dishcloth that was hanging over the faucet. He must have realized my train of thought because he picked it up and handed it to me.

"Thanks," I mumbled, feeling clumsy and awkward.

I actually managed to make the tea without any other significant problems. When his fingers weren't touching me, his eyes smoldered enough to have the same disconcerting effect. I poured two glasses, added some sweetener to mine, and offered some pink packets to him. He declined, picked up both the glasses, and led me to the sofa. I flopped a couple of coasters on the coffee table, and he set the drinks down. Then I ran out of things to keep my hands busy.

Mark sat on the sofa and reached up for my hand. I let him tug me down next to him, thigh to thigh. Jeans and all, I could feel the heat of him against me, could feel every inch of where we touched.

Scooting a little farther away, I turned and put a bent knee between us. "Um... I think we should talk."

He sighed before he moved to face me, put his arm over mine where it rested on the back of the couch, and let his fingers stroke mine. "I still owe you an apology."

"For?" It probably wasn't wise to allow his caresses because they were horribly distracting and this was supposed to be a sober conversation about—

Shit. What were we talking about?

"For letting you believe that I didn't care."

Ah ha! We were talking about him not calling. I had trouble forming a coherent thought when Mark touched me. "Yeah, well...I'm over it."

"No. You're not." His hand covered mine. Warm, slightly calloused, and all male.

"I'm not?"

"No, you're not. I need to make it up to you. How about dinner next weekend?" Those warm fingers wrapped around my hand, making me feel comforted. And horribly giddy.

"That would be nice. It's Fall Break. I'm off on Thursday and Friday." Two days of sleep and peace, and now dinner with Mark Brennan. What more could a thirty-twelve-year old woman ask?

How about some hot, sweaty sex? my stupid and entirely immature thoughts suggested.

"Not yet," I said before realizing I was speaking aloud.

"Not yet what?" Mark scooted even closer.

"Never mind," I replied, feeling entirely stupid.

Pulling my hand away, I moved forward and reached for my tea. Perhaps a few sips of a cold drink would settle my scattered nerves.

I sat on the edge of the sofa, nursing my tea. Mark faced forward again and grabbed his own glass. We just sat there sipping iced tea, and I wondered if he felt as uncomfortable as I did.

"I'm really sorry, Jackie."

I nodded, not sure what to say.

Mark set his tea back on his coaster. Then he turned back to me and grabbed both my hands to pull me to face him. "I'm sorry."

"I know. I forgive you."

Good heavens, this man could sure change my perception of reality. In slow motion, he sat back, pushed a hand under my knees, and lifted me onto his lap. He cupped my face with his palms and stared into my eyes. "Do you? Do you really forgive me? Because I almost made the worst mistake of my life." He closed his eyes for a moment and rested his forehead against mine. When he opened his eyes and pulled back, I could see his pain. "I can't believe I almost let you go."

"I really forgive you."

Mark touched his lips to mine. It was such a gentle kiss, so incredibly tender it brought tears to my eyes.

"Thank you," he whispered as he ended the kiss and rested his forehead against mine again. "I'll make it up to you."

I couldn't leave it at that, not with him thinking I was going to hold this over his head. "No need."

He kissed me again, a little longer, a little deeper. I felt like my blood had turned to liquid heat. This time, when he eased away, I groaned in frustration.

Tired of being the passive player, I gave in for once to what I really wanted. I flipped to straddle him, put my hands to his face, and kissed him. The sexy growl he uttered when he opened his mouth to my insistent tongue sent fire straight to my core.

It had been far too long without feeling wanted, too long without that delicious visceral sensation of anticipation, too long without making love— *really* making love. I snaked my arms around his neck and leaned into the kiss.

No bells ringing in my head this time—at least no warning bells. There were, however, lots and lots of fireworks. Lights exploded in my brain. My heart pounded, begging for more. Sanity fled in a wash of warmth and primitive desire. My body screamed for him in a way I had never felt before, not even when David had actually taken the time to coax my response.

The kiss ended as we panted to breathe.

"God, Babe," he whispered in my ear as he stroked my back. "I want you. I want to pick you up, carry you to your bed, and make love to you all night." His hands settled on my hips, and he rocked his body up, leaving no question how much he meant what he said. The guy was hard as a rock, and I felt a luscious thrill knowing I had pulled that response from his body.

But my pride began to buzz at me like some annoying insect, prompted by years of strict Catholic upbringing. It might have been too *long*, but it was also too *soon*. "I want you too. I really do, but..."

He groaned. "But..."

"I'm not ready yet. I'm sorry, Mark. I am. This is all happening so—"

"Fast. I know, I know. But..."

He rocked his hips again, and the motion sent tremors ripping through me. If he did that again, I wasn't sure I would be able to hold to my conviction.

"Do you like to hike?" he asked.

"I beg your pardon?"

"Do you like to hike? To fish?" he asked with mischief clearly written all over his face.

"I love to hike. Fishing, sorry. Not my thing." I waited to see what Mark had cooked up in that noggin of his.

"I have a really nice cabin in Munising, Michigan. It's close to Hiawatha National Forest. Carly and I were heading up there for the break from school. I'd forgotten it was Fall Break this coming weekend." He kissed my cheek. "Thanks for the reminder. We'll have that dinner you agreed to at the cabin."

"They say memory is the first thing to go when you get older."

He shot me an irritated frown before he smiled with those incredibly white teeth. "My memory's fine, thank you. Will you come with us to Michigan?"

"Really? You want me to go?"

"Yes, I want you to go. Why is that so hard to believe?"

I dismissed the notion with a wave of my hand.

He cupped my face with his hands. "Jackie, you're incredible. You're beautiful. You're sexy. You're smart. You're funny. How can you not know that?"

He almost made me believe him. "Thank you."

"If you don't believe what I'm saying, I have other ways to convince you." A sexy wink.

I decided it was time to move out of this entirely unladylike position. "I could really use some ice cream. You up for Dairy Queen?"

"I'm *up* for you." He wiggled those gorgeous dark eyebrows.

Heavens, could I possibly blush any more than I already was? "I was thinking more about a banana split."

Yeah, that was smart, Jackie. Why don't you just set the innuendo opportunity up on a tee next time?

"I'll let that one slide."

"Thank you. That's very gentlemanly of you." I picked up the glasses, walked to the kitchen, and set them down by the sink. I fished my key chain out of my purse and jingled it. "You coming?"

Why did everything that came out of my mouth sound so dirty?

Mark snorted a laugh. "Not tonight—but I hope I don't have to wait too long." He came to stand by my side, put his index finger to my cheek, and made a noise that sounded like hamburger being seared on a grill. "Face a little warm? Let's get some ice cream. It ought to cool you down."

"Maybe it'll cool you down too." *Take that, Mr. Double Entendre.*

"Doubt it. Especially if you're around."

The man did wonders for my self-esteem.

He picked up my purse and slung it over my shoulder. "Will you go with us? Please?"

I nodded. "Sounds like fun. When do we leave?"

"Thursday morning. Bring your fishing pole."

I groaned as I led him to my garage.

CHAPTER EIGHT

I stumbled across the bedroom grabbing for my robe and mumbling to myself.

It's one in the morning. Who's ringing the stupid doorbell at one in the morning?

Rubbing the sleep from my eyes, I followed the strategically placed nightlights as if they were airport runway lights to the front door. The doorbell hadn't stopped ringing.

"Hold your horses. I'm coming." Pulling aside the curtain, I looked out the transom. "David?"

For a second, I considered not opening the door. There was no good reason for my ex-husband to be spastically ringing my doorbell at such a ridiculous hour.

Then I sighed in resignation. He was still the father of my kids, and I couldn't leave him just standing there on my doorstep. Flipping the deadbolt, I jerked the door open. I smelled the alcohol before he even walked in the house. The odor surrounded him like a thick cloud.

"Phew." I fanned my face. "I sure hope you weren't driving."

"Took a cab." His slurred words.

"I suppose I have to pay for it."

"I paid." His brows knit in thought. "I leasht I think I paid. Geesh, Jackie. I can't remember. Can you take care of it?" He had evidently pickled his short-term memory.

With a disgusted huff, I leaned my head out the door. No disgruntled cabbie was waiting, so I assumed David had taken care of that detail. I shut the door and locked it mostly out a habit. I'd be unlocking it to let him out as soon as I called Ashley to come get her Romeo.

"Why are you here?" I asked.

He stumbled into the great room and sprawled out on my couch, staring at the ceiling. "I need to talk to you."

"At one in the morning? What could you possibly need to talk to me about that couldn't wait until a decent hour?" I sniffed the air again and wrinkled my nose. "And why would you need to talk to me about it while you're drunk?"

"I'm leaving Ashley."

So... There was trouble with wife number two. Morbid curiosity was definitely getting the better of me, but I pushed it aside. Deep down I supposed I would always believe that marriage was supposed to be a lasting union. Even if most people—translate, everyone—had predicted a rocky road to happily ever after, the fact that David and Miss Hamilton County Fair were having problems was really kind of sad.

I arched an eyebrow. "That's my problem because?"

"She hates you," he drawled as he rolled from his back to his side and pushed himself to a semi-upright position. "Shesh jealous of you."

"You're drunk. You've got no idea what you're saying."

I took a couple of steps toward the phone, thinking the ex was delirious.

Ashley is jealous of me?

That was the most ridiculous thing I'd ever heard.

I grabbed the handset and began to punch numbers. "I'm calling your wife to come get you."

For somebody so drunk, he moved awfully fast. He snatched the phone from my hands, clicked it off, and then threw it on the sofa. "I don't wantcha to call...*her.*"

I glared at him, growing angrier by the second. "Just because you and Ashley are fighting doesn't mean I'm the Holiday Inn. Go home, David. I'll call your wife, or I'll call a cab. Doesn't matter to me which."

"She hates you."

"The feeling is mutual."

"She knows I schtill love you." He took a couple of awkward steps toward me.

I had to fight the uncomfortable urge to take a step back. "You're drunk." *And you're entirely full of shit.*

David was close enough to run a wobbly hand down my arm. That used to be the extent of foreplay the last year or so of our marriage. "Jackie...I made a big mischtake."

I swatted his hand away, thinking how utterly absurd this whole situation was. When David had come home and announced that he had knocked up Ashley and "owed it to her and the baby" to marry her, I'd harbored all sorts of elaborate fantasies. I'd even admit to some of them involving David's violent and bloody mutilation, but the most frequent storyline was a version of exactly what was happening now.

Well, not *exactly.* He wasn't drunk as a skunk in my musings.

He would come back, preferably crawling on hands and knees, to tell me he'd been horribly wrong. He didn't want infantile Ashley and her perky boobs and flat stomach. He still wanted me—just good ole me. I would welcome him back with open arms. We would have sex that, for once, was satisfying enough I didn't have to fake an orgasm. Then we'd live happily ever after.

They had been comforting fantasies meant to salvage my shredded self-esteem for being pushed aside for a younger, prettier woman. But that was all those thoughts had ever really been. Fantasies. Because I had to live in the real world where Ashley had married David and had given him a son, fantasies were all they could be.

After the first few months, those silly fantasies faded. *Don't get me wrong. I still wanted the man hobbled and brought to his knees.* Doesn't any woman who feels discarded ultimately wish all sorts of bad karma for the guy who threw her away?

But it didn't take long to realize I was happier without David than I'd ever been with him, and the dreams no longer involved him coming back. They mostly revolved around winning the lottery and rubbing his nose in it.

I might have been sleeping alone every night, and I might have missed being in love—but I'd come to recognize that a one-sided relationship wasn't really a relationship. David might have loved me in his own warped way, but he wasn't *in love* with me. If he had been, Ashley would never have been the irresistible temptation that she was.

A part of me would always love David Ryan, and a part of me would always hate him.

But not a single part of me wanted him back.

"C'mon, schweetheart." He reached for me again. "I mished you so much. Ashley doesn't get me."

"David, I don't think you should be telling me about your wife." I moved around him, got to the sofa, and bent over trying to reach the phone.

He grabbed my shoulders, spun me around, and tackled me to the couch. The stupid cordless was pressing hard into my back, David's sour alcohol breath was in my face, and it took all my self-control not to bring my knee up hard into his groin. "Get off me!"

"Jackie, I've mished you so much." He tried to kiss me.

I turned my head fast enough so all he got was a cheek, which he proceeded to slobber on. "David, so help me... If you don't get off me..." I squirmed and thrashed, trying to throw him.

My ex started to sob. He rolled off me and landed on the floor. Well, partly on the floor and partly on the coffee table. It sure didn't look very comfortable, and he was still crying.

"For the love of..." I sat up and tugged at his arm. "Get up here and sit down."

He slowly worked his way up to sit on the couch, still weeping. "What am I gonna do? Ashley doeshn't love me anymore. I think shesh got a boyfriend."

"Who do I look like? Dr. Phil?" With a heavy sigh, I patted the hands he had clenched in his lap. "Let's go in the kitchen. I'll make a pot of coffee, and we can talk."

***

"Feeling any better?" I asked after David had finished his third cup of coffee.

My ex shrugged from his chair on the opposite side of my small kitchen table. I could tell he was sobering because he was reverting to his normal stoic personality. I could also tell he was embarrassed at the little dog and pony show he'd put on in the other room.

"Do you want to talk about it now?"

"Ashley doesn't understand me." He nervously shifted his coffee cup between his hands.

"Isn't that cliché? Boo hoo. My wife doesn't understand me."

He just glared at me, his usual response to my chastising sarcasm. "I swear, Jackie, the woman's downright stupid. She's not like you at all."

I tried not to smile, but my ego needed to know I possessed some quality that disgustingly perfect Ashley didn't. "Stupid?"

He nodded. Enthusiastically. "We were watching *Seinfeld* re-runs, and she didn't even know what they were making fun of. Remember that episode where the baseball player spits on Kramer and they slow it down like the Zapruder film where Kennedy got shot?"

"Duh."

"Sorry. Forgot you were named for Jackie Kennedy. But do you see what I mean? She didn't even know anything about the grassy knoll or the single bullet." His heavy sigh floated in the air. "She doesn't get *anything* I talk about. She hates my music. She hates my TV shows. She hates that I'm...losing my hair." He sighed again as he splayed his fingers through his salt and pepper hair.

It *was* getting a bit sparse in places. I tried not to smile.

"What exactly did you expect? She's twenty years younger than you." I neglected to add that she was only one year older than Patrick, no longer feeling the need to rub salt in David's wounds. The poor guy was suffering enough.

"I'm tired of people asking if Duncan is my grandson."

I snorted a small laugh before I could catch myself, so I pretended to cough into my fist to try to spare his feelings. "What do you want me to say?"

How about, "Teaches you for screwing around with a younger woman?"

"I miss you, Jackie. I miss our talks. I miss that we share the same memories. I miss that I didn't have to... you know...show off for you in bed. You understood me." He put his hand over mine where it rested on the table.

I pulled my hand back and stared at him. "We didn't *talk*, we *fought*. You don't miss me." *And I don't miss you.*

"But I do. Shit, Jackie, we grew up together. You've always just...been there—almost as long as I can remember. It's hard without you taking care of me." I could tell he was uncomfortable because he got up and poured himself another cup of coffee. He sure didn't need it. His hands were already shaking.

"David..."

"I'm having trouble getting by without you." The chair made a scraping noise on the tile as he took a seat again. "You always knew where stuff was. You always paid the bills on time. You didn't go on shopping sprees for ridiculous stuff like couch purses."

"They're Coach purses, and Ashley just turned twenty-three. Give her a chance. Have you ever even shown her how to balance a checkbook? Have you ever helped her make a budget?"

He shook his head. "I didn't have to show you how to do any of that. She's home with Duncan all damn day and the place is still a mess. I trip over toys, clothes, and–and–*stuff*." David's gaze wandered the kitchen and the great room. "Look how nice this place is."

"Not everyone is as anal retentive as me. And I recall you bitching an awful lot about how messy the house was all the time when the boys were little. Chasing after a growing boy is exhausting. I'm sure she'll get to be better with practice."

He might be nostalgic, but my trip down memory lane was only reinforcing what I had thought earlier. Our marriage had never been paradise.

The house had been livable, but messy. I had paid my share of bills late, trying to juggle way too little money and way too much debt. But through hard work, we'd muddled our way through and lived to tell the tale. That remarkable accomplishment, however, did *not* make a good marriage.

Once the kids hit high school, David and I had already realized we had absolutely nothing in common except for Patrick and Nathaniel. For the last couple of years, I think the marriage limped along like a wounded animal. We had stayed together simply out of force of habit. Neither of us wanted to be the one to admit defeat and take the blame. David's affair wasn't what doomed our marriage. It was just the catalyst that finally forced us to admit the marriage was over.

I was happier now. I had my friends. I had my job. I had my boys. I read to my heart's content. I fiddled with writing books in my spare time, goofy little mystery novels I was sure no one would ever read. Once I'd gotten past the empty nest blues, I enjoyed my life.

I was happier now, even if I was alone.

You're not alone, Jackie. You've got Mark now.

But even if I didn't, I was still better off. I didn't need a man to make my life valuable.

Good God, somewhere in the last couple of years, I'd developed something akin to self-worth. For the first time in my life, I was comfortable in my own skin.

I smiled at the new and incredibly surprising thought.

"You've never even slept with anyone but me, right?" David pulled me back from my thoughts. "*Right?*" he demanded when I didn't immediately reply.

"That's none of your business."

"I knew it," he said with a firm nod. "You've never been with anyone but me. Who's this new guy? Mike?"

I smirked because I knew damn well David knew Mark's name. "He's a friend."

"I don't want you to sleep with him. I–I want you back."

"Bullshit." I wished Ashley would miraculously show up and take her husband home. "I'm a toy you didn't want anymore, but now you don't want anybody else to play with it, either."

"But I love you," he insisted.

"You're the father of my boys. We share a history. I love you too. *But,*" I added when he began to smile, "I'm not in love with you anymore."

Each and every word was true. I had really moved on.

***

I didn't crawl back into my bed until almost three. I sat staring at the clock for a long time, scolding myself for drinking anything with caffeine. But that wasn't the only reason I was still awake. The minutes clicked by slowly, but sleep simply wouldn't find me because I couldn't find the "off" switch for my brain.

I thought about David—about everything he'd said—and the only real emotion I could muster was pity. The man had made an awful lot of mistakes in his life, and I was sure he'd make plenty more. But he was Ashley's problem now.

Thank God.

I thought about Nate and Kathy and wondered how awkward it would be for them if they broke up while Mark and I stayed a couple. Or worse—how awkward it would be if Mark and I didn't stay together while they still went out?

I hated that thought. My mind took a side route as I hoped to hell Nate and Kathy were smart enough to use reliable birth control. I sure didn't want my son having to get married at nineteen like I had.

And I thought about Mark. I thought an awful lot about Mark. Where were we going to go from here?

I never found any answers.

***

Damn doorbell.

The annoying sound seeped into my exhausted brain. I couldn't tell if it was real or just a dream. It rang again. I groaned and rolled over to look at the clock.

7:55 AM.

Fuck that.

I pulled the covers over my head, planning on finding a screwdriver later and removing the stupid doorbell permanently. If that didn't work, I'd find a hammer that would do the job quite well.

The stupid thing rang yet again.

I threw the covers off, mumbled a very unladylike word that I hear from the students on a daily basis in the school hallways, and groped for my robe.

I could hear David stirring in the living room, so I figured I'd find out what the stupid paperboy wanted, brew a pot of strong coffee, and call my ex a cab. He wasn't sleeping on my couch again. He probably had a hell of a hangover.

For some odd reason that thought made me smile.

David's voice was muffled as I went to open my bedroom door. I didn't realize he was talking to Mark until I heard Mark shouting.

"Oh, no!" I sprinted for the front door.

"I told you," David insisted in a scolding voice, "I stayed here last night. Jackie asked me to spend the night with her." He was standing there in nothing but a gray t-shirt, his tightie-whities, and blue socks.

It wasn't a pretty picture.

"*What?*" I screeched as I reached the foyer.

Mark's gaze caught mine, and I could see the naked anger. He was squeezing a small bouquet of pink carnations hard enough the stems were bent.

"Mark, I didn't—"

"Didn't what?" Mark shouted. "Didn't sleep with your ex after you told me you wanted to wait?"

"I knew you hadn't slept with him." David's smug smile made me want to hit him upside the head.

Sweet heavens, what kind of show were we putting on for the nosy neighbors? I could feel their gazes, their stares, and their condemnation.

Get a life.

I needed to soothe Mark. "I didn't sleep—"

"Bullshit." Mark inclined his head at David. "Like he'd lie about *that.* Admit it. You spent the night with him."

Now I was getting angry too. If Mark didn't trust me any more than that, no amount of explanation was going to make him suddenly have faith in me. I should've told him David slept on the couch, but the stupid, sarcastic Jackie came out to interfere before I could wrestle her down.

I gave my eyes an exaggerated roll. "Fine. I spent the night with him."

Mark's free hand was clenched into a fist, and the hand holding the bouquet snapped what remained of it apart. Broken carnations littered my front porch. Then he tightened that hand into a fist as well. I wondered if he was going to punch something. Or *someone.* About the time I was going to make another sarcastic response, something hit me like a heavyweight's punch.

Mark was jealous. The reason he was ranting and raving was because he was jealous of David.

I tried not to laugh in relief, but a chuckle slipped out anyway. He cared for me. Mark Brennan really cared for me.

"What's so funny?" my ex-husband asked, looking horribly annoyed.

"You."

"Me? What the hell do you mean?"

"Have you seen yourself in a mirror?" I decided to ignore David and turned back to the man I wanted, the man whose feelings I actually cared about. "Mark, I'm sorry I got so sarcastic. David was here last night, but he slept on the couch. Seems he and his *wife*—" I stressed the word at my ex-husband, "—are having some marital problems, and he decided to solve them by getting drunk and crying on my shoulder because he didn't have anyplace else to go. I didn't have the heart to kick him to the curb."

David threw me a nasty glare, but he just didn't faze me anymore. I almost giggled at the notion of my newfound independence. I was past letting him get to me.

It was a very liberating concept. What I *did* care about was Mark and soothing his hurt feelings.

The tension in Mark's face had waned, and there was relief in his brown eyes that warmed my heart.

"Why don't you come in?" I asked. "I can make some coffee and cook you an omelet or something." He stared down at the pile of carnations. "Don't sweat it. I'll clean it up later. It was a thoughtful gesture." Turning back to David, I added, "You can call Ashley to come get you."

"I don't get an omelet?" David asked in the tone of a pouting three-year-old.

I just figured he'd been spending too much time around Duncan. "Nope. If you want one, have Ashley cook it."

CHAPTER NINE

"Take some condoms," Julie said before she finished the last of her fast-food dinner.

We only had an hour between the end of the school day with the students and the beginning of parent-teacher conferences that would last until nine o'clock, so Julie and I hit the local Mickey D's and avoided eating healthy for once. We considered the late lunch our just reward for what would be an exhaustingly long day. It had been years since I had a Big Mac, and I was savoring every bite.

At least I was until Julie spit out those three scary words of advice.

"I can't do that," I replied. "It would make it look like—"

"Like you're a grown-up who doesn't want to get pregnant at forty-two or catch a venereal disease," Julie calmly replied, dispensing advice that sounded reasonable and ridiculous at the same time.

"They don't call them venereal diseases anymore. They're sexually transmitted diseases. And I doubt if Mark has any STDs. He was married, for God's sake."

"But you don't know for sure if he fooled around or if he had lovers after she died. It's not just simple stuff now, Jackie. Not like the old days when all you'd need was some penicillin to get over it. There's AIDS. Herpes." Julie calmly gathered her trash.

"Mark doesn't have AIDS or herpes, and I can't get pregnant. I'm on the pill."

Julie shot me a worried glare. "You went on the pill because of him?"

"Hardly, although I might've if I'd needed to. They keep my periods from getting too heavy and stop me from breaking out. You know, they lied to us when they said once we got past adolescence we'd stop getting pimples."

It was another fib grown-ups liked to tell teenagers about how wonderful adulthood was going to be. I remember being twelve and thinking I was never going to grow up—that I was never going to get my period like all the other girls. I would have gladly given it back once it arrived and I realized how much "fun" it was.

"I still think you should take some condoms. You just never know anymore."

I shook my head. "He'll think I was planning to have sex with him."

"You are."

"Yeah, well...I am, and I'm not." I squirmed nervously in my seat. "This is a weird conversation."

Julie tossed me a smile. "Not any weirder than when—"

"I do *not* want to talk about your husband's prostate again."

"Fine, fine. Have a small conversation about erectile dysfunction and people get uncomfortable."

I shot an evil glare that I hoped she realized meant I didn't want to talk about her husband's junk.

"Fine. Jackie, you're not a kid. If you want to sleep with the man, go ahead. Who should you have to justify it to?" She stared at me with those intense, wise eyes. I knew I was in trouble. "You're in love with Mark, aren't you?"

I didn't even try to deny it. Julie would've known I was lying. Yes, I was in love with Mark Brennan. I was stupidly, adolescently, giddily, head-over-heels in love with Mark Brennan.

I finally nodded, but just once and curtly.

We both got up to pitch the remnants of our fast food feast in the trashcan. I got a refill of my Diet Coke to try to bolster myself for the evening with a second dose of caffeine.

"Buy some condoms."

"It would look like I'm expecting him to sleep with me."

"You *are*," she said with an amused grin.

"Yeah, but you don't have to point it out to me. Makes me sound skanky."

"You love the guy, Jackie. There's nothing wrong with it if you really love him."

I snorted. "That's not what we tell our students. Abstinence. Wait until you're older. Remember? That works *so* well," I added with a strong note of sarcasm before slinging my heavy purse over my shoulder.

"Oh, yeah." Julie gave me an exaggerated eye roll. "It works like a charm. I have two pregnant juniors and three pregnant seniors. But you're not a teenager, Jackie. You're an adult. You don't need to make excuses for feeling the way you do about Mark. Being horny isn't against the law. Neither is sleeping with the guy."

"I hate that word. *Horny*. It sounds so...so...*adolescent*." I dismissed the rest of the notion with a shake of my head. "It doesn't matter anyway. His daughter will be there. That's not exactly conducive to romance."

There was no way I'd allow Carly to get sucked into that kind of situation. It had to be a nightmare for the poor girl as it was to have her teacher dating her father. My falling into Mark's bed sure wouldn't make it any more bearable for her.

I was not going to sleep with Mark at that cabin. It wasn't fair to her. "Besides, she'll be a great chaperone."

"Take some condoms anyway. You never know what'll happen." Julie groped through her purse and retrieved her car keys.

"I'll think about it."

***

"She's not coming?" I asked for the third time.

Mark was loading my bag in the trunk of his Honda, and I stood in the driveway, absolutely unsure of my next move.

"I told you, Carly wants to spend some time with Kathy. She really misses her, and since Kathy's going to be home this weekend, Carly wants to stay. I hope you're not too disappointed. You get to see her every day at school." He slammed the trunk and took my hand. "Maybe she's smart enough to realize I want to be alone with you."

I was in serious trouble. I was going off to a romantic cabin in the woods with Mark, and I hadn't gotten around to buying those condoms Julie had recommended. "Maybe we should stay. You probably want to spend time with your girls."

"It's so nice this weekend—probably the last warm one we'll get this season. Let's go." He squeezed my hand and gave me a puppy dog look with those big, sad, brown eyes. Mark probably knew I was putty in his hands.

"But..."

"Jackie, don't you want to go with me? We'll have some alone time. We can...talk."

"Oh, I'm sure we'll...*talk*. That's what I'm afraid of."

A naughty smile spread from his lips to color his whole face. "You're afraid of me? I'm big, but I'm not *that* big."

I laughed despite myself. "I cannot believe you just said that." I could feel the heat radiating from my cheeks.

"I got you to laugh didn't I?" He took my other hand. "Babe, we won't do anything you're not ready to do. I know that making love would be a big step for you."

I nodded at the obvious. "I imagine it would be a big step for you, too. I mean Elaine was probably—"

"Stop," he said, giving my hands a quick, firm squeeze. "Rule number one—let's not talk about anyone except us. Let's talk about now, not about the past. No Elaine. No David. It's just Jackie and Mark and what's happening between them. Okay?" His eyes searched mine.

I could feel the rush of freedom whistling over me like a cool spring breeze. The shackles of the past were springing open, leaving nothing to bind me to a dead marriage and nothing to bind him to a dead wife. "That's a really good rule."

He brushed a quick kiss on my lips. "So you'll go? It's beautiful up there. Most of the leaves have probably fallen, but there are deer, foxes, and raccoons, too. You'll love the cabin—and I'll love having you all to myself. No kids. No school. No cops. Just us."

"It sounds like paradise. Let's go."

                                    ***

"It's so beautiful." I took in the landscape surrounding the cabin. Not really a cabin, more like an enormous log house. I never realized cops made enough money to afford something like this.

Mark handed me my bag, snatched his own, and slammed the trunk shut. "I love it up here. I time share with several other cops in my precinct," he explained, obviously reading my mind. Detectives could be creepily perceptive. "Just looking around takes all the tension away." He took my duffle back and walked toward the front door. "We could go for a walk and stretch our legs after that long drive and all."

"That would be great." I arched my back, trying to remove the collection of painful knots that had formed there. "I need to hit a bathroom first."

And grab a handful of Tylenol for my poor aching body.

When did I get so old that traveling wore me out?

Dropping the bags, he opened the door and held it for me. Then he followed me inside. "Down that hall," he said with an incline of his head. "Third door on the left."

He was coming out of a bedroom when I opened the bathroom door. I figured he'd put our luggage in the same room, but I wasn't going to argue the notion that we would be sharing a bed. I wanted him. I'd wanted him for a long time. I could feel my core tighten at the mere thought. I savored that delicious shiver of excitement that I hadn't felt in far too long—years to be precise.

I followed Mark into the kitchen.

He opened the refrigerator. "Just like I thought. Empty."

"I'd hope so," I said with a chuckle. "I can't imagine how disgusting anything someone left here the last time he visited would be by now."

"Point taken. We'll have to hit that little Mom and Pop grocery later."

I wasn't thrilled with the notion of getting back into a car after the long drive that had eaten a lot of the day. "Yeah, but...can't we wait a little bit?"

"Of course," he replied with a sweet smile. "I'm as sick of the car as you are."

I leaned back against the big kitchen island. "We could go for a hike."

Mark took a few steps and stood in front of me, placing both arms on either side of the counter, effectively trapping me exactly where I wanted to be. "We could." He kissed my forehead.

"We could go fishing."

"We could." He kissed my nose.

"We could go watch birds."

"We could," he said before he kissed each cheek.

"We could—"

His mouth settled on mine before I could even complete the scatterbrained thought.

His kiss was so warm, so consuming. Every nerve tingled, from the hair on my head down to the tips of my toes. My heart beat in a steadily increasing rhythm that echoed in my ears. There would be no long, agonizing wait to see which one of us would make the first move. No worry about what each little touch meant. No stupid guessing games.

This was it.

And I wanted it to last forever.

As he pressed his hard body against mine, I drowned in his scent, his feel, and his touch. He deepened the kiss, stroking that talented tongue across mine. Every cell in my body responded with an agonizing want—an almost paralyzing desire.

I threaded my arms around his neck. He replied by lifting me by the waist and setting me on the countertop. Instinct made me wrap my legs around his hips and pull him closer. His breath was a bit ragged when he ended the kiss. My ego liked that a lot.

"I feel like I've waited forever for this," Mark whispered in my ear. "You have no idea what you do to me."

His words raised shivers up and down my skin. Then he buried those heavenly lips against my neck, starting the process all over again. I arched into him. He growled in response.

His hot breath against my neck, strong hands stroking my arms, and firm muscles pressing against me were more heady than a stiff shot of whiskey. He found the zipper of my jacket and slowly eased it down, probably knowing he was driving me crazy. I pulled my hands back and returned the favor.

I marveled at the newness and savored the experience like a virgin who wasn't afraid of what was to come. I knew what was going to happen—or at least I *hoped*—and I embraced every satisfying piece of the puzzle.

Clothing was in the way—garments that were too thick and entirely too hard to take off. Somehow he'd tugged my shoes off. Don't ask me how. I was too busy trying to work his sweatshirt over his head.

Those incredibly masculine hands slipped up under my shirt as he pushed it up my torso. The light brush of his palms across my bra caused a couple of gasps. First mine, then his. I raised my arms to make his task easier. Anything to get those hands busy doing something more important than taking off my shirt. He needed to be touching me again.

For the first time, I rejoiced in my age, in Mark's age. We weren't a couple of kids fumbling around in the backseat of some car—frenzied, hurried, and left entirely frustrated. With age came grace and control. We teased. We tantalized. We enjoyed. He was slow and predatory, despite the overwhelming passion I felt in each kiss and each touch. I wasn't afraid he wouldn't wait for me, and that freed my own response.

Damn, I was glad I'd worn my red bra. I'd bought it at some silly lingerie bridal shower for a young teacher, thinking no one would ever see it. Best thirty bucks I ever spent.

Mark kissed me again in a deep, sharing exchange of breath and warmth and passion. With my legs holding him so tight he had no chance to escape, he put his arms around me and lifted me off the counter.

He shuffled us down the hall with me clinging like the ivy on the big wall at Wrigley Field. Somehow we got close to the bed, and I let my legs down. They were weak and trembling, but I stood my ground.

Mark kicked off his shoes before he crouched in front of me. He smiled up as he took off each of my socks and threw them over his shoulder. His hands settled on my waistband. Popping the button, he dragged the zipper down. As he stood back up, he pushed his hands between my hips and my jeans and worked them off my body.

Not to be outdone, I mimicked his actions, first letting my fingers slide slowly over that glorious erection that I was amazed his jeans could hold. I'd thought he was joking about his cock being big. Shit, I never figured I'd be so shallow as to admire a guy for *that* particular trait. But I did, licking my lips in anticipation. Jeans descending over his hips revealed a pair of light blue boxers that I planned to remove pretty quickly.

Mark jerked down the covers and picked me up before he set me on the bed. It took every ounce of self-control not to cover anything he could see with my hands. Although it was rapidly growing dark, there was still too much light to make me comfortable, because I was convinced he wouldn't like what he saw.

He stretched out beside me, rolled to his side, and propped his head up. Then he just stared at me.

I reached for the sheet.

His hand shot out to catch me by the wrist. "Don't. It's been so... You're beautiful, Jackie. Please don't deny me the chance to see you."

The man set my blood boiling saying things like that. He tugged at me to roll on my side and face him before he put the fingertips of his free hand against my cheek.

Mark traced a slow, lazy path from cheek to neck, which caused an uncontrollable, ticklish giggle on my part. His hand followed my collarbone to my shoulder and down my arm as he watched me with those intense eyes the whole time. He made a detour to my belly button where he circled it lazily, then his fingers moved up my stomach.

That hand made its way to my breast, which was already tightening in anticipation. I could feel the heat of his palm through my lacey bra. I absorbed it, savored it, needed it—but I also needed that damn lingerie out of the way. I reached behind my back and popped the clasp with one hand. Mark grabbed the bra and tossed it off the bed.

His dark eyes stared at me in the waning light. Then he moved so fast I let a surprised squeak escape when his mouth settled on my bare breast. I buried my hands in his hair and arched up. He gave me a satisfied male chuckle and shifted his attention to laving the other breast. Pleasure zipped from my nipple to core.

I couldn't stop the sounds—the guttural moans and excited gasps tumbling from me with surprising frequency. I didn't care an ounce about how I sounded—didn't want to think at all and possibly drown out the maelstrom of sensations Mark sent scorching through me.

All I wanted was to *feel*.

His growls excited me and stirred the woman inside me. I was wet, warm, and past ready. "Mark, please... I need—"

"I know what you need. Patience, sweet Jackie," he whispered against my skin.

But I couldn't get any kind of grip on my control. This was *so* not me—so not the way my body had always reacted to David's touch. So downright terrifying. I'd never felt raw desire pound through me with such intensity and crippling sincerity. My fingernails dug into his shoulders. I needed that anchor to keep me grounded.

He chuckled again and kissed his way down to my panties, which he proceeded to remove with surprising dexterity. There was no hurry, no trying to meet his own needs while ignoring mine. His hand found the part of me that throbbed in anticipation, the part that wanted him so desperately. He separated my folds and then eased a finger inside me.

"Oh, God..." My fingernails raked his shoulders.

I welcomed his touch, shamelessly pushing into his fingers, wanting the strokes to be deeper, faster.

Mark seemed to instinctively know exactly what I needed and had no problem providing it in luxurious quantities. He added a second finger as his thumb tortured my sensitive nub in a rhythm that had me teetering on the edge of orgasm.

My muscles tightened, begged for release from the exquisite torture. "Mark, *please...*"

"I'm right here, babe. Don't fight it. Let me love you. Please." He dropped his head to my breast to suckle and tease.

His fingers picked up the cadence of my hips. And then it happened. I came in waves of bliss and searing heat, moaning like a banshee the whole time.

When had my body learned to do *that* so quickly?

Somewhere in my scattered thoughts, I figured I'd have to write Oprah and ask.

Mark wasn't done, not that I wanted him to be. He tugged off his boxers and rolled to cover me. His body fit mine perfectly. The weight of him lying on me, the heat of his erection against my stomach, and the press of his muscular chest to my breasts were all perfection.

"I have condoms," he whispered against my ear before he kissed my neck. He gave me playful, stinging bite that he soothed with a lick. "I need to go get them from my bag."

A thrill ran through me. He'd wanted me enough to plan ahead. Knowing he'd been so considerate only made me want him more. "No, you don't," I replied in the same hushed tones, terrified talking too loud would break the spell of whatever voodoo Mark had been spinning. "I'm on the pill."

"You're not worried about—"

I couldn't even let him finish the ridiculous notion. "No, I'm not. You were faithful to Elaine. I have not a single doubt of that. The only man I've ever slept with is my ex, and it's been years. We don't need condoms."

He evidently didn't need to hear it twice. His knee pushed my legs apart as he kissed me. I wiggled my hand down to wrap it around his cock. He hissed his approval. Then I guided him home.

I'd forgotten the feel, the utter joy of joining a man's body with mine. Bliss. Rightness. Completeness. His low growls made me smile. The rhythm was slow, luxurious, sliding slowly in, pulling slowly out. My hands wandered his broad back and then settled on that heavenly butt. I guided, encouraged, and praised in mindless words.

Mark's mouth settled on mine, his tongue sweeping in with each thrust of his hips. Each push was faster, deeper, driving me out of my mind. I could feel the peak again, muscles tensing and straining, before I shattered. Lights, sounds, sensations pounded through my body and my mind. He was a heartbeat behind, driving into me and collapsing with a satisfied grunt that sent a small wave of delightful spasms through me.

Mr. Yummy is a very talented man.

I planned to fully explore the extent of his gifts for the rest of the weekend.

He chuckled in my ear. "Am I crushing you?"

"Nah."

"I'm not sure I could do much about it if I was. God, Jackie. You... you..." He shook his head.

"I what?" Insecurity kicked in before I could stop it. Damn it, I wished I could turn that annoying part of my personality off.

"You were wonderful. Perfect."

"Perfect? Really?"

Shut up, Jackie! You'll ruin everything!

Mark pushed himself up on his elbows and kissed my nose. "Perfect." He eased away and rolled onto his back.

Normally, I'd have gotten up, gone to the bathroom, and gotten dressed. But I didn't want to leave. I snuggled up against him as he dragged my arm across his chest. There wasn't any awkwardness like I feared. No shame. No feeling like I'd just made a huge mistake. No apologies because it wasn't enjoyable for either of us.

It had been a damn long time since I felt this good. For the last several years of my marriage, I'd started to believe there was something wrong with me. Maybe I was frigid. Maybe I was defective. Maybe I just wasn't pretty enough for my husband to waste time with any type of foreplay or the cuddling I desperately needed afterward.

Then I got angry.

It wasn't my fault!

David had been selfish. He hadn't cared about my needs or my wants or...*me*.

Fuck him. Let Ashley deal with him and his premature ejaculation and selfish lovemaking.

I had a real man now—a man who'd actually been more concerned with my enjoyment than his own, who'd coaxed two incredibly mind-melting orgasms from my middle-aged body. I had a man I was pretty sure wasn't going to stop at two. I cuddled up a little closer and smiled in sated contentment, marveling at what a lucky woman I was.

"I'm starving," Mark said. "Want to see if there's anything in the pantry. We're not dressed to head to town," he added with a chuckle.

"I suppose not, with public decency laws and all that nonsense. Think there's anything here?"

"Probably. Staples at least. Maybe some cans of something edible. What do you say?"

I nodded. He kicked off the sheet. I squealed and grabbed it, practically ripping it from the bed and wrapping it around me like a cloak.

Mark just shook his head and smiled. He grabbed his boxers, slid them on, and held out his hand.

I shook my head. "I'll meet you in the kitchen in a minute. I need to head to a bathroom."

"Fair enough. I'll go see what I can find to eat."

After a hasty cleanup, I grabbed an over-sized t-shirt from my duffle, donned it, and slid my red undies back on. By the time I got to the kitchen, Mark had a small smorgasbord spread out on the island. Crackers, peanut butter, jelly, cereal, and I could hear some popcorn making a racket in the microwave. "Sweet. No shopping."

"It'll last us a little while. I plan on being too busy to head into town until later." He let a leering gaze sweep my body, sending heat through me. "*Much* too busy. You look great in that."

"Why, thank you." I pulled the edges of my shirt out like a skirt and curtsied. "This li'l ole thing? I just threw it on."

The microwave beeped as the smell of hot popcorn wafted through the kitchen. Except maybe for chocolate, popcorn was my favorite food, especially if I had a good glass of white zinfandel to go with it.

"Smells delicious."

He took a few steps toward me, buried his nose against my neck, and inhaled. "Yes, you do."

Was this man for real?

Feeling a bit embarrassed at the attention, I started rooting around the cabinets for a bowl for the popcorn. He sighed, and I hoped it wasn't in exasperation, although I would have understood it if he had been frustrated with me. It wasn't as if I didn't know I could be a bit trying at times.

But I am what I am.

I grabbed an enormous ceramic bowl and put it on the counter as Mark opened the steaming bag and poured the popcorn into it.

"Was there any soda left in the cooler?" I asked.

"Yeah, there are a few I think. There was one thing in the fridge that looked interesting." He opened the door and pulled out two Michelobs.

"Perfect."

He popped them both open, set them next to the popcorn, then grabbed me and lifted me to sit on the counter. Settling in a comfortable position between my legs, he kissed my forehead. I was quickly growing used to that wonderful little gesture that made me feel special. I let a passing thought slip through my brain that he must really like this particular position. Perhaps I'd have to explore just how much after I downed my beer to instill some false courage.

Sliding the bowl over, he started feeding me kernels of popcorn, and then he'd take a bite for himself. In between, I sipped my beer, letting it go straight to my head.

After a while, Mark pushed the popcorn aside, took the almost empty brown bottle from my hand, and moved it out of the way. His hands worked their way from my knees up my thighs. He leaned in and gave me a long, slow, dramatic kiss, tasting like beer and salt. My body responded instantly.

I laced my fingers through his hair, kissing him deeply, with our tongues caressing and moans coming from both our throats. He found his way to my panties, and I took my hands away from his hair long enough to brace myself up so he could pull them away. They hit the floor, followed almost instantly by my oversized t-shirt and the blue boxers.

Mark gave me a wicked smile, reached for the black raspberry jelly, and popped open the lid. Dipping one finger inside, he took a small glob of jelly and smeared it around my nipple. I opened my mouth to say something— probably something really stupid—when his mouth covered my breast as he licked and sucked away the jam. It was so naughty, so scrumptious. I almost came on the spot.

And my mother always told me never to play with my food.

He kissed me again. I could taste the lingering sweetness in his mouth.

Wrapping my legs around him, I realized what a perfect height the counter was, hoping he intended to use it wisely. As he eased his cock inside me, I let a satisfied gasp escape my lips.

After a few moments of easy movement, I wanted more. I wanted it rough, and I wanted it *now*.

Mark must have sensed my needs as he picked me up and fairly slammed my back against the wall, saying something about "better leverage." He pounded into me as my body absorbed and savored each thrust. I let myself drown in the eddy, the whirlpool pulling me to a mind-melting release.

Somewhere in the Michigan woods, I'd found a little slice of heaven.

CHAPTER TEN

It had been an awfully long time since someone woke me with kisses. Okay, it had actually been never. Mark was pressed against my side, slowly rubbing circles on my bare stomach while he tickled my face with soft kisses. How easy it would be to get used to this.

I smiled and rolled into his arms, still hardly believing I'd slept entirely nude. He pulled me closer and tried to kiss my lips. "I've got morning breath," I whispered against his shoulder as I ducked his attention.

"So?"

"You don't care?" Not only did I probably have funky breath, my short hair was surely standing up in fifteen different directions, especially considering how active we'd been the night before. The only time we hadn't been naked was for a quick trip for food. When we got back to the cabin, we'd left a trail of clothes right back to the bedroom. I had to look like a disheveled—

"You're thinking too hard again, babe."

I laughed at that, stopped hiding against his shoulder, and kissed him, morning breath and all. And it was wonderful.

Mark playfully pressed his pelvis toward mine and realized that the sun wasn't the only thing that rose that morning.

"Again?" I asked, not entirely sure how I'd like him to answer.

I really wanted a shower and an enormous cup of coffee. We had, after all, been up quite a bit of the night, and I was sure I looked terrible with day old make-up and raccoon eyes. We'd been a bit too busy for me to wash it off.

I suddenly didn't give a damn because he didn't give a damn. He wanted me anyway.

With a growl, he kissed the spot where my shoulder meets my neck. I was always so ticklish, I couldn't help but giggle. "Seriously, Mark. I'm not sure I'm up to it again."

He pressed against me and gave me a naughty smile. "I'm up to it."

"I can see that. Do you want me walking around bowlegged all day?"

Another kiss on the same spot elicited another giggle. "Fine. Later then. I could use some coffee anyway."

He threw the sheet and blanket aside and walked gloriously undressed toward the bathroom, his erect cock bobbing with each step. I hoped he hadn't heard my appreciative and entirely immature sigh. That ass was perfection.

Hard muscle. Flawless. So was his front. I could actually feel myself blush just admiring him and thinking how much he looked like some gorgeous Calvin Klein model.

How in the hell had I made a man that looks like that want me?

You're thinking too much, Jackie.

When he came strolling back from the bathroom, I jerked the sheet up to hide my own nudity. The cover of darkness had taken away some of my normal timidity, but the morning light made all of my imperfections way too obvious.

Reaching into his duffle, Mark pulled out some clean boxers. My stars, I loved a man who wore boxer shorts. There was simply nothing attractive about tightie-whities. At least I had always thought so, until I pictured Mark in a pair. Yeah, I'd have to rethink that whole notion. Of course, Mark would be sexy in a potato sack.

He took a seat on the edge of the bed and gently ran his hands over my shoulders. I squeezed my arms hard against my side to hold the sheet up under my armpits. He ran a finger across my collarbone, tucked it between my shrouded breasts, and deftly pulled the sheet down. I squealed and reached for the blanket, but Mark grabbed my shoulders and held me back. Then—with a slow and deliberate gaze—he stared at my body. I could literally feel my blood warm to his perusal. I closed my eyes, not wanting to see his reaction, knowing my breasts weren't nearly as firm as I wished, that my waist had all but disappeared with time, and that those stretch marks two pregnancies had left on my lower abdomen hadn't faded as much as I had always hoped.

"You're so beautiful."

My eyes snapped open as I framed some sarcastic retort. "Yeah, right, and—"

His kiss stopped the sour words. Not a simple kiss, but the kind he had drugged me with last night. The man was as addictive as meth.

As he pulled away, I cupped his cheeks in my hands. "Wow." I forgot all about the sheet.

A smug smile crossed his lips. "Two choices. You get up, get dressed, and have some breakfast with me—or I pick you up and carry you into the kitchen, and we eat naked."

"I'd hate to have you see me naked and ruin your appeti—"

He kissed me before I could finish the sentence. The man refused to let me say anything derogatory about myself. He had entirely disarmed me. A long kiss later, I nodded, got out of bed, and grabbed my abandoned clothes. Messy hair and all, I sat across the kitchen table from Mark and ate the omelet he made.

While he cleaned up the aftermath of our meal, I popped in the shower and then got dressed. The air had a definite chill, and I shivered as I fished my blow dryer out of my duffle bag. I figured my typically uncooperative hair would make me look an awful lot like Buckwheat, so I dried it and arranged it best I could since I forgot my hair gel.

I was shaking a little bottle, preparing to slap on a heavy layer of foundation when Mark came up behind me and wrapped his arms around my waist. He put his chin on my shoulder and smiled at me in the mirror.

"Don't bother, babe. You're prettier without it. No one around but me, and I love you just the way you are." I could see the anticipation, the longing in his eyes.

I love you.

Damn it all anyway.

Mark had said the three words that could send me running faster than a fox being chased by a hound. A man's love never brought me anything but heartache. Why couldn't we just have fantastic sex and not muddy the water with declarations of things he didn't really feel?

That guard of mine snapped right back into place, bringing with it the sarcasm that was its constant companion. "You sound like Billy Joel."

His reflection frowned back at me, and he squeezed my waist almost too tight. "You don't have anything to say to me?"

I love you too. More than you could possibly know.

But the man was going to stand there for a very, very long time if he was expecting me to lay my heart bare simply to have it shredded and handed back to me on a platter.

David had taught me a brutal lesson that I intended never to forget. Men confuse love and lust. They say the former when they really mean the latter.

No, thank you. I wasn't going through *that* again. I wasn't about to tell him how I felt. I would get hurt.

"Jackie?" Those brown eyes were getting darker. I'd forgotten Mr. Yummy had a temper. Judging from his expression, I was just about to find out to what extent that temper could flare. "After what I said, don't you want to say *anything?*"

I shoved my make-up back into the case without applying any. "I know. How about we go for a hike? Maybe we can see some deer."

Mark turned around so fast he almost knocked me over.

I reluctantly followed him into the bedroom, hoping there wouldn't be a storm.

Grabbing his duffle bag, he muttered under his breath the whole time he pulled out clean clothes and threw them on the still unmade bed. I couldn't catch everything he was saying, but I sure got the gist of it.

I was cold. I was unfeeling. I was stubborn.

Gee, Mark. Haven't we met before? I'm Jackie Delgado. The most stubborn woman you're ever likely to know.

"I'm not cold," I finally grumbled. I rooted around in my bag for my birth control pills. Not that I'd need them anymore.

Mark took his clothes into the bathroom and slammed the door hard enough to make the pictures on the wall jiggle. I decided I needed to put some space between us for a little while.

I tugged on my boots, grabbed my jacket, and set out for a long, long walk. I needed to clear my head, and I needed some fresh air. If I didn't get the hell out of there, he was going to wear me down. I was going to confess all that I felt, and I was going to get hurt again because he couldn't truly love me.

Even though most of the trees had shed their leaves, the woods were still beautiful. I loved the tall trees, the autumn sunlight, and the clean smell of outdoors. I hiked hard and breathed deeply, hoping to untangle the mess of thoughts that were weighing on me.

Now what?

I knew I loved the guy—had almost started loving him from the moment he pulled his car over on our first date to scold me. I'd loved him from the moment he slid that butter across the table when I'd pushed it out of my reach. I'd loved him from the moment he first kissed me.

I brushed away a few tears and damned myself for forgetting my iPod. Without music blaring in my ears, all I could do was think.

His voice echoed in my head. *"You're thinking too hard again, babe."*

Sorry, Mark. It's what I do.

I began to list the reasons why he couldn't possibly love me.

"I'm past my prime." Okay, that was bullshit. Last night proved it.

I'd never enjoyed making love so much. I'd never felt my body respond so readily and so warmly before. It was the best sex of my life. I might have always joked that I looked old, but I had to honestly admit I wasn't *that* bad. No gray. No major wrinkles. I might not be model thin, but I wasn't exactly ready for a gastric by-pass either. My intellect was as sharp as a chef's boning knife, and I could still make people laugh when I tried. I had a lot of good years left.

Maybe Mark appreciated all those qualities.

I tried again. "He still loves Elaine."

That wasn't a good reason. It wasn't as if I should have expected him to walk away from her grave and act like she had never been a part of his life. If he was like that, I couldn't possibly love him. Mark had room in that huge heart of his to keep her memory and still be with me. Last night proved that too. I refused to give in to the nagging voice that whispered, "It was just lust." It wasn't just lust. Mark and I had connected on a very special, very emotional level. Of course, he still loved Elaine. But he could love me, too.

The devil's advocate in me refused to shut up. *Your personality will wear him out. It'll kill his love just like it killed David's.*

Then it hit me hard and fast. *I* hadn't killed David's love for me—*David* had.

His mid-life crisis had been more important to him than I'd been, than our marriage had been. It was my own insecurity that wanted to blame me. It wanted to blame my boisterous nature, my changing body, and my domineering personality. What did those have to do with David's need to feel young again, to fuck a girl young enough to be his daughter?

Not a single, solitary thing.

"It wasn't all my fault," I said to the trees. Then I shouted it. "It wasn't all my fault!" I suddenly felt free.

Mark's voice sang in my head. *"I love you just the way you are."*

Had he meant it?

Could Mark possibly love me as much as I loved him?

Because, God help me, I did. I loved him more than my own life. I wanted to wake up with him every morning exactly the way I had today. I wanted to fall asleep snuggled up with him every night. I wanted to grow old and wrinkled with him. Visions of grandchildren floated through my emotionally overwrought brain, grandchildren we would share and spoil.

"But am I brave enough to tell him?" That was a tougher question, so I decided to ponder that while I hiked a little longer.

I glanced up to the sound of an obviously active woodpecker. That moment of inattention was more than enough for a clumsy person like me. My friends liked to joke that I could trip over the crack of dawn. My ankle rolled as I trod over a tree root. I was sprawled on the ground before I really knew what happened.

The sharp pain in my ankle stole my breath away and brought tears to my eyes. On my hands and knees, I flopped over to sit on my butt as I felt the ankle already beginning to swell inside the boot.

Damn. Damn. Double damn.

Desperately wanting to take the boot off to relieve the increasing pressure,

I resisted the misguided urge. I struggled to remember the right things to do for a badly sprained ankle.

The same thing had happened to me when David was in college, sometime after Patrick was born, but before we had Nate. That was so long ago it was hard to bring it all back. We'd been walking to one of David's intramural basketball games, and I had tripped where grass met sidewalk. He helped me into the gym, propped my foot on a chair, and played his stupid game. *Then* he drove me to the E.R. That much I remembered.

But the only thing I could recollect about treating the injury was that it took several hours to get an expensive x-ray only to be told my ankle wasn't broken and there really wasn't much they could do.

Ice and elevate. Hard to do when you're sitting on the ground in the middle of the woods with no way to get back to civilization.

I didn't want to cry, but no one was around, so I indulged myself for a couple of minutes. Wiping away the tears, I straightened my spine and tried to think of what to do.

I needed something to use like a crutch. I let my gaze scan the area. Nada. "Damn it."

My ankle throbbed in time with my rapidly beating heart, swelling until I was sure the boot would split open.

"Jackie? Where are you?"

I couldn't believe it. Mark had come looking for me. I shook my head to make sure it wasn't just some hallucination brought on my pain and frustration. "Over here! I need some help!"

Hearing his footsteps, I shouted again.

He came jogging up. He skidded to a halt in front of me and crouched down. "Jackie! What happened?"

"I sprained my stupid ankle," I said, feeling clumsy and more than a little embarrassed. I'd run away from the cabin like some stupid kid. "I twisted it on that." I pointed at the offending tree root. I winced when he touched the boot.

"It's swollen already," he said, giving my thigh a pat. "Not good."

Knowing he sure didn't deserve the sharp edge of my tongue, I bit back a sarcastic retort to his statement of the obvious. "Yeah. It hurts like hell."

"I'm going to have to carry you."

Snorting, I shook my head. "You'll get a hernia."

His responding snort didn't sound at all like amusement.

I looked into his eyes.

Oh, yeah. Mark's temper was full flight.

"You sure know how to piss me off, you know that? You're a piece of work, lady."

I could have given back as good as I was getting, but I was smart enough to realize I deserved his anger. I just bit my tongue and sat there.

He ran his hand from knee to ankle. "Nothing looks broken, but I haven't seen that ankle yet. I hate to take the boot off. If I—"

"I know. I know. If you take it off, you'll never get it back on. Look, you can't carry me."

"So help me, God, if you say something about your weight—"

"I could weigh as much as Carly, and it *still* wouldn't work." Mark seemed to be reining in his anger, so I tried to explain. "It's just too far. We need to find something I can use as a crutch."

Before I could protest, he reached down, gripped my hands, and pulled me to my feet. Well, at least to my *foot*—my good foot.

He turned his back and bent his knees. "Put your arms around my neck. We'll piggyback."

"Mark, you can't—"

"Jackie," he said before he took a deep breath. I thought I heard a slow count of ten. "Put your arms around my neck."

"Fine," I snapped before I did as he asked.

He put his hands behind my knees and pulled me on his back. After he got me settled, he began to hike back toward the cabin.

"Let me know if you need to put me down."

"If I put you down, it'll be in the damn lake. Cool that hot Spanish temper."

"Now we're resorting to ethnic insults?" I was growing a little angry at the implication that this was all *my* fault. *He* was the one who said those three stupid words that started this whole mess. "It's your fault I got hurt."

He skidded to a stop. I heard a ten count again.

This whole situation suddenly seemed horribly amusing. I bit my bottom lip to keep from laughing.

Funny—whenever David and I would fight, it got ugly. Fortunately, it was never physical, although I was known to throw a knick-knack or two at his head, and I had a nasty door slamming habit. Mark and I were, for all intents and purposes, fighting. But all I wanted to do was laugh.

"You're damn lucky the lake is the other direction," he said with a note of humor to his voice. He started walking again.

"Damn lucky," I said with a chuckle.

It didn't take long at all to get us back to the cabin. I had to admire that type of strength.

Mark set me down in the main room, and I hopped on my good foot until I let myself fall into the chair. He was immediately there, taking a seat on the coffee table and propping my injured foot on his lap.

Slowly untying the laces, he slid my boot off as I dug my fingers into the arms of the chair and sucked in my breath. He gently ran his fingers over the ankle that appeared to be about the size of a softball. "I really need to take the sock off. Or do you want to do it?"

"None of the above?" My whole leg throbbed from knee to toes. "Can't I at least have a stiff drink first? Bite on a leather strap or something?"

He laughed, the sound rumbling in that broad chest, making me smile despite the pain. "I'll be gentle." And he was. He made a pained face when he looked at my foot. "Ouch. Already bruising. That's going to be pretty ugly in a couple of days. You should probably have it x-rayed."

"Nah. It's not broken. Just sprained. Is there any ice in the freezer?"

"I'll check." Mark started to get up, but I reached out and grasped his elbow. "What?"

"I'm sorry, Mark. I–I shouldn't have run out like that. I knew I'd pissed you off, and I just needed to get some fresh air. I wanted to give us some space."

With a curt nod, he went into the kitchen. I could hear him moving things around, and he came back in with one of those flexible blue packets you freeze and then put inside a cooler. "Better than ice." He sat back down on the coffee table and folded it over my injury. "We should go home."

Tears flooded my eyes before I could stop them. "I ruined everything."

"You didn't ruin...*everything*. Last night was still fantastic."

I sniffled and nodded. "I wish I could explain it so you'd understand."

With a shrug, Mark took off my other boot. He got up, grabbed a throw pillow from the sofa, and settled my injured ankle on it. He sat next to my foot on the coffee table, holding the cold pack and idly stroked my calf through my khakis. "Don't you love me, Jackie?"

I love you with all my heart. "Did I ever tell you I was only nineteen when I got married?"

"What does that have to do with my question?"

"David—"

He shook his head. "You're breaking the first rule."

"I know, but hear me out. Please."

Mark gave me a quick nod.

I heaved a deep sigh and dove in headfirst. "David was the first guy—the *only* guy—I ever loved. He was the only man I'd ever slept with. I think marrying your first love isn't necessarily the right thing to do. You never have to face that...that...*hurt*—that horrible hurt that comes with losing your first and only love. I went through my entire adult life thinking that my life was his, and when he left me, I thought I didn't matter if I couldn't be with him." Mark started to say something, but I cut him off. "My life wasn't my own because he was my beginning and my end. I thought we'd be together forever. I never learned how to get over a lost love. Something every teenager learns, I never did."

"Angela Kramer."

"I beg your pardon?"

"My first love. Angela Kramer. She broke up with me the week before the junior prom because Scott Fitzpatrick had a Camaro." Mark sighed. "She broke my heart."

I took a deep breath, hoping I was getting through to him. "I'd never had my heart broken until the year I turned forty. My husband of twenty-one years came home and told me his secretary was pregnant with his child—his twenty-fucking-year-old secretary. I was suicidal." I couldn't believe I had finally admitted that frightening reality to myself, let alone aloud and to Mark. "I'm not sure I would have lived through it if it weren't for Patrick and Nathaniel."

Mark's dark eyes locked with mine, and I was so intimidated that I almost glanced away, fearing he would discern the depth of my feelings. "I'm not going to leave you, Jackie."

Tears brimmed my eyes again, spilling over onto my cheeks. "No one ever means for something like that to happen, but—"

"I'm not going to leave you, Jackie. I love you."

I just shook my head and let my chin drop to my chest. "You can't know that."

His heavy sigh floated through the air, settling on my heart like a tremendous weight.

I love you, Mark.

I'd admitted it to myself. Why in the hell couldn't I say it to him?

"You don't believe me. You think I'm just like that bastard ex-husband of yours. Not all guys are like that. Some of us mean what we say and do what we promise." He stood up, came to me and put his finger under my chin to force my head up. "I love you, Jackie Delgado. I won't look for other women. I won't fool around. I promise." He caught one of my tears with his thumb. "I'm breaking my own rule, but I need you to know something. I was married to Elaine for sixteen years, almost seventeen. And I never strayed. *Never.* I don't make promises I can't keep."

"But—"

"Just shut up and listen to me for a minute."

I nodded and sniffed back some more tears.

"When Elaine got sick, I had well-meaning friends—guy friends—who thought I might be...lonely. They tried to set me up with women, but fuck that. I didn't care how sick she was, I wasn't going to some other woman just to have sex. Sex is great, but without love that's *all* it is. Sex. I didn't have sex with you, Jackie."

I laughed before I could stop myself. "Silly me, I thought we did."

His hand cupped my cheek as I turned my face into that wonderful, loving palm. "I made love to you because that's exactly what it was—an expression of my love. I'm a one-woman man. I'll always be a one-woman man. And *you're* that woman. *I. Love. You.*"

I started to cry again. God, I felt like a stupid yo-yo. Cry. Laugh. Cry. It spilled out of my lips before I could even stop it. "I love you too."

"Told you so."

Time to laugh again. Then Mark bumped the coffee table and I hissed at the resulting pain.

"I'm going to get our stuff together and throw it in the car. We're heading back home, and we're going to get that ankle x-rayed." He ran his fingers lightly down my leg. "I suppose sex is out of the question." He wiggled his eyebrows.

I picked up my sock and threw it at him.

CHAPTER ELEVEN

Mark pulled the Accord into the garage, then came around and helped me out. After getting me settled on my new crutches, he grabbed our duffle bags and cleared a path for me into the house by holding open doors and kicking shoes out of the way.

I was so tired I could barely see straight. The ankle had throbbed all night as it continued to swell and turn some disgusting shades of blue and purple. I tried to tough it out, insisting I didn't want to ruin our trip, but by supper it was obvious the mini-vacation was over. Hard to feel sexy or enjoy the wilderness when you're in that much pain, and we couldn't even cuddle because I had my ankle propped up on pillows. Neither of us had gotten much sleep, and we left hours before dawn to get back home.

"I still wish you'd let me take you to the hospital," he scolded.

I teetered on my crutches, put my injured foot on the floor to regain my balance, and grimaced. "I don't need an x-ray, and I sure don't need to spend four hours in some E.R. for them to tell me it's just a sprain." I sounded as grumpy as I felt. Tired and in pain were a bad combination. "The crutches are enough. Thanks for stopping at the pharmacy, and thanks for buying me the ibuprofen. I need a handful right now."

Mark grunted a reply that I figured was caveman speak for, "You're welcome."

"Dad! You're back early!" Carly called from where she sat on the barstool, eating what looked like Fruit Loops. She fixed her eyes on my crutches. "Ms. Delgado? What happened to you?"

"She sprained her ankle. Where's Kat?" Mark asked.

I followed his gaze to two enormous Nikes he had kicked aside by the door and realized very quickly exactly who they belonged to.

Oh, shit.

Nate suddenly appeared in the hall, blushing all the way as he tugged on his t-shirt.

Oh, shit. At least his jeans were still on.

Carly confirmed what I had already figured out. "Nate stayed over last night, but I wasn't supposed to tell you."

Oh, shit.

"We were watching movies, and I–I just feel asleep on the couch." Nate used that sheepish voice he always trotted out when he was caught with his hand in the cookie jar. "You're home early."

Nate really needed to learn when to keep his mouth shut.

How had I missed his car? It wasn't in the driveway, and I hadn't taken inventory of the ones parked on the street. Of course, I hadn't known there was a reason to check them for a familiar, weathered black sedan.

Mark's ruddy face and clenched fists told me he was trying to contain a potential nuclear meltdown. Nate was in for it. So was Kathy. My problem was I didn't know where I fit into this whole ridiculous nightmare. My personality split right down the middle and began to tug me in two different directions. Was I going to react as Nate's mother or Mark's girlfriend? Even worse was how would Carly's teacher handle all of this?

Just call me_"Sybil."

Mark's hard gaze eventually settled on Kathy. She would be victim number one. "Young Lady," he began as I saw her wince, "you've got a hell of a lot of explaining to do." He inclined his head toward Nate. "Did he stay here all night? In your room?"

Kathy wrung her hands, clearly tongue-tied.

"*Well?*" Mark shouted. "Did he stay in your room?"

"Yes," Nate replied, followed quickly by, "sir. But nothing happened. We just wanted to hold each other."

Oh, Nathaniel. You're lying through your teeth. You always tug on your right ear when you fib.

I saw the mushroom clouds in Mark's eyes and tried to reduce the number of ensuing casualties. "Nate, you need to go home. We'll talk about this when I get back."

Mark's fatherly indignation was redirected at me. "That's all you're going to say to him? Your son took advantage of my little girl."

"I'm not your little girl anymore," Kathy shouted, finally finding her voice—her very loud voice. Stomping her foot like a child detracted from the overall message. She stopped wringing her hands and stepped closer to Nate, threading her arm through his and interlacing their fingers. The intimate, loving gesture made my heart ache for them. "I'm Nate's girlfriend."

I'd never seen Mark so angry, and, despite how much I loved my son, I understood Mark's reaction. I also figured I needed to get Nate out of there. *Fast.* "Nate, go home. Now." This situation needed someone to diffuse the potential for a nasty, ugly argument.

Nate stared at the crutches for a moment and then at me, but I shook my head in response to his unasked question. There was enough to deal with at the moment. I could explain the stupid sprain to him later. He gave me a quick nod and pulled away from Kathy before he shoved his feet into his shoes, grabbed his jacket off the coat rack, and left through the garage.

"Mark, I think I should go too." Then I stupidly realized my chance for a ride had just walked out the door. If I wanted to go home, Mark would have to drive me.

"You need to stay here for a day or two," he said in the same scolding voice he'd used with his daughter.

I bit back a sarcastic retort.

Carly, who'd been watching the whole episode with wide-eyed astonishment, came to stand next to me and adopted a motherly tone. "You can't go home, Ms. Delgado. You need someone to take care of you." She picked up my crutches and moved them out of my reach. "Dad, why don't you carry her into the family room? I'll get some ice for her ankle."

"I should really go home," I insisted. "Carly, do you think you can catch Nate for me?" She didn't budge.

"I told you, Jackie," Mark scolded, "you should stay here, at least for tonight. You can't get up your stairs. Hell, you can't even walk."

Kathy's face quickly flushed crimson as she wagged her index finger at her father. "Oh! So it's fine if *your* girlfriend spends the night, but if *my* boyfriend stays—"

His interruption was swift and loud. "It's not the same thing!"

"Bullshit," sweet, little Kat replied.

"She's hurt," Mark said through clenched teeth.

"She wasn't hurt when you two went to the cabin. Did you sleep on the couch there, Daddy, or in the spare bedroom? Did you?" Mark glared at her. "I didn't think so."

Score one for Kathy.

This was going to get worse before it got better. Carly was staring at her feet, and I wasn't sure it was my place to step into the mix now that Nate was gone.

Boy, oh boy, was he ever going to get it when I saw him again.

Then I realized I was being a hypocrite. Nate was an adult, albeit a young adult, but an adult nonetheless. What he and Kat were doing wasn't really any different than what Mark and I were doing. He obviously didn't feel the same way. I guess being a parent of a son is different from being the parent of a daughter. Shit, David would probably be patting the kid on the back.

Kathy and Mark had stopped shouting at each other and were now trying to set a record for time spent in an angry stare down. He finally uttered a curse and strode over to me. He scooped me into his arms before I could protest and marched me into the living room. I heard footsteps stomping down the hall followed by the slam of a bedroom door and assumed she'd removed herself from our company.

Setting me down on the sofa, he returned to the kitchen. I could hear him rummaging around, slamming cabinets and digging through things until he returned with a big plastic bag full of ice. I tried not to wince when he propped my foot on the coffee table and put the compress on my ankle a little bit more forcefully than necessary. I wasn't about to scold him as he went back to the kitchen.

Mark said something to Carly before she came to sit on the end of the sofa. I leaned forward to shift the ice to the worst of the swelling.

"Ms. Delgado?"

"Hmm?" I looked around for a pillow, but the only one I could find was on the far chair.

"Do you think Nate and Kathy had sex?"

Holy shit.

She actually asked me that.

Aloud.

"Well, Carly...I don't know. But if they did, I'm sure it's not anyone's business except theirs."

"The hell it's not!" Mark came into the room, carrying a glass of orange juice and two ibuprofens. He handed them off to me. I was touched that—despite the high drama surrounding our arrival—he remembered I needed something for the pain. "Here, take these. I'm going to make some coffee."

"Thank you."

He just grunted a response and went back to the kitchen.

"I think they had sex," Carly stated as casually as if we had been discussing the chance of precipitation. She fixed those big, brown eyes on me. "You and Dad are having sex too, right?"

I choked on my orange juice, barely able to keep from spewing it across the room.

Now what?

A legal scale suddenly appeared in my thoughts as I weighed my options. I could lie to her. But Carly was perceptive enough to see right through it. The girl was fourteen going on forty. If I told her a lie, not only would she know it, but I'd also look like an absolute moron and a bald-faced liar. She'd never trust me again.

I could tell her the truth. But it really wasn't something I thought I should be discussing with a fourteen-year-old.

Damn it all anyway.

"Well, um...Carly. Your father and I are—"

"In love," she said with a quick nod.

"And people who are in love—"

"Want to show each other how much they care," she said, finishing my thought. "Mom told me sex is wonderful, but it's better to wait until you're married. She said sometimes people don't wait, but that doesn't make them bad."

Mark took a couple of steps into the room and evidently heard the conversation because he quickly turned on his heel and retreated back to the kitchen.

Coward.

"Kathy and Nate probably didn't want to wait. Mom said when you have sex too soon in a relationship that it can kill it. You should love each other first." Carly slid a hair band off her wrist, pulled her hair into a ponytail, and tied it. "Having sex becomes more important than learning to love. I think Mom was right."

"I think she was right too," I replied.

"Dad loved Mom so much, I didn't think he'd ever fall in love again."

The girl was the epitome of honesty.

She twisted her ponytail around her finger. "But I think he's in love with you."

I shifted uncomfortably, trying to move the ice that was now hurting more than helping. I always hated icing an injury almost as much as the injury itself, but I had to admit I was more uncomfortable having this type of conversation with Carly.

Elaine had obviously had "the talk" with her daughter, and I wasn't sure Carly needed a surrogate mother—especially one who was now sleeping with her father.

"And you love him." Her words were a statement, not a question. "I think he loved you right from the start. I could see it. You, too. You loved him too." The kid was insightful beyond her years. "I suppose it's okay if you two spend the night together." She leveled her gaze at me, with her eyes serious and her mouth drawn thin. "Just don't let it mess you two up. Okay, Ms. Delgado?"

"I really think it's all right if you call me Jackie now."

A smile tugged at the corners of her mouth. "I promise not to at school."

Mark must have decided it was safe to come back into the room. He'd probably been listening for a break in the intense conversation. He carried two mugs of what I fervently hoped was strong coffee. "Cream and sweetener." He handed me a cup bearing Garfield's image.

"Thank you." He settled on the arm of the sofa, sipping his coffee. "Your daughter and I were having a nice little chat."

"Girl talk." Carly got up and headed back to the kitchen.

"Girl talk, huh?" Mark asked after she had left. "I think she misses her mom."

"I think so too. Elaine did a great job raising those girls."

He snorted. "Looks like she didn't get everything important across to Kat."

I sipped the coffee, trying to think of what would be the most appropriate thing to say. Then I found some courage. "Mark, they're not babies. I know you don't approve. I don't, either—but Nate turned nineteen last week. I assume Kathy's the same age."

"Just turned nineteen too. She's a baby."

"She'll always be your little girl, but she's a young woman with her own life now. It's hard to let them go. I know."

"Your kids won't turn up pregnant with the guy running out the door the minute he finds out."

I took major offense to the inference that my Nate would knock up Kathy and leave her high and dry. "My boys would never do that to a girl."

"See? Even you called her a *girl*."

I had to think about that for a second. I guess our kids will always be our kids. "Point taken. Look, I don't think they should be...you know...getting physical. But at some point they've got to make those choices for themselves. I think my boys learned something from my mistakes, and I hope to hell they don't follow in my footsteps."

He sipped his coffee, obviously contemplating my words. "I don't like it," he finally grumbled.

"I don't, either."

"How's the ankle?"

"Nice way to change the subject. The ankle's sore. Do you think you could take me home? Nate will be there, so I won't be on my own. I think you need some alone time with Kathy and Carly."

"Jackie, you can't even walk."

"Nate can help me. Please, Mark. Please. You need to spend time with your daughters, and I really need to sit Nate down and try to talk some sense into him." I handed him my now empty coffee cup. "I'm exhausted, I hurt like hell, and I want to catch a long nap."

He nodded. "I'll get your crutches."

***

Patrick's car was parked next to Nate's in my driveway.

"Shit," I mumbled under my breath.

Mark was still a sore point with my oldest, and I really didn't think any of us needed another confrontation today.

"What's wrong?" Mark asked as he turned off the Honda.

"Both my boys are here."

"That's good. They can help you if you need anything." He crawled out of the car and came around to my side. "Can you stand up?"

I nodded and awkwardly got to my feet. Instead of reaching in the back seat to get my crutches, he immediately scooped me into his. He kicked on the door leading into the house until it suddenly opened to reveal Patrick. I watched my son's eyes flash with barely contained fury.

"What in the hell happened?"

This day just kept on giving. "I sprained my ankle. Think you can move so Mark can put me down?"

Patrick moved aside.

Mark carried me into the living room and deposited me on the couch. He grabbed a pillow, put it on the coffee table, and propped my foot up. "Want some ice?"

"No, but I need it anyway." I glanced up to find my oldest staring holes through me.

Patrick jerked his thumb at Mark. "What did he do to you?"

"I sprained my ankle, Patrick. Mark didn't do anything to me." I had a flash to how Kat must have felt when she was getting the inquisition from Mark. Why was I defending my life to my child? "I was hiking and I tripped over a tree root."

Patrick shot a glare at Mark when he returned with a bag of ice that he set on my ankle. "You had no business going away with this...this...*guy*."

"I don't see how that's any of your business, son," Mark said in a stern voice that told me he'd reached his limit.

Patrick's scowl could melt metal. "She's my mother and—."

"I'm old enough to know my own mind," I interrupted. "We'll talk about it later, Patrick. Mark?"

"Hmm?"

"Thanks for everything. Why don't you go home and get some rest? It was an awfully long night." My face instantly flushed, realizing how dirty what I'd just said probably sounded to my son. "We didn't get much sleep." *Oh, yeah, that made things better.* "My ankle throbbed all night. Mark was getting me ice and—"

"I'll bet," Patrick snidely replied. "I'll bet that's *all* he did. Get you ice."

Watching Mark set his stubborn jaw, I figured the best thing to do was diffuse the time bomb by getting him to leave. But I really didn't want him to go. I wanted his arms around me. I wanted him to get me my ibuprofen and ice when I needed it. I wanted him to make me forget the pain with a kiss or two.

I had been a horrible coward for most of my adult life—always taking the path of least resistance instead of pushing for what I wanted, what I needed. Whenever David and I made plans, we always ended up doing exactly what he wanted to do. I guess after years of never getting what I wanted and never winning a single battle, I'd lapsed into a state of learned helplessness. I simply gave in.

Well, I wasn't going to give in now. If I wanted Mark around, then, damn it, Mark was going to be around.

"Patrick, sit down. We need to talk."

"You want me to go?" Mark took my hand, his anger seemingly abated.

"No. I want you to stay. That's the point." I glanced over at my oldest. "Patrick?"

My son stared back at me, folding his arms over his chest.

"Mark and I are going to be together. You're just going to have to get used to it."

There. Better to lay it all on the line.

"But, Mom..."

"No. No, *but, Mom.*"

"You don't even know this guy."

Nate sheepishly entered the room. "And he hurt you. And he's Kat's dad. It's just too...*weird.* I mean, a woman your age... It's gross." He stared at his shoes.

I rolled my eyes. "Thanks a heap, Nate."

Mark's grip on my hand tightened—he was fighting to hold his temper in check.

Perhaps this hadn't been a good idea after all.

That's what I get for trying to be brave.

"Yes, I'm Kat's father," Mark finally said, breaking the stilted silence. "I wasn't happy with what we stumbled across this morning at my house, but we can talk about that later. Your mother isn't over the hill. Not by a long shot. Right now I need you guys to understand that I love her and I—"

Both Nate and Patrick started shouting, drowning each other out so I couldn't understand either one of them.

I put two fingers to my lips and blew a loud whistle.

They stopped yelling and gaped at me.

Mark arched an eyebrow and glanced my way.

"Enough. Mark is here. He's going to be a part of my life now, so you better get used to the idea." Patrick started to say something, but I cut him off. "I know you don't like it, Pat. But I'm a grown-up. And I love Mark."

"Really?" Nate asked, barely above a whisper. "You *love* him?"

I nodded.

My tenderhearted son suddenly understood. I could see it all over his face. He took a couple of steps and held out his hand to Mark.

Mark shook Nate's hand. "You better be good to her," Nate said with more sternness in his voice than I could ever remember hearing before. "You better not hurt her again."

"I won't. I made that mistake once. I won't do it again."

Patrick snorted. "That's why she's on crutches."

He wasn't going to be nearly as easy to win over. Mark was smart enough not to poke that sleeping dog by trying to shake Pat's hand.

"I'm exhausted," I said with a yawn. "Is the high drama over for the day? Because I really need a nap."

"Here or your room?" Mark asked.

Patrick snorted again, still standing there with his arms crossed over his chest.

"Catching a cold there, son?" Mark asked.

"I'm not your damn son."

"Patrick David Ryan. I didn't raise you to be rude."

He turned on his heel, stomped to the door, and slammed it as he left. A few minutes later, I heard tires squealing as Pat drove away.

I didn't complain when Mark carried me to my room. He propped my ankle up on some pillows, lay down beside me, and covered us both with my afghan. Then he curled up against me, threw his arm across my belly, and was contentedly snoring in a few minutes.

Dear God, what a mess.

My oldest son hated my boyfriend.

My boyfriend was pissed because his oldest daughter was sleeping with my youngest son.

And the only person who seemed entirely satisfied with the totally baffling situation was my boyfriend's youngest daughter.

Calling Jerry Springer!

As I felt sleep start to work its magic and scatter my thoughts, I smiled.
I loved Mark. And Mark loved me.
Life had definitely taken a turn for the better.

CHAPTER TWELVE

"You're having everyone at your place?" Abby asked, sounding incredulous.

"I thought you hated to cook," Suzanne chimed in.

"I do, but this is a chance to try to smooth out some of the rough edges," I replied. My friends' reticence was starting to shake my confidence. "The kids need to get to know each other a little better, and maybe if we try to act like a family..." I shrugged, wondering if even *I* believed that having the four kids together with Mark and me for a nice traditional family Thanksgiving might make things any better.

What exactly was I wishing for? Was it to meld our two separate groups into one? It wasn't as if Mark and I had ever talked about moving in together or about having a future together. We were taking it one day at a time—yet in the recesses of my mind, I speculated about the next step and the next.

It wasn't going to be a smooth road.

Patrick still resented any attention Mark gave me. He'd had a month to get used to it, but he was his father's son in so many ways. Stubborn, arrogant, and always thinking he knew what was best for everyone else. He wasn't out and out rude to Mark. Well, he wasn't rude *all* the time. But he wasn't friendly, either. At least they only saw each other on weekends.

Nate had accepted Mark without a struggle, which was a bit surprising since Mark was still obviously unhappy with Nate and Kathy's relationship. The kids both tended to stay in Bloomington, preferring to call us rather than visit. I missed seeing Nate as much as Mark missed seeing Kathy.

The one weekend they came home, Kathy had a hard time concealing her resentment of me, barely speaking a few words in response to any of my attempts at pleasant conversation. Did she think I was trying to replace her mother in Mark's life? Or did she just not like me? Maybe she simply thought it was too bizarre to have your father dating your boyfriend's mother. Either way, Kat was going to be another obstacle I'd have to clear.

Carly embraced our relationship wholeheartedly. She had no trouble calling me "Ms. Delgado" at school and "Jackie" at home. She implied she'd like Mark and me to move in together, constantly dropping hints about how expensive it must be to have two houses when we only needed one. And she pointed out diamond ads in magazines as if Mark wasn't smart enough to figure out that we belonged together without her helpful advice.

God love her.

"That's the way we all became the Brady Bunch," Abby sang, clapping her hands.

Julie rolled her eyes. "I think you should take them all to a restaurant like you've done with your boys the last couple of years. You hate to cook." She frowned. "This could be a nightmare, Jackie."

"Thanks for that heaping dose of confidence." I pushed what was left of my salad around on my plate. "Look, I've already got all the groceries. I'll make the pies and noodles tonight. Everything else, I can just get up early and work on before everyone gets there."

"When did you take the turkey out of the freezer?" Suzanne asked before she sipped her Diet Coke.

"I'll take it out tonight."

She put her soda can down and stared at me with wide eyes. "You mean you haven't defrosted it yet? How big a turkey did you get?"

"I think it was fifteen pounds or so. I don't remember." I was suddenly alarmed at her reaction. "Why?"

"Because they usually need several days to thaw."

"No, they don't they..." *Great. Just great.* "Days? They need *days*?"

Suzanne, Julie, and Abby all nodded.

Shit.

Julie patted my hand. "Best you can do is pull it out of the freezer when you get home and defrost it in some warm water. Read the label, Jackie, or Google the directions. It's not that tough. Is Nate coming with Kathy? That must be weird." She gathered up her lunch debris and piled it on her brown tray.

"It bothers Mark more than it bothers me. I think they're good together. I'm more worried about Pat. He boils over every time he spends any time with Mark."

I wasn't sure Pat would ever come around where Mark was concerned, just like I wasn't sure if Mark would ever come around where Nate was concerned.

I had a bad flashback to the type of family Thanksgiving the Delgado family would endure each November in my childhood years, with aunts and uncles bitching and moaning, and Grandma Delgado thoroughly drowning in all the preparations that most of my relatives took for granted. Once the beer and wine began to flow, there was at least one fistfight over the outcome of some stupid football game.

What in the hell had I been thinking trying to get both of our families together and hoping we'd work past our differences?

My heart was so full of Mark, I wanted my boys to love him too. But I wasn't being fair to them. They already had a father, and Mark didn't need to be thrust at them like some surrogate. Yet I wanted their acceptance—needed their acceptance—of Mark in my life.

It wasn't fair to his girls, either. I knew Carly loved me—just like I loved her. To her, I wasn't Elaine's replacement; I was Mark's girlfriend. But I wanted Kathy to at least *like* me. As it stood, we were no better than casual acquaintances.

Why did this always seem so easy on television and in the movies? Why couldn't it be as easy as it was for the fucking Brady Bunch?

Abby brought me back from my thoughts. "I can come help tonight, if you'd like."

"Thanks, Abs, but I think I've got it all under control."

***

The droning smoke alarm wouldn't shut up and neither would Jellybean.

I grabbed his cage and dragged it out of the living room so the poor bird could get some fresh air. Nate stood on a kitchen chair, trying to pull the blaring alarm from the ceiling. As I came back into the kitchen, the noise pounded in my head and the smoke filled my lungs. No real fire, but the turkey was toast.

I'd been so busy running back and forth to the stupid grocery store to get the ingredients I'd forgotten that I overlooked the damned turkey still in the oven. It had been there since five in the morning because I had neglected to take it out of the freezer the night before and it needed several more hours to cook than what I'd planned. It probably wasn't much help that I'd jacked the oven temperature so high.

"Shit!" I cupped my hands over my ears. "Can't you get that thing turned off?"

Nate finally gave it a hard tug, and the alarm came off in his hand. After he jerked the battery out, blessed silence filled the smoky room. He shrugged. "At least we know it works."

The door from the garage opened and in strolled my oldest. "Jesus Christ on a pogo stick. What happened in here?"

"Mom burned the turkey."

Patrick laughed at me, and I was tempted to throw something at him. "Mom shouldn't be cooking. I think there's some law against it."

"Bite me, Pat."

I pulled the pan full of charcoal that used to be poultry out of the oven and dropped it in the sink. I sprayed some water over it to make sure it wouldn't spontaneously ignite. Tears welled up in my eyes. My first Thanksgiving with Mark and his girls, and I'd ruined it.

Pat came and put his arm around my shoulders. "We can get by without turkey."

"But it's Thanksgiving," I said with a dismal sniffle. "You have to have turkey on Thanksgiving."

He nodded at the bowls full of food piled up on the table and countertop. "We've got plenty. Look—there's noodles, dressing, green beans, yams." He walked over to the refrigerator and opened the door. "Salad. Jell-O. A gazillion pies." Pat grabbed a beer and raised it so I could see. "And plenty to mellow the mood."

"Put that back," I scolded. "It's too early for beer, and I hate knowing you're old enough to drink. Makes me feel ancient." I brushed back the few remaining disappointed tears with the back of my food-coated hands, wondering how awful I looked. "You really think it'll be all right without the stupid turkey?"

Pat nodded as the door opened again.

"What happened here?" Mark walked into my hazy kitchen, fanning his face to dispense the lingering smoke. Then he looked to the sink and the charred carcass before he burst out laughing.

I wanted to smack him. "I burned the stupid turkey," I confessed, sounding entirely pathetic. "I'm sorry."

He came over and kissed my forehead. "It's fine, babe. I hate turkey anyway. Makes me sleepy."

Patrick smirked. "I'll bet it makes you fart, too. I heard it affects old guys like that."

Kathy had followed Mark inside. Nate immediately moved to her side and brushed a quick kiss on her lips, drawing a stern frown from Mark.

Carly breezed in, took a good, long look around, and started organizing things like a drill sergeant. "Well, it looks like we're ready to eat. Kat, you and Nate get these bowls moved to the table. Dad, you take that...*thing* in the sink out to the trash."

He saluted and got about his job.

"Pat?" she asked.

Patrick snapped his heels together. "Yes, commandant?"

Carly giggled. "Would you please get some plates and silverware?"

He smiled at her. "Yes, ma'am."

Of all of the unusual family dynamics this odd situation had produced, the relationship between Carly and Patrick was the most fascinating. They acted like an authentic brother and sister would, as if they'd grown up together. They teased, they antagonized, and they genuinely liked each other. They made me very, very happy with their immediate acceptance of each other.

If only the rest of us could manage to emulate them.

By the time Carly was done barking out orders, we were seated around the dining room table, eating a vegetarian Thanksgiving feast. At least there would be plenty of dessert. I hadn't screwed those up. I'd made six kinds of pie, afraid I wouldn't hit everyone's favorite. And I'd used the extra dough to make cinnamon treats. I wanted this Thanksgiving to be perfect. Our first, family holiday was supposed to be *perfect*.

We ate and chatted and laughed. Things finally seemed to be going well, and my heart was full of happiness.

Mark hit his glass with his spoon.

Five pairs of curious eyes turned his direction.

"Now that we're all finished making absolute pigs of ourselves, I've got an announcement."

"You're moving to Alaska," Pat said under his breath. "Have a safe trip."

Mark chuckled. "Sorry to disappoint you, Son. Actually—" he reached over to take my hand and cradle it in his, "—I've made a really big decision, and I wanted to share it with all of you."

I arched an eyebrow at him because he sure hadn't mentioned anything about really big decisions to *me*.

Mark released my hand, shifted to reach into his pocket, and pulled out a small, black velvet box. My heart stopped beating and my mouth felt like it was suddenly stuffed with cotton balls. He set the box gently in front of me, slid out of his chair, and got down on one knee.

I choked back a sob. This wasn't happening. It couldn't be happening. Not so quickly. A dream. This was just a dream. I stared at the little box and put my shaking free hand to my lips to try to stop any pitiable sound from escaping.

I had always fantasized about being proposed to in some romantic way. David asked me to marry him sitting in his car in the middle of the obstetrician's parking lot. Of course, my pregnancy had forced his hand, but it hadn't been a proposal as much as an accepted circumstance beyond our control. My engagement ring had cost less than a hundred bucks, and he'd always made me think I was damn lucky to even get one.

"Jackie," Mark said, staring up into my eyes. "I love you. I'll always love you. I'm asking you to marry me. Here, in front of the people we love most in the world, I'm asking you to be my wife."

Patrick shoved his chair back and hopped to his feet. "You've gotta be kidding me. Mom, it's too soon. You haven't even known him that long."

Carly jumped up and began to wag her index finger at Patrick. "You need to leave them alone and let her make up her own mind. They love each other."

I glanced over at Nate and Kathy, who both looked entirely too shocked to say anything, exchanging a nervous stare only they understood.

And me?

I was a catatonic mess, sitting there like an enormous statue, having no will to move. I couldn't even squeak out a word. Not a single word.

Mark was smart, though. He was obviously learning how to handle me when I became a basket case. Probably because I was giving him plenty of practice. Pulling my hand to his lips, he kissed the back of it.

"I know it's a big step," he said.

I let out a nervous laugh.

"And I know marriage hasn't always been good to you. But I'm not David. I'm sturdy. I'm faithful. I don't make promises I can't keep. I love you, Jackie."

"I–I know. But..." I glanced up at our four kids.

It wasn't just my life or Mark's that would be changing. There were drastic implications for every person sitting at that table.

Mark's dark eyes grew a little stormy, and I could see he was afraid—afraid I might say, "No."

He was serious. The man really wanted to marry me.

I couldn't leave him dangling there without any reassurance that I loved him in return. I reached out and cupped his face in my hands. "I love you too, Mark. I just... What about our kids?"

"What about them?" he asked with a shrug. "We have our own lives, Jackie. I know this would be a change, a big change for everyone. But we'll make it work. I promise. We'll make it work." He pulled one of my hands away from his face and kissed my palm. "Will you marry me?"

Patrick's hands were tight fists. "Mom, you can't—"

I shot him a stern glare.

"Fine. It's your life."

"Yes. Yes, it is." But I still couldn't accept Mark's proposal.

What in the hell was wrong with me? I loved this man more than I thought possible, more than I ever loved David, more than I'd ever loved another human being. Why couldn't I shake the insecurity, the fear that he'd leave me someday for someone younger, or prettier, or—

"You're thinking too hard, babe."

I laughed at that, although it was a nervous chuckle that probably sounded more like a whimper. "Mark, I just... I don't..." I started to cry again, feeling like I'd spontaneously developed a severe case of bi-polar disorder.

Mark got to his feet, grabbed the black box, and shoved it in his pocket. He tugged me to stand, bent down, and in one swift move had me thrown over his shoulder like a sack of grain before marching down the hallway.

"We need a few minutes alone," he growled as he carried me toward my bedroom.

The kids just gawked at us as we retreated.

I wasn't sure whether to be thrilled or insulted at being hauled away. He didn't put me down until he was in my room. He kicked the door shut behind us.

"All right. We're alone now. You can talk freely. No more audience."

"Gee, thanks." I had to swallow the stupid, self-defensive sarcasm that was fighting to fall from my lips.

He sat on the bed and patted the space next to him.

I sighed and went to sit at his side, fervently hoping he wouldn't touch me. I couldn't think straight when he touched me.

"Tell me what's bothering you."

"It's such a big step," I mumbled, realizing how ridiculous I sounded stating the obvious.

"Yes, it is." Mark sat there for a second, lost in contemplation. "But if I've learned anything from what happened to Elaine, it's to grab for what you want—not to wait for later to try and find happiness. Because there's not always a later to look forward to."

I nodded, feeling a lump forming in my throat. "But it's so–so...*quick*."

"I could get shot tomorrow."

I put my trembling fingers to his lips. "Don't say that. Don't even *think* it."

He kissed my fingertips before I dropped my hand back to my lap.

"Don't you love me?" he asked, searching my eyes for an answer.

"Of course, I love you. I do."

"And I love you. We're great together. You make me laugh when I thought I'd forgotten how. You make me mad. You make me insane. And you make me want to tear your clothes off and make love to you every minute I'm with you."

I was blushing at his words, but they were sure nice to hear. "Ditto. Straight down the line. Ditto."

He leaned in and kissed my lips, sweetly and gently with no demand. "I want to marry you. I want us to make that crazy group of kids sitting out there waiting for us a family. A *real* family."

"A family. Do you really think we can? After all the rotten things that have happened to all of us, do you really think we can?" I asked, hardly believing any of this was happening.

"I'm sure as hell willing to try."

"Show me."

He gave me a deep, stirring kiss. As he eased away, he asked, "Does *that* show you?"

I giggled like some silly teenager and figured that's what happened when you've spent too much time in their company. "I meant the ring. Show me the ring."

Mark fished in his pocket to pull out the black velvet box. Popping it open, he set it on his palm.

The ring was exquisite. A simple band of gold with small diamonds surrounding one, very large teardrop stone. I reached for it with trembling fingers.

"Carly helped me pick it out."

No wonder she'd been giving so many funny smiles all week. Every time she'd come into class or caught my eye in the hall, she'd grinned until those braces winked in the fluorescent lights. I just chalked her strange reactions up to being a typical goofy teenager. Now, I realized she'd known all along that her father was going to propose. "You did good. She did good."

He plucked the ring from the box and reached for my left hand. "Jackie, will you marry me?"

"Yes." I nodded like a bobblehead someone had just jostled. "Oh, yes. I'll marry you."

An enormous grin lit his face, and he slid the cool metal over my ring finger. It was a perfect fit—just like Mark and me.

I pulled him into a passionate kiss. All I really wanted in the world at that moment was to strip him and hop all over him like some lust-crazed wanton. His response to our kiss told me he felt the same way.

For the first time, he pulled away before I did. "God, babe, I want you, but..."

I nodded my understanding, but I had to acknowledge how disappointed I was. "I know, I know. But, damn it, I want you now." I sighed. "The kids are right down the hall."

"Hell, their ears are probably pressed to the door," Mark added. He kissed me again, quickly, but sweetly. "Tonight. We'll have tonight."

"Tonight," I repeated a bit breathlessly. I held up my left hand and admired my new engagement ring. "It's beautiful, Mark."

"Just like the woman wearing it." He stood up and pulled me to my feet. "Let's go tell the kids."

We walked back into the dining room hand in hand.

Carly was the first to react, letting out an excited squeal. "She's wearing the ring! She's going to marry him! Sweet!"

Patrick folded his arms over his chest and leaned his chair back on two legs, but he kept his thoughts to himself.

Nate gave me a beaming smile and then looked over at Mark. "Congratulations."

Mark nodded. "Thank you."

Kathy sat there stoically for a moment. Those dark eyes of hers were locked on me, probing, looking for something she needed to see that I wished I could show her. She finally heaved a sigh that I tried not to take as disappointment on her part. "When?"

"When?" I repeated, a little confused at the question. "Oh, when will we get married? I don't know."

I hadn't even thought about it—hadn't dared to speculate. While I'd always hoped and prayed that Mark and I would be together, I'd never let my fragile ego do anything as daring as anticipating that he would propose or that we would ever marry. Plus, I was still a little gun-shy on the whole idea of "happily ever after," even if it was with Mr. Yummy.

"Soon," Mark said with a strong, clear voice that warmed my heart. "Real soon. Christmas break?" He arched an eyebrow.

"Christmas break?" I asked. Things were happening too quickly.

My mother's old sermon of "marry in haste, repent in leisure" was nagging my brain. Sometimes I wished the damned thing had an "off" switch. Why couldn't I just be happy? Why did I always have to think something bad was going to happen if I was happy?

"Oh, Mark... I can't possibly get things together that fast."

"Sure *we* can. Hang on." Carly popped to her feet and hurried out the door to the garage. She came back a few minutes later, humming to herself and holding a thick notebook. "I've been doing some research."

Mark laughed and clapped me on the shoulder. "She decided she wants to be a wedding coordinator when she grows up. You ought to see all the books and magazines she has in that basement room of hers."

"Quit teasing," Carly scolded. "This is fun, and I'm getting good at it."

Laying the book on the table, she flipped through pages of magazine cutouts and pages printed from websites. I wondered just how long she had been working on this important little project. How long had Mark been planning to propose?

"Here or in Vegas?" she asked.

"Here," I replied. "Vegas weddings always seem so...cheap. I don't want Elvis to marry us."

Mark laughed and nodded.

"Fine." Carly turned to another page in her notebook. "Here. Do you want a church or the courthouse? You know, we could even go to the cabin in Michigan. That would be pretty." She put a finger to her cheek and then she shook her head. "Nah. Too much snow."

I put an arm around her shoulder and looked at her collection. She was an industrious young lady, and I marveled at the time and effort her work must have taken. I loved her wholehearted acceptance. "This is wonderful."

"See, Daddy? I told you she'd want my help."

Mark ruffled her dark hair.

She shot him an annoyed glare and smoothed her bangs back in place.

Patrick dropped his chair back on all four legs and stood up. He grabbed a couple of dirty bowls from the table and hauled them to the kitchen. Nate and Kathy started to help in the clean up. Not a one of them said a word.

There was still plenty of trouble in paradise.

CHAPTER THIRTEEN

Abby hadn't stopped clapping since I told my friends the news at lunch the following Monday.

"How are you going to pull all that together in three weeks?" Julie asked.

I knew her well enough to read the nuisances of her expression. She didn't think this was a good idea at all.

"Carly is helping. You'd be amazed how well she's got this all planned out," I replied. "We're having a really small ceremony at my house, in the family room."

"*Your* house," Julie said with a rueful chuckle. "Geesh. Have you even thought about what you'll do after the wedding? Who'll be moving in with whom? Who's going to have to sell? Who pays the health insurance?"

I stopped my forkful of lettuce mid-air. No, I hadn't thought about any of that. I'd been so busy thinking about dresses and flowers and licenses that I realized Mark and I still had an awful lot of planning to do. I dropped the fork back onto the plate, having suddenly lost my appetite.

I tried to cover my apprehension with a lame joke. "Oops. I guess I've got some more stuff to let Carly deal with."

Julie was angry, and for some reason that hurt. Didn't she want me to be happy?

"Don't 'oops' me, Jackie." I heard her breathe an annoyed sigh like she always did right before I got a lengthy lecture. "You're rushing into this awfully fast. I know you think you love the guy, but—"

I waved my hand to stop her, trying not to sound as annoyed as I was rapidly becoming. "I don't *think* I love Mark. I love him. I know this is quick, but we're both old enough to know what we want. You could try being just a little bit happy for me—or is that too much to ask from my friends?"

"We *are* happy for you." Suzanne patted my hand.

It seemed condescending gesture, so I pulled my hand away and opened a packet of crackers so I wouldn't seem too rude.

Abby looked confused. "Why are we fighting? What's wrong with Jackie getting married?"

"She didn't even want to *date* the guy in August," Julie replied, still glaring at me across the table. "Now—twelve weeks later—she wants to *marry* him?"

"That's not fair," I snapped. "It was a blind date. I didn't know it would be Mark. And we did go out. And we fell in love."

"He's rushing you," Julie countered, the pit bull part of her personality asserting itself. She had a good hold on the notion that I was doing the wrong thing, and she wasn't going to let it go. "Guys who lose their wives feel some weird drive to get remarried really fast. I read about it on some website."

"Me, too," Suzanne chimed in. "Oprah said if they had a happy marriage, they dive right back in within a year. But it doesn't always work as well the second time."

"Elaine died more than two years ago," I said, hoping this topic would drop soon.

Abby let a heavy sigh hang in the air. "I think it's romantic. Even if it is awfully fast. You love him, Jackie? Don't you?"

I closed my eyes for a moment and massaged my forehead with my fingertips. I knew I should have expected this. They were my friends, and they were obviously looking out for what they thought was in my best interests. Had I been sitting in any of their chairs, I would've given all the same advice, pointed out all the same pitfalls. But I was the one who was being badgered, and my already emotionally overwrought mind couldn't take much more.

I sighed. "Look, I appreciate all the concern, but I'm marrying Mark on Christmas Eve. Please stop trying to talk me out of it." Julie opened her mouth, but I cut her off. "If you're not going to say something nice, please don't say anything." That did it. She was pissed. I was amazed steam wasn't literally pouring out of her ears. "Julie, I'm sorry. I didn't mean—"

"I'm not running your life, Jackie. I won't say another word. Not another damn word. Just don't come crying to me when things go sour."

"I appreciate that vote of confidence," I sarcastically replied. "Think he'll leave me for a younger woman too?"

What the hell was wrong with me? Julie and I never fought. We were always on the same team. I loved her like a sister.

"I think we all need to go to neutral corners for a few minutes." Suzanne shifted her gaze between Julie and me. "We're all friends here. Remember?"

"I'm sorry, Julie," I said, feeling extraordinarily stupid and more than a little immature.

She gave me a curt nod that said this was far from over.

I nodded back and finished my lunch without another word to any of them.

I didn't have to wait long for Julie to finish what she'd started. She met me at my classroom door right after last bell.

I offered the olive branch. "Julie, I'm so sorry. I didn't mean to jump down your throat at lunch."

"I know. You're under a lot of stress. Do you want to talk about it now, or are you still in your defensive mode?" She sat down in a student desk and stared up at me.

"Shields are down right now," I replied with a soft, nervous chuckle. "You just took me by surprise." I turned another student desk around and faced my best friend. "I guess I hoped you'd be happy for me."

"Oh, Jackie. I *am* happy for you. But I'm concerned, too. You've only known Mark since August. That's not very long, and... Well, I know you don't have much self-esteem. I don't want you marrying Mark if you're only doing it because you're grateful for the offer. You know, I could really kill David for doing what he did to you—making you feel like you're not worth anything."

I took a long, steadying breath. "I'm not marrying Mark because I need a self-esteem boost. And I'm not marrying Mark because David dumped me."

"Really?"

"Really. I'm marrying Mark because, for the first time in my life, I'm in love—a mature love that gives and takes. He's good for me, Julie. And he's good *to* me."

"Need any help with wedding plans?" she said, brushing away a tear.

I could feel one slipping down my own cheek. "Sure. Carly and I are going dress shopping this weekend. Want to come?"

"Maybe. Will you ask your mother and father to come for the ceremony?"

I hadn't even thought about that. I hadn't even told them I was *dating* Mark, let alone *marrying* him. Mom would take one look at him and tell him he was too good for me.

"I'll invite them, but they won't come—not back to Indiana in the dead of winter. Besides, I think they'll be content if I just email them some pictures."

"Have you met his parents yet?" Julie asked.

"Not yet. They're living in Florida." I chuckled. "I wonder if they're in the same retirement complex as my parents."

***

As the days before the wedding passed in a dizzying blur, Patrick called almost every night, hoping I'd changed my mind and that I might at least wait a few months.

Every night at supper, Carly filled me in with updates on the wedding plans. She'd booked the judge, the florist, the cake, and the reception caterer. Mark started calling her "J-Lo." I wasn't sure she got *The Wedding Planner* reference because she told him to quit telling her that her butt was big.

Nate and Kat had all but disappeared, and of all the family issues, their continued silence worried me the most. Nate had always been the kid who needed to touch base with me often. I wasn't at all used to being shut out, especially when he got this quiet. Silence usually meant something was wrong. He didn't return my messages, and I was getting more and more frustrated.

As Carly and I cleaned up the supper dishes, Mark came back into his house after running the trash outside, put his arms around me, and started tickling me. I almost dropped the last of the plates I was putting on the top shelf before I collapsed against him in a giggle fit. Carly smiled over at both of us.

"I can't believe we're getting married next weekend," he said when he finally stopped torturing me.

"Well, you *are,*" Carly replied in a parental voice that brooked no argument. "Everything's ready." She lost herself in her thoughts for a moment. "Except we need to pick our dresses up from the lady doing the alterations on Thursday."

"And you need to go study for your biology final, young lady," I scolded, hoping she realized I was mostly teasing.

"If I get another high test grade, my friends will never let me live it down. They think you give me good grades 'cause you're marrying my dad," she grumbled.

"We know better," I replied. "We know you study, and we know that you're way too smart to only be fourteen. How many days until your birthday?"

She flashed me her braces. "Fifteen days 'til I'm fifteen. I really need to go study. Faith has probably sent me a million text messages." Carly disappeared down the basement stairs to her bedroom.

I knew it was probably time for me to be heading back to my own house. In the weeks that had passed since Mark proposed, I'd developed a habit of spending the evenings with him and Carly, then I'd go back home before it got too late. But it was getting harder and harder to leave.

If he wasn't called out on the job, he usually slept at my place on Fridays and Saturdays. My frazzled nerves needed to see him more often. I knew it was my ridiculous insecurity and my fear that he might suddenly change his mind about marrying me, but I needed his reassurances that he still loved me. Not that he'd given me any reason to feel anything but loved.

Maybe I was just needy.

"I guess I better go." I wondered if I sounded as dejected as I felt.

"Stay," Mark said as he came behind me and wrapped his arms around my waist. "We can watch TV."

I closed my eyes and leaned back into his embrace. "I have papers to grade." He kissed my ear, then ran that incredible tongue around the ridges. Shivers raced over my body. "Carly is here. We can't—"

"Carly is studying. Do you think she's going to disappear after we're married? We're going to live here, Jackie. She'll get used to it. Hell, I think she's already used to it."

"We're going to live *here?*"

Julie had been right. I really needed to sit down with Mark and make some important decisions—decisions like where we'd live, what we would do about insurance, what would happen to our kids if something happened to one of us. It had simply been so much easier to ignore all that adult stuff and plan a pretty wedding. What we should have been doing was planning our life together.

Now my lack of attention was coming home to roost.

"I assumed. I mean, my house is paid off. Don't you have a mortgage?"

"Yeah, but my garden's there. And all my stuff's there. Where would I put it here?"

"We'll make it fit, babe." He kissed my neck. "Everything about us fits. Perfectly."

I normally loved his cute little innuendos, but I was having a hard time keeping my panic at bay. "Can't we be serious for a second? I don't want to sell my house. I might... I might need to... What if things don't work out?" I couldn't believe I'd said that aloud, but once out in the open, the notion needed some serious consideration.

Mark came around to stare down at me. "You still don't trust me, do you?"

I shrugged before I could stop myself.

"You can be such a piece of work. You still think I'm only in this for some short-term kicks, don't you? You want to keep that house so you have someplace to go when I leave you."

I stood there as quiet as a mute.

"Don't you?" he shouted, causing me to wince.

"I just don't see why I should sell my house. We can move some of my things here—"

Mark stomped out of the kitchen into the family room and plopped down on the couch. Grabbing the remote he began to flip through channels too fast to even know what he was watching. "I'm getting tired of you not having a lick of faith in me."

"I have faith in you!"

He scoffed and kept changing channels. His agitated breathing was loud enough for me to hear.

I stamped my foot. "I do! I have faith in you!" I knew I was shouting, but the lid had blown off the pressure cooker, and there was no containing the explosion. He wanted to know what was wrong, then, damn it, I'd tell him. "I don't have faith in *me!*" Words tumbled out of my mouth—there was no stopping them. "You're too good a man to be stuck with someone like me. I'm stubborn. I'm temperamental. I'm... I'm... Argh!" I threw my hands up in frustration.

Mark threw the remote at the chair and walked over to me. Fists firmly planted against his hips, he glared down at me.

I rattled on. "I'm such a bitch when I want to be. I'm getting old. Things are sagging all over the place. And you're... you're... still so handsome. So... so... *perfect.*" Shaking my head, I felt the torrent of words finally sputter to a halt.

He tugged me into his arms. "I'm not perfect." A chuckle rumbled his chest. "At least not *all* the time."

I snorted and shook my head. "No, you're not."

"I'm stubborn, too."

With a sniffle, I nodded and let a small, nervous laugh escape my lips.

"I'm temperamental, too."

I nodded against his chest. He smelled like Polo Black again. God, I loved that cologne on him.

"Nobody's perfect, Jackie." He pulled away to kiss my forehead. "Not even me. Except in bed."

I had to laugh at his ability to relate any conversation to sex.

Mark hugged me a little tighter. "I know you're scared. And I know trust takes time, but I need you to understand. I'm not leaving you. You won't ever have to go back to your house because I'm not leaving you."

"I trust you, Mark. I do."

"How about we keep the house for now? Would that make you happy?"

Suddenly, it didn't matter. Selling my house didn't matter. The insurance didn't matter. Where we lived didn't matter.

Mark mattered.

I didn't need a safety net because he was walking the tightrope right beside me. If we fell, it would be together—because, for once, I wasn't alone. "I'll call the realtor tomorrow."

He kissed me. One of those deep, consuming kisses that always made me forget myself. In a daze, I let him lead me upstairs to his room. It was our room, really. I had left so much of my stuff behind, I could have moved in and never have to go back to fetch anything from my house.

Pinning my back against the door the moment it was shut, Mark took total control. I rejoiced in his insistent hands on my body, covering my breast, cupping my butt. Warm kisses against my neck, my ear, and covering my mouth, demanding my response. Clothes fell away in small piles, some ripped, and some discarded. When we were gloriously naked, he wrapped his arms around my waist and lifted me. Shuffling across the carpet to the bed, he dropped me on my back so my legs hung over the side.

He didn't even give me a chance to protest, but fell to his knees and buried his mouth between my legs. Separating my folds, his tongue tickled my sensitive bud before he drew it between his lips and sucked.

Had anything ever felt so glorious? I writhed and moaned, and when he stabbed his tongue inside me, I finally grabbed a throw pillow to hold over my face to keep from screaming too loudly. Hopefully, Carly was listening to her music. At least she was in the basement.

In all the years of my marriage, David had never done that for me, never given me such a wondrous gift, although he'd expected similar attention from me. He told me a blow job was his favorite birthday present.

Mark was right. He wasn't David, and judging Mark as the same type of man was an insult.

I would never make that mistake again. *Ever*.

The man was thorough, loving, and he had me bucking beneath him in a very short time. I shouted my orgasm into the corduroy pillow and could hear his satisfied chuckle over the noise of my own heartbeat echoing in my ears. But he wasn't done.

Mark tugged the pillow out of my clutches and tossed it aside. Then he lifted me by the hips and entered me in one, dominant thrust that rattled my teeth. The man instinctively knew when I liked it rough, and, man, could he deliver. If he hadn't covered my mouth with one of his hypnotic kisses, I would have had to grab the pillow again.

He created such a flurry of sensations. The taste of me lingering on his lips, the glory of him driving into me so hard and fast, the delicious heat of his body pressed to mine. I hadn't even come down from the first release before he sent me soaring back over the moon with him following only a moment behind.

I didn't even mind when he collapsed on me like an enormous lump. It was nice to know I could do that to him—that I could make him so sated he couldn't hold himself up.

Mark groaned and rolled to his side. We just lay there side-by-side with our legs hanging over the end of the bed.

"God, we're greedy," he said with a chuckle. "I can't keep my hands off you."

"Like a couple of pigs at a full trough." Rolling to my side, I threw my arm over his strong chest. "But I don't plan on stopping any time soon. You've spoiled me, you know."

"Spoiled you?" He turned his head enough to look into my eyes.

"Spoiled me. You're so...so...*good* at this, I expect it to always be satisfying. I don't have to pretend."

"David wasn't—"

"You're breaking rule number one," I interrupted before I began to giggle as his hand wandered up to tickle my ribs. "Stop. Stop."

With a wicked smile on his lips, Mark rolled over and began to torture me with tickles. "Say it. Say I'm the best ever. Say it."

"Yes!" Tears ran down the corners of my eyes. "You're the best. You're the best."

He stopped tickling me and kissed my forehead. "Told you so."

CHAPTER FOURTEEN

Carly shot me a frown. "Quit picking at the flowers or there won't be anything left of your bouquet."

"Sorry." I pulled my hand out of the cascade of silk roses I'd been clutching in my hands like a lifeline. Glancing down at the floor, I noticed bits of baby's breath and red petals lying in a small puddle at my feet. "Sorry," I said again, giving Carly an apologetic look. "You look awfully pretty."

She flashed an enormous smile. "Thank you. So do you."

Standing there in her tea-length red dress, she looked a lot older than fourteen. She'd wanted a strapless, but I insisted on something less revealing. At least this dress had capped sleeves and only revealed a little shoulder. Kathy was supposed to wear one exactly like it, but she hadn't come up to see me before the ceremony, choosing instead to stay at her father's side.

"Jackie, leave the bouquet alone."

"Sorry."

Three seconds later, I was picking at it again.

I should have expected the attack of nerves. I was getting married, for pity's sake. It was something I had sworn I would never ever do again. I had a vivid memory of a summer lunch with my friends where I pledged I wouldn't be a wife again. I didn't want the hassle. I didn't want some man to run my life, to call the shots, to make me hate myself again.

But Mark Brennan wasn't "some man."

Carly came over, took the roses from my hands, and handed me a huge wad of tissues. "Shred those instead." She was definitely fourteen going on forty.

"Are you going to be a psychologist when you grow up?" I asked with a nervous chuckle.

"There are enough crazy people in this family, I oughta consider it," she replied with a smile. Then she glanced at her watch. "Won't be long now. Relax."

The bedroom door opened to reveal my frowning oldest son. Patrick was so handsome, so grown up in his black suit, ready to stand in for my father. Mom and Dad said they might visit in the spring and to have a nice wedding.

And people wondered why I had low self-esteem.

My heart was heavy, knowing Patrick didn't approve of this marriage. No matter how much his acceptance meant, his disapproval wasn't going to make me change my mind. I hoped he would follow through and give me away when the time came.

"You ready?" Pat asked, not a note of emotion in his voice. He might as well have been leading me to the Green Room at San Quentin.

I placed a hand on his arm. "Pat..."

He shook his head. "I don't want to argue."

"I don't, either. I wanted to thank you."

His eyes widened. "Thank me?"

"I know this is hard for you, but I want you to know how much I appreciate you being here, giving me away." I stood on tiptoes to kiss his cheek.

He blushed and stared at his shoes. "You know how I feel, but I couldn't not be here for you." His eyes finally found mine, and I could see the little boy for a quick second—the little boy who was always going to be there was hiding just behind the man he'd become. "Mark's an okay guy. I just want him to be good to you. I love you, Mom."

Tears formed up in my eyes. It was way too soon for tears. I tried to choke them back, but a couple leaked out anyway. "I love you too."

I dabbed at my eyes with the shredded tissues. No black blobs were left behind, so at least my waterproof mascara was holding. Thank heaven for small favors.

"We need to go. The judge is here and Mark is waiting." He opened the door and gave me a sassy smile. "It's not too late to call it off. Sure I can't change your mind?"

I shook my head. Taking one, last look in the mirror, I felt pretty for one of the few times in my life. My ivory dress brushed the floor. Light caught the bits of beads that dotted the skirt, making them sparkle. I adjusted the off-the-shoulder sleeves, smoothed the front of the dress, and took a deep, steadying breath. It didn't help calm me much.

Pat escorted me from the bedroom. Lifting the hem of my dress I started down the stairs before I suddenly realized I'd left my bouquet. Carly was right behind me, holding my roses.

"Got your back," she said with laughing eyes and a grin full of braces.

One day those dark eyes and that beautiful smile would devastate some poor guy, and his life would never be the same.

"Thanks." I made my way down the steps.

When I reached the ground floor, I stopped to take in the whole setting. Carly had done a beautiful job planning this wedding.

The family room was awash in Christmas and candlelight. Carly and I had decorated for the holiday, even though no one was really living here now. I'd moved in with Mark the day after I put the house up for sale. We'd sold the couch, recliners, and tables, so the room was empty. It was a perfect place for a small gathering.

There was a Christmas tree in one corner, covered in red and gold bows, lights twinkling in the dim room. Garlands of pine covered the fireplace mantle and glowed with the light from a dozen red candles. Soft music floated around us.

Julie, Abby, and Suzanne were there. Julie looked a bit misty-eyed as she leaned against her husband's arm. Abby was beaming. So was Suzanne. They would *finally* be able to tell everyone they were trying to fix up on one of their blind dates that they'd made a successful match. I took strength from having my friends close. It was almost like having real sisters.

I nodded to a couple of police officers Mark had introduced to me one night at dinner. I felt bad that I couldn't remember all their names. One escorted a woman I assumed was his wife. She gave me a goofy little half wave that reminded me so much of myself, I instantly liked her.

Mark stood next to a local judge I'd met when I had her twins as students a few years ago. The blond judge smiled at me and nodded, clutching a small white book.

I nodded back as I threaded my arm through Patrick's and let him lead me to my groom.

Kathy took her place at Mark's left, looking spectacular in her red dress. Nate stood at her side. Patrick and Carly would be my attendants. It made a nice little mix for the new family we were creating.

Mark took my breath away. He'd chosen a dark gray suit and a solid red tie. The red rose boutonniere Carly and I had made was pinned to his lapel. He smiled at me with those handsome brown eyes and sparkling teeth.

I realized—probably for the millionth time since I met him—that I was a very lucky woman.

I saw the appreciation of the way I looked in his eyes. His gaze scanned me from head to toe, and his smile grew even wider. Even here, in front of everyone, I warmed to that smile. A quiver of excitement and feeling of rightness flowed through me.

Mark was going to marry me. It was really happening.

Patrick stopped in front of the judge as our children and guests gathered around us. Twenty of our closest friends formed a sheltering semi-circle. I was happy we were here. A church wouldn't have been nearly as intimate.

"Who gives this woman to marry this man?" Judge Honeycutt asked.

"My brother and I do," Patrick replied in a voice with a small catch to it that choked me up.

Taking my hand, he gave it an affectionate squeeze and then set it in Mark's waiting hand. It was probably the hardest thing Patrick had ever done. He was already sniffing in that masculine way he always did when tears threatened. I could feel my own eyes growing moist.

Mark drew my hand through the crook of his elbow and gave it a loving pat. "You look stunning," he whispered.

"So do you," I whispered back.

The ceremony proceeded per tradition, with the standard questions and the usual answers. I had a hard time paying attention, because all I could think about was Mark. The warmth of him beside me, the gentle weight of his hand covering mine, and the rumble of that baritone voice as he responded to each question with no hesitation. Then came the time for the vows we had both decided to write for each other.

He'd asked me if he could say something and if I wanted to say anything other than the customary vows. Thinking I had plenty of time to prepare, I'd agreed.

But I'd resorted to an uncharacteristic bout of procrastination. The problem was that I had too much to say, but I also had too little. How could I possibly sum up everything I felt for Mark Brennan in a few words?

I started writing the silly vows a hundred different times, but each attempt ended up in wadded paper being pitched across the room. Not until the morning of the wedding had I finally decided what to say. A small folded paper was tucked in my bouquet, waiting at ready in case my memory fled. I hoped I hadn't accidentally left it amongst the rose petals I'd nervously plucked.

Judge Honeycutt closed her little book. "Mark and Jackie have written their own vows. Mark, would you like to recite your vows to Jackie now?"

"Good a time as any," he said before his eyes grew serious, penetrating to my very soul. "Sweet Jackie. You've changed my entire world. I've never met a woman so full of love, so full of life. Every time I'm around you, I feel like I have to catch my breath. You never stop moving. Or talking."

Several people in the small crowd chuckled. I couldn't blame them. Yet I didn't take his words or their amusement as criticism as I always had before. He meant what he'd said as an endearment. A tear fell from my lashes.

"And I love that about you. I love that you sing aloud to the radio and that you always mess up the lyrics. I love that you eat peanut butter right out of the jar. I love that you always think about everyone else before yourself. I love that you laugh the same time you cry. I'm damn lucky that I found you, and I couldn't imagine life without you. I promise to be faithful. I promise to be there through good times and bad—no matter how bad things might get. As long as I draw breath, I'll be by your side."

I thought my heart would burst. Mark knew me—he knew me almost better than I knew myself.

Suddenly the words I had written seemed inadequate.

"Jackie?" the judge asked. "Would you please recite your vows to Mark?"

Reaching deep down, I let all I felt for that wonderful man tumble from my mouth, fervently hoping the words would come out right. "Mark, you're my rock. My stalwart. I've never known a man I could trust the way I can trust you. You're always there when I need you. No matter how hard I tried to push you away, you didn't budge. I love that stubbornness. I love your bad jokes. I love that you turn everything I say into a double entendre. I love that you always do a really bad impersonation of William Shatner to make me laugh when you know I'm sad."

Carly let out an enormous laugh that sent a ripple of chuckles through the crowd.

"I love that you're always there for your girls, too. I promise that I'll be there for you—just like you're there for me. Through the good times and the bad, through sickness and health, through living on a cop and teacher's salaries and putting four kids through college, and through gray hair, wrinkles, and grandkids. I'll be there. I promise."

He kissed the back of my hand and smiled.

The rest of the ceremony went by in a blur. We exchanged rings, we answered a few more of Judge Honeycutt's questions, and then she pronounced us husband and wife. Mark kissed me deep and long, and I remembered sighing in response.

Hugs were exchanged with our children as I wondered what it would be like to be a family again. Patrick made nice and shook hands with Mark. Kathy hugged me, although she seemed a bit stiff, and I tried not to let the fact that she obviously hadn't accepted me ruin the wonderful evening. Carly greeted me with a wonderful smile and a hug that squeezed the breath right out of me. Mark and Nate shared one of those hugs guys always use that was more a slap on the back than an embrace.

After a tour of the room, shaking hands, getting more hugs, and drying a few tears, Mark and I were ready to cut the cake. Instead of the customary white cake, we went with red velvet, keeping with the crimson theme. His hand covered mine on the silver knife as we sliced a couple of small pieces.

I'd always figured the way a bride and groom fed cake to their partner was a good indication of how much overall respect they had for each other.

I'd been to weddings where the couple rudely smeared cake and icing all over their new spouse's face, and I never expected those unions to last too awfully long.

Mark quickly ate the piece I fed him and held the piece he gave me so I could take a small bite. Then he smiled and put the rest of it in his own mouth before he kissed me. He tasted like icing, and it's widely known that I'm an icing junkie. Adding my new husband's lips to the taste only strengthened the addiction.

The *hors d'oeuvres* came out as the waiters Carly had arranged started mingling among our guests. Her promise of twenty dollars and any leftover food had bribed three of her friends into helping. Patrick, Kathy, and Nate poured the drinks. Mark kept me close at his side as we made small talk and drank champagne from the bride and groom glasses. He tried to get me to eat some of the appetizers, but they tasted like sawdust.

I started to throw back the champagne like shots of whiskey, wishing they were every bit as strong. I was buzzed, but not quite enough to calm my jittery nerves.

Mark threw me a disapproving frown a couple of times, but I just shrugged in response.

Kathy was sipping champagne from a fluted glass Nate handed to her. I figured one glass of alcohol wouldn't hurt before realizing everyone else was now holding a drink too. It was time for the toasts. Mark wrapped his arm around my waist and held me closer.

Nate picked up a fork and hit his glass until the smattering of conversation died down. While my youngest wasn't a shy person, he hated speaking in public. Since he'd assumed the role of best man, Nate was going to have to give a toast.

"Um... well..." Nate cleared his throat and tried again. "Patrick and I want to welcome Mark into the family." Kathy elbowed him in the ribs. "Oh, and Kat and Carly, too." He raised his glass. "Have a nice, long marriage."

Why did that sound so much like a judge passing sentence on a convicted prisoner?

Carly, my maid of honor, took over. Raising her glass of grape juice, she smiled at her father. "Daddy, Kat, and I are happy to have Jackie around. She made my dad smile again when I was afraid he'd forgotten how." She took a sip from her flute as the guests did the same.

Mark and I clinked glasses and drank champagne. He leaned in and kissed me. "Can't wait until we can get out of here so I can get you alone."

My thoughts were in tangles. This was supposed to be the happiest day of my life. So why was I trying to drown myself in alcohol? Just this once, why couldn't I simply enjoy feeling good and being happy?

Because he married you, my brain whispered. *It's all downhill from here.*

"That's not true," I mumbled, before furtively looking over to see if Mark had caught me talking to myself.

He seemed too busy chatting with a friend to have noticed.

Oh, yes, it is true. Now that's he's got you, he doesn't have to try anymore. He'll get bored and discard you just like David.

I stopped the waiter as he walked by and grabbed another glass of champagne.

***

"I hate leaving the kids to clean up," I said as Mark held the door open. "Are you sure they won't come back here?"

"Carly said they were staying at your house at least for tonight. Patrick was supposed to bring Uno. Could turn ugly." He grinned. "I imagine they'll be here tomorrow. I mean, it's Christmas, and they're all greedy."

Stepping into our house, I was rendered speechless as I took a good look around. The lights were out. A fire crackled in the fireplace, giving the room a warm glow. The Christmas tree sparkled with multi-colored lights. A bottle of champagne chilled in a silver ice bucket on the kitchen island where two fluted glasses stood at its side. A bowl full of chocolate-dipped strawberries sat next to two small plates. Soft music filled the air, compliments of the stereo.

Carly was truly a miracle worker. I had no idea how she managed to pull all this off while she was at the wedding, babysitting the nervous bride.

Mark helped me out of my overcoat, and then hung it next to his on the coat tree. Coming behind me, he wrapped his arms around my waist and pulled me back against him. "How are you feeling tonight, Mrs. Brennan?"

Mrs. Brennan. It was such a lovely name but a shame it wouldn't be mine for long. "I'm...fine. And you Detective Brennan?"

"Never better. Want some champagne?"

God, yes! "That would be wonderful."

It took him a few moments to remove the wrapping on the bottle, and he struggled to get it open.

"Having a little trouble popping the cork?" I asked.

"My cork always takes a long time to pop," he replied with a naughty smile. "Wouldn't want to rush you." With a big tug, the cork came free, hitting the ceiling, and bouncing somewhere in the living room. "Shit." The champagne spilled from the bottle in a burst of bubbles and foam.

I grabbed the glasses and tried to catch the overflow. Mark put the bottle down, grasped the kitchen towel that was sitting by the sink, and dropped it over the spill.

"Don't you think we should clean it up?" I asked.

"It'll still be there later."

After we had full flutes, I carried them into the living room and stood in front of the fire, watching the flames lick greedily at the pieces of wood.

Someone had moved the coffee table to one side, and a couple of quilts and a few pillows were spread out on the carpet in front of the fireplace. A lot of thought had gone into this honeymoon.

Thank you, Carly.

Mark followed with the bowl of strawberries and the plates. He glanced down at the pile of bedding on the floor. "That's interesting. I think someone assumed we wouldn't make it to the bedroom." He put everything down on an end table and took a glass from my hand. "They were right. A toast."

I held my glass up. "To what?"

"To us. To a long, happy life together. To OfficeMax. To ice-skating. To—"

I took over. "To cabins in Michigan and raspberry jam." I felt a blush spread across my face.

I drank the champagne in one gulp. Mark did the same.

He went to the kitchen and brought the bottle back. He refilled both our glasses. I drank the liquid down in one big swallow.

"Easy there. I don't want you drunk."

I held the flute out to him. "More."

What was I so nervous about? It wasn't as if we hadn't had sex before. Great sex. Fantastic sex. Mind-blowing sex. Why did I suddenly feel the need to get blitzed out of my mind?

Because marriage ruins everything, my thoughts taunted. *He doesn't have to try anymore, and he'll get bored with you.*

"Shut up," I mumbled at my stupid brain.

"I beg your pardon?"

"Nothing." *Just thinking too much again.* Holding out my empty glass, I asked, "More please."

"You sound like Oliver Twist. Want to switch to Jell-O shooters?" he asked with an acerbic smile as he refilled the flute.

I drained the glass.

"All right, that's enough." He took the empty glass out of my hand and set it on the table next to his. "What in the hell is wrong with you?"

I really needed some more champagne. The mind-numbing buzz was fading too quickly. Was there any zinfandel in the kitchen? "Nothing."

Knitting his brows, he frowned. "I know you better than that."

"Nothing's wrong," I repeated.

I thought I heard a slow ten count.

"Jackie, babe, what's wrong?" Mark asked again as he took my hands into his.

I didn't want to tell him, didn't want him to think I'd lost faith in him, until I realized that was exactly what I was doing. I was losing faith in him and in me—for no good reason.

We were married now. *So what?* I still loved him and still wanted him. Judging from the front of his trousers, he felt the same.

I finally let it go. Standing there in that room—a little champagne-buzzed and nervous as a cat in a room full of rocking chairs—I let it all go. I let go of all the pain, all the insecurity, and all the uncertainty.

Mark Brennan was not David Ryan. Mark Brennan wouldn't stop loving me if some twenty-something swung her hips in front of him. Mark Brennan wouldn't become a selfish lover. Mark Brennan kept his promises.

I felt the weight of fear and worry melt away. "Nothing, Mark. Honest."

The best thing I could do was distract him. Pushing my hands up his chest, I helped him shrug off his coat. It fell to the floor, and he kicked it aside.

He reached for me.

I dodged his hands and held up an index finger to stop him. "Not yet. Patience."

He smiled at me, that saucy smile that always made me so hot. "Fine. I'm putty in your hands."

I ran my fingers across the front of his pants, loving the hardened cock that greeted my palm. "Oh, no. There's nothing *soft* about you."

I unbuckled his belt and pulled it free before turning my attention to removing his tie and shirt. His bare chest shone like gold in the firelight. I ran my fingers through the patch of dark hair that covered his pecs, loving the total masculinity of him. I got his shoes, pants, and socks off in short order.

Standing there in nothing but boxers, he looked like some Greek god. Or at least he would as soon as I got him naked. How odd it was being there in my wedding dress, while he was next to nude. I felt a primitive thrill tumble through me.

Mark started to say something, but I put my fingertips to his lips to stop him. Then I backed up a few steps and tried to find my bravado.

The high heels were first to go, but I didn't just kick them off. I hiked my dress up to my thigh and put my foot on the coffee table. I ran my hand down my leg before slowly taking the shoe off, and then I repeated the actions with the other leg. With my feet back on the floor, I turned my back to Mark. "Think you could unzip me?"

I felt his warmth against my back as the zipper was slowly dragged down. His lips caressed my bare shoulder as his hands came to rest on my hips. The front of the dress fell forward, and I caught it to keep it in place. Turning around, I backed up a step. "Tell me what you think."

I let the dress fall in a pool at my feet, revealing a strapless bra and a full set of thigh-high stockings complete with white, lace garters. I passionately hoped I appeared as sexy as I felt.

Mark growled and took a step toward me.

"No, no, no," I said, holding a finger up again, stopping him in his tracks.

"Jackie..."

"No. Not yet. Patience." I walked a slow circle around him, letting my fingers caress and slide over that heavenly skin, reveling in the fact that I had the poor guy so worked up.

"Jackie..."

"Yes?"

"I want you."

Relishing the huskiness in Mark's voice, I stepped in front on him and took a good, long look at every inch of him. "I can see that."

"Now."

I slipped my arms around his neck and kissed him long and deep. He rumbled his approval deep in his chest. When I pulled away, he groaned. Finally, I dropped to my knees.

I took those boxer shorts down, and awed at the thick cock that bobbed at me, demanding my attention. With no prelude, I took him deep into my mouth—my wedding present to him.

His fingers threaded through my hair, and I savored each moan, each throaty sign of his approval. He thrust his hips forward. "You're killing me, babe."

All I did was hum in response. It was heady stuff, realizing how much I could affect him, how much my doing this meant to him. I felt naughty. I felt downright wicked. And loving him heated my body as much as anything I'd ever done. I was wet and oh so ready...

His hands slipped under my arms and jerked me to stand. I had to laugh at his impatience. The man knew his way around women's undergarments. He popped the garters and slowly slid each stocking down my leg, kissing my body until I felt tipsy. The panties and bra joined the rest of the abandoned undergarments.

Mark pulled me down to my knees as he dropped to his. He embraced me and lowered me to my back, drugging me with deep kisses.

Settling himself between my thighs, he supported his weight as he stared down into my eyes. "I love you, Jackie. I'll always love you."

The emotions roiling through me caused tears to roll from the corners of my eyes. This moment was everything I had ever wanted in my life, all I would ever need. "I love you, Mark." He slid inside me as I gasped my appreciation.

Nothing had ever felt so fulfilling, so right. The slow rhythm quickly became frenzied. My hips rose to each of his thrusts.

He breathed hard in my ear. "Oh, God, Jackie..."

I couldn't find a single word, couldn't do anything except feel the blood pounding through my veins, while the core of me throbbed and demanded satisfaction. Pleasure raced over me in spasms and waves.

Mark gasped my name in my ear and shuddered.

I forgot all about the notion that marriage ruined everything, and that silly notion never floated through my mind again.

CHAPTER FIFTEEN

"Happy Valentine's Day," Mark said as he waltzed in the door. He had that mischievous look in his eyes and was obviously hiding something behind his back.

A glance at the clock yielded a pleasant surprise. It was nice to have him come home at a fairly normal time. I'd quickly learned detectives kept odd hours. Mark was constantly being called to crime scenes. The stupid criminals of our fair city didn't seem to have much respect for allowing Detective Brennan nor his poor schoolteacher wife the proper amount of sleep.

Mark threw his jacket over the coat tree and started to remove his shoulder holster, so I looked away.

On the mornings when we got ready for work together, I had a hard time watching Mark strap on that gun. I wondered if I would ever get used to knowing he might be in danger. I coped by constantly reminding myself that detectives weren't on the front line and weren't answering patrol calls or responding to alarms. He seldom talked about work, and I didn't ask. From my point of view, denial was the easiest way to function.

Do all cop wives have the same apprehension?

I'd always been afraid of weapons. It didn't matter what kind—guns, bows, swords, bazookas. My father and his brothers hunted, so it wasn't as if I wasn't used to seeing them. For some odd reason, I always felt a cold grip of fear whenever I saw an instrument that could kill something. Or *someone.*

My boys had grown up watching all the ridiculous action flicks that macho young men indulge in, but I blamed their father. David always told me I was overprotective if I protested whatever Bruce Willis or Mel Gibson movie they chose. I hated weapons. I hated blood. I hated pain. Why combine all three and call it "entertainment"? But—as with many arguments from my years with David—I'd always lost.

Seeing that shoulder-strapped gun on Mark only meant one thing to me. It meant that he could get hurt. As he went around the corner, I hoped it was to put the gun away in the small gun-safe he kept in the utility room. I tried to shake the feeling of apprehension and dried my hands on the kitchen towel. He came back into the kitchen, and I went to give him a proper Valentine's greeting. Before I got close enough to kiss him, he whipped a long-stem red rose from behind his back to present to me.

"Pretty," I said, standing on tiptoes to kiss him. "Thank you. You'll get your present later," I added with a naughty smile.

He wolf-whistled and Jellybean echoed the tune. "That sounds promising."

"It is. Let's just say it involves red silk and lots of strategically placed lace."

My husband had turned me into a sex maniac who liked to browse the lingerie section of every store to try to find something I figured he'd like. Perimenopause was now being very, very kind to me.

He whistled again—drawing another song from our bird—and gave me a long, promising kiss. I grabbed his heavenly butt and gave it a squeeze. As I went back to the stove to stir the fettuccini, the phone rang.

"I'll get it." Mark kicked off his shoes and headed toward the cordless.

I listened to his side of the conversation and finally realized he was talking to Kat. He was trying to figure out why she was heading home in the middle of the week, but from the tone of his voice and his insistent groans, he was rapidly getting frustrated with her.

Kathy had been home the weekend before, but she'd been sullen and moody, staying in her bedroom rather than coming out to spend time with the family. Nate hadn't come home at all.

There was trouble brewing.

Mark hung up the phone. "Kat's on her way home. Something's up, but she won't tell me what. She'll be here in a few minutes."

"What's wrong?" I asked.

"I don't know. She sounded upset."

"Teenage girls *always* sound upset."

"We do not," Carly said with a laugh as she came into the kitchen. "Can I go to Faith's house? We've got a project due in history, and her mom said she'd get us dinner."

"I was making dinner for us," I said, stirring the Alfredo sauce.

"And it actually smells good this time," she said before she must have realized how it sounded. "Sorry, Jackie."

I gave her a lopsided smile. "It's fine. Cooking isn't my thing, but this stuff is idiot-proof. All I have to do is heat it up."

Mark snorted a laugh.

I shot him an angry glare. "You're never going to let me live Thanksgiving down, are you?"

"I was thinking about the pot roast last week."

"That was the crock pot's fault, not mine. And it's rude to bring it back up again."

"How about the lasagna you fried on Sunday?" Carly piped in.

"Watch it, kid. You're going to fail biology."

She grinned at me and flipped her ponytail over her shoulder. "Can I go?"

"Fine," I said. Then I wonder if I'd overstepped my bounds.

In the weeks we'd all been living together, Carly seemed more and more like one of my own. I was beginning to treat her that way. I'd been signing field trip slips, handing out lunch money, and teaching her to drive. But I didn't have the right to grant permission when her father was standing right there.

I sheepishly glanced over at Mark. "Sorry."

"Why? You haven't burned anything." He paused, and I was sure it was for effect, so I waited for the other shoe to drop. "Yet."

I swatted at his arm. "I meant about answering Carly. That's her father's job."

"No. That's her *parent's* job, and since you're her stepmother—"

I scrunched up my face to show him my distaste. "I hate that word. Makes me sound like the evil stepmother in *Cinderella*." Then I processed what he'd said. "You don't mind? I guess I'm used to bossing her around at school."

Carly laughed at that. "She's really mean at school. The kids in the hall are afraid of her."

"*I'm* afraid of her," Mark said before he leaned over and brushed a quick kiss on my mouth.

Kat came stomping in from the garage with tears streaming down her cheeks. I realized she must have called using her cell phone while on route. Mark went over to greet her, and she threw herself into his arms before she began to wail.

The drama queen was home.

Carly's gaze caught mine, and we both rolled our eyes.

Stroking the back of her head, Mark gave me a pathetic glance that told me the male in him had no idea how to deal with the hysterical teenage girl clinging to him. I took pity on his predicament.

"Kathy," I said, rubbing circles between her shoulder blades. "What's wrong?"

"Your son!" she shouted, pulling away from Mark and throwing her purse on the kitchen counter. "Your stupid son is what's wrong!"

Mark rolled his eyes. "Lover's quarrel." He took a couple of steps toward the family room.

I figured he'd make a run for it and force Kathy and me to sort this out without his help. He wasn't getting away that easily. "You coward. Get back here." Turning to Kat, I asked, "What happened?"

"He... he..." She hiccoughed a couple of times and wiped away some tears. "Nate's an asshole."

Mark nodded.

I thought about throwing something at him.

"Why's Nate an asshole?" I asked. I didn't really want the details, but Kathy was just as stubborn as her father. This wasn't going away until we talked it out. My defenses were already up and I wanted to blame Kat, not Nate.

These family dynamics were still more than a little odd.

The door from the garage opened again. I wasn't surprised in the least to see my youngest come charging inside. At least he was here to defend himself.

"I knew it! I knew you'd run home to your daddy!" Nate snarled, his temper was in full flight. Nate didn't lose it often, but when he did, he could be every bit as loud as his mother.

God help us all.

Kathy shot him a scowl that might have brought a lesser man to his knees. Nate, on the other hand, didn't seem fazed in the least. I tried not to let my pride in him shine through.

I glanced out the window to see both of their cars in the driveway. "If you two were going to come all the way from Bloomington to argue, you could've at least carpooled. We can't afford your gas bills."

At least my husband smiled.

"I don't want him here!" Kat screeched, pointing at Nate. "Make him leave, Daddy!"

"This is my house too." Nate kicked off his shoes and threw his coat over Mark's.

"No, it's not. It's my dad's house." Kat heaved her own doffed jacket at the poor overloaded coat tree that appeared to be on the verge of collapse.

They started to squabble like the Hatfields and McCoys, and I was just about to intervene when I caught the whiff of something burning. "Shit." I headed back to find my Alfredo sauce turning a wonderful shade of brown.

"I hate to miss the show, but I'm going to Faith's house," Carly announced. She dug into the coats—several of which tumbled to the floor—until she retrieved her letter jacket. She made a hasty retreat as I envied her escape.

Racing around the kitchen to try to prevent yet another smoke alarm incident, I poured the ruined sauce down the garbage disposal. The fettuccini had boiled down to a big lump of dough because I hadn't been there to stir it. The whole time I worked on clean up, Mark sat at the kitchen island and listened to Nate and Kat squabble.

"You're irresponsible," Kat scolded. "You always expect me to clean up your messes." She turned toward us. "He's lazy! He's...he's...*immature!*"

"Well, you're a freakin' basket case," Nate countered. "Always moody, bitching about everything." He decided to expand his audience as well, turning to shout at Mark and me. "She cries every five minutes! How am I supposed to deal with that?"

Kathy whipped around to face Nate again, who turned and glared right back at her. "You never think about me," she bellowed, "or about *us*. You just take and take and take." She wagged her index finger at him.

"Yeah? Well...well... You know what you are? You're a...a... *succubus!*" Nate put his hands on his hips and scowled down at her like Mark had a habit of doing with me whenever we had a disagreement.

I figured the height difference always gave the guy a strategic advantage. The posture was intimidating. The only trump card in a woman's hand was weeping. Most men couldn't stand tears.

Mark walked over to stand next to me. "A succubus?" he whispered.

"A woman who sleeps with a guy and then drains his life force," I explained as I watched the last of the ruined dinner disappear down the garbage disposal. I wondered if I could've burned anything—even a tossed salad. "I think he's taking a literature class this semester. Must've broadened his horizons."

"Ah." He stared back at the kids who were still bickering. "Think we should get involved?"

"The last thing we need to do is get between them. Which side would you take? I mean if you go with Kat, you'll piss off Nate, which pisses me off." He smiled and tweaked my nose, knowing I was only kidding. "You side with the other Y chromosome, your daughter hates you. No win situation, detective." I put the last of the dirty dishes in the dishwasher, shut it, and hit the button to start it. "So what do we do?" I asked.

"I don't know about you, but I'm calling for pizza."

***

I knocked on Kathy's door with the back of my knuckles.

The things she had shouted at my son had struck a familiar raw nerve, and I wanted a chance to talk to her privately. Nursing a frightening theory, I decided to go on a fishing expedition as I tried to ignore the knots that were rapidly forming in my gut.

"It better not be Nate," Kat shouted through the door.

"It's Jackie. May I come in?"

A few long seconds passed. "Fine. Whatever."

The room was dark except for the glow of the computer monitor. The speakers were blaring Alanis Morrisette's "You Oughta Know" loud enough I was sure Kathy meant for Nate to hear it. It was the ultimate go-fuck-yourself song. I'd played it at least a million times during my divorce.

I walked across the room to turn the volume down.

Kat had thrown herself across the bed and was hugging a teddy bear as she stared at the ceiling. She looked so damned young.

"Is there anything I can do?" I asked, glancing down at her.

She'd obviously been crying. Her eyes were red and swollen as she sniffled every couple of seconds.

"I don't want to get in between you and Nate," I added, "but maybe someone with a cooler head can help."

She scoffed and hugged the teddy bear a little tighter. "No one can help me."

I remembered a time I felt exactly like that.

Shit.

I sat down on the foot of the bed. "I know it seems that way, but I'd like to try."

A tear worked its way from the corner of her eye, tracing a path across her temple to fall on the comforter. "You can't help. No one can."

Alarms started blaring in my head, and for once they weren't coming from smoke detectors. No, this time the alarms were triggered by a frightening case of *déjà vu*. It was not just my own history repeating itself, but the history of dozens of girls I'd been teaching over the years.

The helplessness in her voice, the utter despair, the lashing out at everyone might be normal for most teenage girls, but they weren't for Kathy. She was quiet, strong, and never prone to flights of melancholy. She might have liked her moment of high drama every now and then, but this response just wasn't her.

Something was definitely wrong, and in the pit of my stomach, I instinctively knew exactly what it was.

"Have you taken a test yet?" I finally asked, holding my breath and hoping I was entirely wrong.

She didn't even flinch. "Yeah. It had a big blue plus sign. How about that?"

God damn it anyway.

"Oh, Kat." I reached for her hand. She didn't pull away. Another tear leaked out.

The first response I considered was to blister her ears with a nasty lecture, but what good would that do? The horse had already run out of the barn— closing the door now would be futile.

My second considered response was to give her a sound shake. The only thing that would solve was venting my considerable frustration.

I decided on a course of action. It would have to be one baby step at a time. "Okay. So you're pregnant. What are we going to do about it?"

Kathy sat up and threw the stuffed animal aside. "You'll tell Nate, won't you? And Daddy. Oh, my God. You'll tell Daddy." She flopped onto her stomach and began to sob into her pillow.

I instantly shook my head, even though I knew she couldn't see me. I reached out and rubbed her back. "No, I won't."

I had no idea where I'd found the calm, but I knew it was exactly what she needed right now. She needed another woman, not a couple of men who would either turn entirely catatonic or blow their tops. There would be plenty of time to tell them later and face the apocalypse. Kat needed her mother.

I would have to suffice. "We won't tell either of them until you're ready."

Rolling to her side, she looked up at me. "Really?" She sniffed back a few tears. "You won't tell them? Promise me you won't. *Swear* you won't."

"I promise I won't tell Nate or your father. Not yet. But we'll have to tell them sometime."

She nodded. "I know, but... I can't. I just can't. Not yet."

"Right now, we need to think about what you want to do."

I was on autopilot. The teacher in me had listened to many a girl cry on my shoulder about her lack of options in an unplanned pregnancy. But there *were* options. The poor girls just needed to get past the initial hysteria and weigh their choices carefully before they made up their minds. I owed Kat no less consideration. I had to divorce myself from my personal involvement in this situation.

Divorce. A funny choice of word because that's exactly what I was setting myself up for.

My mind started screaming at me. *Mark will hate you. Nate will hate you too.*

But Kat needed me now—she had no one else to turn to. Mark and Nate would just have to get over it. Neither of them had ever been a frightened nineteen-year-old girl who was pregnant and felt as if her future had instantly ended with a positive test. I had been. I'd lived the anger and the fear and the humiliation. I promised myself I'd smooth it over with Mark and Nate later.

"You need to see a doctor to be sure," I said. "Those tests are good, but they're not perfect. How far along do you think you are?"

She sniffled some more. I grabbed a tissue from her nightstand and handed it to her before I realized how wet my own face was getting.

When had I started crying? I grabbed some tissue for myself and dabbed at my eyes.

"Not very. I'm only three weeks late."

"Then we don't have to decide anything yet." Time. We had time. "Have you even thought about what you want to do about the baby?"

"No abortion. Absolutely not," she said, flopping back on her stomach.

I breathed a huge sigh of relief. I didn't believe in abortion, but it was Kathy's choice, not mine. My heart would have broken if I knew that Nate's child—my grandchild—wouldn't be allowed to survive. But just because those were the beliefs I held didn't mean they were necessarily Kat's.

"I'm going to take a personal day tomorrow." I rubbed her back again, trying to give her something to hold on to—something to help her not panic. "We'll go see Dr. McNeff. When we know for sure, we can sit down and talk about what you want to do."

Kat nodded into her pillow.

"It'll be all right, Kat. I know it doesn't seem like it right now, but it'll be all right."

She slowly rolled to her side and sat up. "I don't see how. My life is over."

I shook my head. "Your life is *not* over. My life wasn't over when I got pregnant with Patrick when I was nineteen. It seemed that way at the time, especially since David and I weren't married."

She looked at me wide-eyed. "You–you got pregnant before you got married?"

I nodded. "I got married *because* I got pregnant."

"Patrick's dad didn't hate you? He didn't blame you?" She scrubbed her tears away with the back of her hand.

"If you're worried that Nate will stop loving you, you need to quit. I know my son. He's got a heart as big as all outdoors." I reached out to tuck a stray strand of hair behind her ear. "He won't blame you. He's too much like me. He'll blame himself."

Kathy threw her arms around me and hugged me so tight I wasn't sure I'd be able to draw a breath. "Thank you, Jackie. Thank you. I didn't know who to talk to. I was so...alone."

"Well, you're not alone now." I hugged her back. "It's okay, honey."

She shook her head and pulled away. "No, it's not. I was so mean to you. I just didn't want Daddy to get married again. I didn't want him replacing my mom."

"I didn't replace your mom, Kathy."

"I know that now. I'm sorry for being so mean. Do you forgive me?"

"Of course." I gave her a pat on the shoulder and stood up. "Pizza's here. Do you want me to bring some back here or do you want to eat with the family?"

"I don't want to see Nate."

"Fine. I'll bring you some pizza and a soda."

"Thanks, Jackie."

"You're welcome, honey." I closed the door softly as I left her room.

"What is it? PMS?" Mark asked when I returned to the kitchen.

He and Nate had done a good job on the Domino's, and I grabbed a plate to get a slice or two for Kat before the men devoured the whole thing.

I'd lost my appetite.

"Why do all you stupid men think PMS causes everything?" I snapped.

Mark cocked his head and stared at me. "Where did that come from?"

It came from the fact that your daughter is pregnant and my son is the father—and I can't even talk to you about it!

"Sorry. I'm just a bit frazzled."

"Maybe she's got PMS too," my youngest said with a small chuckle.

I tossed a nasty scowl his way, and he dropped his gaze to stare down at his plate.

"If I hear one more word about PMS, so help me someone's going to pay."

CHAPTER SIXTEEN

"Do you want to go get some lunch?" I asked Kathy as we walked out the front entrance of the doctor's office.

"I want to die." She stared down at the sidewalk and then the asphalt of the parking lot. I didn't figure she was admiring the view.

"Stop it. We're going to get through this, Kat." I clicked the alarm off and opened the door to the big red monster, thinking I should stop setting the alarm and maybe someone would do me a favor and steal the stupid minivan. "I really think you need to tell Nate now. Your father, too."

She slid into the passenger seat and buckled her seatbelt. "I know. I'm just not ready. Not yet."

I could see the tears in her eyes again, and I understood. I'd cried a lake's worth of tears when I had found out I was pregnant with Patrick. I'd been terrified of telling my mother and embarrassed to tell my father. When I finally worked up enough guts to clue David in, his response had done little to spare my feelings. He blamed me and ranted about how I'd ruined his life. After he finally pulled himself together, he told me he would marry me in a way that made me feel as if he was doing me an enormous favor.

I hoped when Kathy finally told Nate that he would handle things with much softer kid gloves.

"He'll hate me." She stared out her window.

"No, he won't. He was there too, you know. I hate to ask, but didn't you two use any birth control?" I started the van and eased out of the parking space.

She nodded but kept gazing out her window.

"So what happened?"

"It broke."

"Ah. I can't even guess how many kids are toddling around out there because of a broken condom," I said, hoping to lighten the mood before realizing how lame I sounded. "Nate should know you're pregnant. He should be a part of making this decision."

"What decision? I won't have an abortion. I won't give the baby up for adoption. Looks like I don't have much of a choice, do I? There isn't any *decision* to make." She brushed away a tear. "I'll have to quit school."

"No, you won't. In fact, that's the *worst* thing you could possibly do."

David and my parents had practically demanded I drop out of college and be a full-time mom, telling me there would be time to go back to school later. The reason I was a teacher was because of my stubborn refusal to stop living my life just because I was having a child sooner than I'd planned. It had taken years of night school, but I'd made it. Kat deserved no less of a chance.

"You need to stay in college," I insisted. "There are day-care centers, and Nate won't leave you high and dry."

"He'll want to get married."

"I imagine he will."

"I don't want to marry him—at least not because of the baby."

I empathized. Pulling into the driveway, I noticed Nate's car was gone and hoped he'd gone back to the university.

"Coast is clear," I said as I shut off the van. I turned to face Kat. "It's up to you now. I promised I wouldn't tell Nate or your dad, but you'll have to. Soon. They love you, honey. You need to tell them."

She nodded and sniffed back some threatening tears. "This weekend. I'll tell Nate this weekend. Then—when we decide what we're going to do—I'll tell Daddy."

                                   ***

I slid between the flannel sheets and waited for Mark to come home from whatever crime scene he was attending. Even with the cozy linens, the bed was always too cold when he wasn't in it with me.

Guilt weighed so heavily on me that I was on the verge of tears. I tried in vain to remind myself that I had nothing to feel guilty about. I was helping Kat during a difficult time—a time when she needed a strong woman to see her through. If only I actually believed that was all there was to this whole situation.

I sure wasn't going to be sleeping much—probably not tonight or for the next several nights. I figured there would be no sleep for me until Kat made up her mind to talk to Nate and to Mark.

I wasn't feeling guilty because of the promise I'd made her, and I didn't necessarily wish I could take it back. What was killing me was the lie of omission, the fact I was duplicitous with my beloved husband. Mark valued honesty above all else, and here I was keeping a very important piece of information from him.

I tried to reassure myself. *You're not lying. She'll tell them. Soon.*

The affirmation didn't help much.

As I lay there, I worried about Kat and the road she would now have to travel. At least it wasn't the 1950s where everyone would condemn her. The social stigma of unwed pregnancy had all but disappeared. Hell, because we had so many student mothers at my high school, the administrators were seriously discussing adding day-care so the girls wouldn't have to quit school. And last week, a colleague at the middle school told me one of her sixth graders was pregnant.

A sixth grader! What was happening to our kids?

I traveled down memory lane, trying to make it less bittersweet, but failing miserably. Patrick had been born when I was barely twenty. At least I had been out of high school. But I had gotten damn sick and tired of the behind-the-hand comments from the girls I knew, and some people were rude right to my face. With the self-esteem issues I've always had, it had been easy to believe that everyone condemned me. All of my friends had been sexually active, and the only difference between them and me was that I got caught. There but for the Grace of God...

Still, the embarrassment had been smothering.

When I'd married David, I restored a little bit of pride. And I'd been a damn good mother. Of that, I had no doubt. Patrick and Nathaniel had grown up to be smart, caring, and independent. If a parent's job was to eventually make herself unnecessary, I'd been a resounding success. My boys were men now. Autonomous. But it hadn't been easy.

Getting pregnant so young had stolen my youth as David and I struggled to pay for both of our colleges and the expense of two growing sons. I went from nineteen to forty overnight. It was no wonder David had eventually gone after a younger woman. Perhaps he was trying to recapture his own lost youth. A mid-life crisis had marked the perfect time for him to at least *try*.

I suddenly had a whole new insight into my ex-husband that took away some of the lingering sting to my pride that came from him leaving me for Ashley. I actually laid that ghost to rest with a sense of understanding and closure.

Now—at forty-two—I'd finally come into my own. I was damn good at my job. I had a great relationship with both of my sons. I was in a fantastic marriage that was based on affection and mutual respect. I'd learned the secrets of my own body, and I enjoyed my sex life more than I'd ever dreamed possible.

For the first time in my life, I loved myself.

The weight of guilt crashed down on me, so suddenly I gasped. I feared Kathy's pregnancy, and my promise to protect her secret could cost me everything.

Looking over at the clock, I knew it was going to be one of "those" nights—one of those interminable nights of watching minutes click by and calculating just how much sleep I would get if I immediately fell asleep.

*I can still get six hours if I just fall asleep...*now. *I can still get five and a half hours if I just fall asleep...*now.

When the alarm buzzed, I stared at the digital clock with blurry eyes and swore I had just drifted off. With a quick estimate, I guessed I might have managed about four hours of restless sleep. Mark's side of the bed was undisturbed, and I worried about him. Grabbing my cell phone from the nightstand, I opened it, searching for the usual text message he sent when he pulled an all-nighter. It was waiting patiently for me.

Out being a cop. Love you.

I hauled my exhausted body out of bed and forced myself to face the school day.

***

"I'll tell him tomorrow, Jackie. I promise," Kat's voice buzzed in my ear. I'd called her right after school on Friday. "I know it's hard that you can't tell Daddy, but..." I waited for her to finish the thought. She never did.

"Then you're staying in Bloomington for the weekend?"

"At least for Saturday. Nate's taking me out to eat and to a concert, and I'll tell him after."

I was being impatient—but with each passing hour, I increasingly feared Mark's reaction. The longer it took to tell him, the more intense his ultimate anger would be. "You two can come home on Sunday, and we can all sit down and talk about this."

"I don't know, Jackie..."

"Kat, you *have* to tell your father. I know you're embarrassed, and I know you're afraid he'll be mad at you. But you can't keep him in the dark. I'll cook us something nice for lunch, and we can all talk."

"That's not a good idea. You cooking, I mean."

I wished I could scowl at her. "We'll get take out."

"Fine. We'll see you Sunday," Kat said. "I've got to run. I've got a class in ten minutes."

"See you Sunday."

***

Mark eased himself from my body, rolled to his side, and tugged me into his arms. "Now can you tell me what's bothering you? You've got to be more relaxed. Was that two orgasms, or did I squeeze out a third?"

"Just two. Quit being greedy." I snuggled up against him and closing my eyes. "It's not attractive."

"I could've sworn I heard—"

I swatted his chest. "Fine. Two and a half."

"Three."

"All right, all right. It was three. Geesh, you've got an ego."

"Told you so."

I snuggled a little closer, needing to feel secure in his arms. Long, slow minutes passed.

"Jackie?"

"Hmm?"

"Everything okay?"

I nodded. I could tell he was waiting for me to say something, to say...*anything*. My silence must have seemed deafening to him.

Right after we made love was always the time when we talked, sometimes for hours. I didn't have anything to say because my brain was filled with Kathy and Nate and their baby—the three people I couldn't talk about.

My grandchild. Kat was carrying my grandchild.

I felt ancient. I felt excited. I felt anxious. I needed to talk to Mark, to share this news with him, to plan the future.

Just one more day. He'll know tomorrow.

I wanted to see if he thought I'd be one of those cool grandmothers who everyone tells she couldn't possibly be old enough to have grandchildren. I wanted to laugh with him about how wonderful a grandfather he would be. I wanted to know if he wanted Nate and Kathy to have a boy or a girl.

My thoughts darkened with the fear I'd been carrying around over how upset he would be when the kids told him tomorrow. He'd be angry with me for not telling him. That lingering dread had lent a note of desperation to my desire. Mark must have felt my need because his response was intense and passionate. As I lay there in his arms, entirely sated, I knew what he wanted from me.

But I just couldn't say anything.

"Jackie? You asleep already?"

I shook my head against his shoulder.

"What's wrong, babe?" Mark hugged me a little tighter.

"Nothing's wrong, I'm just...tired."

I don't want to lie to you. Please don't ask me anything else.

"You're still worried about Kathy and Nate, aren't you? They've got to work this out themselves. I can't imagine how awkward it'll be when they break up—at least for a while. It's not like they can stay out of each other's way."

He chuckled, the sound rumbling his chest and tickling my ear. I wanted to laugh too, but I had nothing to laugh about.

Mark continued his dialogue. "I doubt they'll be together much longer after that little show they put on earlier this week. What do you think? Maybe you and Carly and I should start a pool. Pick the date of their break up."

"That's a bad idea."

"She *can* talk," he said with a laugh.

I wanted to cry.

"Jackie, what's wrong?"

The phone rang. I was saved by the bell.

Mark grabbed the handset. "It's Nate's cell." He handed me the phone.

"Nathaniel? I thought you were going to the concert."

"Mom, I need you and Mark to come down here. Now."

"Why on earth would you—"

"Kat's in the hospital."

CHAPTER SEVENTEEN

Mark and I hurried into the waiting area of the Emergency Room. The nauseating hospital smell hit me instantly. Coupled with the eerie sense of foreboding, it was enough to make me want to turn around and run for the exit. Of course, simply getting to the hospital had been an ordeal.

The ride to Bloomington had been tense. He'd driven way too fast, and I'd worn out the imaginary brake on my side of the car because of all the times I thought he got too close to the cars in front of us. He'd fired question after question that I couldn't answer, and I knew he was entirely fed up with my quiet.

My detective obviously didn't deal well with the unknown.

The trip had seemed interminable as I'd silently stared at the passing cornfields and shrugged my shoulders to each of Mark's increasingly loud questions. I was pretty sure I knew what was happening to Kathy, but I wasn't about to blurt everything out to her father until we saw her. I'd made a solemn promise, after all. Plus, Kat could have a broken arm or hot appendix. Nate hadn't been very forthcoming with details. He just told us she was going to be fine, but that she wanted us there. And I knew Nate needed us too, especially if the trip to the E.R. had anything to do with the baby.

Trying to ignore the disinfectant smell, I looked around the waiting area and saw Nate sitting in a chair with his elbows propped on his knees, hands laced through his hair.

"Nate," I said as we reached him, putting a steadying hand on his shoulder. "How's Kat?"

My son turned his head to glare up at me with anger and hurt clear in his eyes. The shock was recognizing that he was directing both those emotions right at *me*.

He knew.

Nate shrugged my hand away. "Why in the hell didn't you tell me?"

Damn it all anyway.

I should have forced Kathy to tell them both—but I'd made her a promise, and I hadn't broken it. I just hoped Mark and Nate could understand and forgive me one day.

I stroked my son's head.

He jerked away. His rejection hurt like a hard slap to my face.

"I promised her, Nate," I said. "I promised Kat I'd let her tell you."

"Tell you what?" Mark asked, clearly confused and already pissed off. His gaze shifted between mother and son, and I could tell he sensed a conspiracy.

He narrowed his eyes at me. "What's wrong with my daughter?" His voice had taken on a hard edge, and I couldn't tell if he was yelling at Nate or me.

Probably both.

"She's having a miscarriage." Nate got to his feet and stared down at me with so much condemnation in his eyes I wanted to weep in response.

"A what?" Mark shouted. "She's having a *what?*" I watched the emotions play across my husband's face. Shock. Confusion. And then rage.

"A miscarriage," Nate replied. "She was pregnant, and she lost the baby."

Mark moved so fast, I didn't even have a chance to stop him. Grabbing a couple of fistfuls of the front of Nate's shirt, he pinned my son to the closest wall. "You son of a bitch. What did you do to her?"

"Don't call my mom a bitch." Nate managed to reply in a flat voice that seemed a bit peculiar considering the fact he'd just been slammed against a wall.

He wasn't fighting back, which told me that he was angry with himself for what Kat was going through. He blamed himself, and he probably thought he deserved a good smack or two. He was evidently going to let Mark provide the punishment.

I put myself between them, wanting desperately to get Mark to let my son go. "Mark, stop it." I tugged at his arm. It was like trying to move an anchored steel beam. "Not here. Please, not here."

His arm remained straight as an arrow, but his gaze shifted from Nate to me.

I deserved *some* of fury flowing my way, but not *all* of it. I'd done the right thing by Kat when she had needed me most. When Mark got over his shock, surely he would see that.

"She was going to tell you tomorrow," I insisted.

"But you already knew, didn't you?"

I stood there, trying not to fight back and feeling the prying stares of everyone in the waiting area.

"*Didn't you?*" he shouted loud enough to make me flinch.

"Just for a couple of days."

"And you didn't tell me? You didn't think I needed to know my own daughter was pregnant? Damn you, Jackie."

I wanted to shout right back at him. I wanted to tell him I had been helping his daughter, damn it. My own anger was quickly rising in response to his, and those suppressed defensive shields—the ones I had tucked away when I married Mark—were slowing creeping back into place.

He shouldn't be *yelling* at me. He should be *thanking* me. I'd taken care of his daughter when she really needed someone. I'd done all the right things to help her through this. And what did I get in return?

Damn me?

Damn me?

Damn him!

"Let Nate go." I grabbed at his arm again. He didn't budge an inch. "Let go of my son!"

A security guard was taking long strides to reach us, and Mark was going to be in a world of hurt if he didn't get that temper under control pretty damn quick.

"Look, I know you're pissed, but this isn't the place for us to talk. Let him go, Mark," I begged as I tugged at his arm. "Let him go. Now."

Mark snarled and pulled his hands away from Nate's chest.

Nate slowly eased away from the wall.

"Everything okay here?" the rent-a-cop asked when he reached us. He bore that air of self-importance that people who had no real power often sport. I could tell the guy irritated Mark as much as he did me.

"You all right?" The uniformed man looked Nate up and down.

"I'm fine," Nate replied, giving his shoulders an exaggerated roll and straightening his shirt.

The security officer eyeballed us for a few more moments. "If I let this here go, I won't have no more trouble from you folks?" He gave Mark a stern glare I figured was supposed to intimidate him.

Mark scowled right back at the man. I could see the carefully contained fury in my husband's eyes and hoped the barriers would hold for a little while longer. For my part, all I wanted to do was correct the guard's abhorrent grammar and send him on his way, figuring there was a vending machine waiting somewhere in the hospital where he could get himself another snack and add another inch or two to that enormous waistline.

"No more trouble," I replied. "Emotions are just running a little hot. That's all."

The security guard nodded at me. Then he hiked up his sagging pants and walked over to the reception desk. He said something to the lady sitting behind it—probably telling her to call him if the white trash he'd just expertly handled got rowdy again—and he left the waiting room.

"Stay here. I'm going back to see my daughter," Mark said as he walked over to the reception desk.

I followed, trying to control my annoyance at having been dismissed like some child. "Maybe I better go back too."

"Oh, I think you've caused enough trouble," Mark sneered before he asked the receptionist where Kat was. He listened attentively, and then he leveled a glare at me. "Take your son and go home."

"Don't be silly. I'm not going anywhere," I replied with a condescending wave of my hand that didn't help cool Mark's anger.

I was every bit as anxious to see Kathy as he was, and I wasn't about to leave her with only her father to lean on. His temper was getting the better of him, and right now she probably needed some TLC. I doubted her enraged father could provide much.

"Neither is Nate," I insisted. "Look, I know you're angry, but—"

"Angry? *Angry?* I'm so far past that..." He stopped, huffed a few breaths out of his flared nostrils, and drew his lips into a grim line. "You're a piece of work, lady. You know that?" He turned to go.

I grabbed his arm.

He stared down at me, throwing daggers with his eyes aimed right at my heart.

"Kat made me promise. She was going to tell you and Nate, but she just wanted to think it all through first. She was scared—scared to tell Nate and scared to tell you. Please don't shout at her when you go back there."

"I think getting parenting advice from *you* is a colossal waste of time." He pulled his arm away and jerked his thumb toward where Nate stood. "I mean, look how great your son turned out."

"What the hell is that supposed to mean?"

"He goes and gets some innocent girl pregnant and—"

"They were both there, Mark. It takes *two* people to make a baby."

"I'm going back to see my daughter." He punched the big button, and the double doors opened. He strode through them and disappeared in the treatment area.

"I'll be here if either of you need me," I called after him, hoping he would hear.

Nate was sitting with his head in his hands again when I went to take a seat next to him. I put a comforting hand on his shoulder.

He sat up and brushed it away.

"Nate, I'm sorry. I know this is hard. You're both so young..."

"What would you know about how I feel?" he scoffed.

Because I was nineteen when I got pregnant with your brother, Nate. Remember?

I reined in my sarcasm. "Think about that for a minute."

He stared over at me for a few moments. "Fine. Maybe you *do* understand."

The anger seemed to ebb right out of him as it was rapidly replaced with hurt. I felt entirely helpless, only able to watch him and listen.

"You know what sucks?" he asked. "She didn't trust me enough to tell me. I love Kat so much, and she wouldn't even tell me she was pregnant with my baby."

"She was going to—after the concert."

I saw the flicker of hope in his eyes. He loved Kathy and wanted to believe she loved him in return. "Really? She was going to tell me?"

I nodded. "Right after the concert. Then she was going to come home with you tomorrow and tell Mark. What happened tonight?"

He put his elbows back to his knees and rested his forehead against his hands. He might as well have been talking to the carpet. "We were eating at The Chuckwagon, and she just...doubled over and started crying. Then I noticed that..." Nate turned his head away, obviously embarrassed.

"She was bleeding?"

He nodded. "I drove her right here. She wouldn't even let me call an ambulance. When we got here, I stayed with her for a couple of minutes, but then she told me to leave. She didn't want me with her."

"Nate, I'm so sorry."

His head snapped up, and our gazes locked. Nate looked like he was drowning—like a young man who was being pulled down by a relentless undertow and was tired of fighting it. "I want to come home. I hate it here. I hate classes. I hate the profs." Nate got up and started to pace. "I hate the dorm. I hate not having you around when I need something. The only thing I had here was Kat. And now she... she..." He shook his head.

I heaved a sigh, feeling entirely inadequate to help my son. He wasn't a child anymore. I couldn't fix this for him. It was time for him to put some starch in his spine. "College can be rough, but you've got to tough it out. Finish the year here, then we can talk about transferring somewhere else—somewhere a little closer if you want."

"Rough?" Nate shook his head again, this time adding a rueful laugh. "I'm in the ninth circle of Hell."

I couldn't help but roll my eyes at the exaggeration, and a hesitant smile twitched on my lips. Nate always liked his melodrama, and his usual personality was starting to assert itself.

He would be all right.

I refused, however, to indulge him in any pity. "We need to take things one step at a time. Let's help Kat through this, then we can talk about everything else."

"She won't let me help her through this. I want to be back there with her, but she doesn't want me."

I stood up and started pacing next to my son. "I know, but she's hurting. She doesn't know *what* she wants. When Mark comes back out, I'll see if she'll let you go back."

"I just can't seem to wrap my mind around it. I was going to be a father. Now I'm not."

"Jackie?" I turned around to see Mark. His face now read of hurt, the anger seemingly evaporated. "What?"

"Kat won't talk to me. She wants you."

***

I peeked around the curtain.

Kathy was lying curled up on her side with her back to me. An IV was pumping next to her bed, humming softly every few seconds. She appeared so fragile—so young—in the green hospital gown. I was overwhelmed with sympathy. The poor girl had been through so much so very quickly.

I went to the bed and put my hand on her shoulder. "Kat?"

She rolled to her back. One look at me, and she started crying. "I lost the baby."

"I know, honey. I'm so sorry."

Sitting up, she reached for me.

I sat down on the bed next to her and hugged her close, stroking her hair as she cried against my shoulder. I could feel the tears rolling down my own cheeks.

After several minutes, she pulled away and leaned back against the pillow. "I couldn't talk to my dad."

"I understand, but you need to face him. You can't hide from this forever. He's just worried about you, Kat. So is Nate."

She breathed a long, shuddering sigh. "I know. I just... They both hate me now." She pulled her knees to her chest and hugged them.

"No," I replied with a shake of my head, "they don't. They both love you. We *all* love you. We'll help you get through this."

A doctor who appeared barely old enough to shave came into the cubicle, making me feel ancient. Doctors were supposed to be older than me, not younger—especially not *that* much younger. Plucking the chart from the end of Kat's bed, he flipped it open before he started to make notes.

"How are you feeling now, Katherine?"

Kat shrugged. "Better, I guess. Kind of crampy, but the stuff they gave me helped some. Makes me sleepy though."

The way-too-young-to-practice-medicine doctor smiled and made a few more notes on her chart. "We can adjust the dosage if the pain gets worse. I've got your test results." He glanced over at me. "If you'd please excuse us for a minute."

Kathy shook her head. "No. She can stay. She's my mom."

She's my mom.

My chin was quivering, and my eyes were pooling with fresh tears. I'd finally earned her trust, and I doubted she would ever know how much that meant to me.

But what had Kat's trust cost me?

Don't think like that, Jackie.

"The ultrasound shows you miscarried, but there are no products of conception remaining." He stated all of that with an air of matter-of-fact that told me he assumed we knew exactly what he was talking about.

He was wrong.

"Want to put that in English, doctor?" I asked.

"It means she shouldn't have any complications. She miscarried completely. I don't think we'll have to do a D and C." He glanced back at Kat, who looked confused again.

At least this I understood. "That means you won't need surgery, honey. That's good news."

Dr. Adolescent nodded. "But we want to keep you for a few hours to keep an eye on the bleeding."

"Can I still have kids?" Kat asked, staring at her knees and blushing dark red.

I realized how embarrassing the situation must be for a girl her age. Over the years, I'd become desensitized to doctors discussing the private parts of my anatomy or seeing me naked. Hell, I could have an entire conversation with my gynecologist while I was trussed up in stirrups or with a radiologist, who was smashing one of my breasts entirely flat for a mammogram.

Kathy was still shy because she hadn't experienced two births where everyone and their cousin were staring at your hoohah while you tried to squeeze out a baby who seemed to have a head the size of a bowling ball.

"This shouldn't hurt your fertility," he said. "Lots of first pregnancies are miscarried—especially in the first trimester." He hung the chart back on the end of her bed, clicked his pen closed, and shoved it in his lab coat. "We're going to admit you to a day ward for a couple of hours." He glanced at the clock. "If everything looks good, then your mom can take you home in the morning."

***

Mark and Nate were actually talking when I went back to the waiting room. I was so relieved to see them sitting together, I didn't want to interrupt and break the spell. Mark patted Nate on the back, and I almost started crying again at the conciliatory gesture between my husband and my son.

Unfortunately, I couldn't leave them alone to continue to work through their differences because I needed to talk to them both about Kat. I sighed and walked up to stand in front of them.

Mark stared up at me from where he sat. His anger had ebbed, and his features appeared less strained. This hadn't been easy on him. It hadn't been easy on *any* of us.

I wanted to reach out to him, but I felt coldness in his gaze that pinched all the way to my heart.

"How's she doing?" he asked.

I gave him a hesitant smile.

He didn't offer me one in return, but I tried not to read too much into that.

"She's going to be fine," I said. "The doctor wants her to stay for a little bit longer, then we can take her home. I think I'm going to take her back with us instead of taking her to the dorm. She really needs a few days of rest, and it would help if I could take care of her. I'll email her teachers."

"I'm going home too," Nate said.

I shook my head.

So did Mark.

"No, you're not," I said firmly, hoping he wouldn't fight me on this. I couldn't let him walk away from his responsibilities, no matter how tempting it was to want to let him come back home and just be my little boy again.

Nate needed to grow up.

I needed to let him grow up.

Now was as good a time as any. "You have classes on Monday, and right now, I think Kat needs some alone time. There'll be plenty of time for you two to talk this out later. Maybe even next weekend."

He gave me a short stare down, trying to change my mind.

I stared back, letting him know that simply wasn't going to happen.

Nate finally nodded. "Can I see her at least?"

"I think she'd like that."

Nate hopped to his feet and headed through the big doors leading to the treatment area.

I sat down next to Mark and folded my hands in my lap. I desperately wanted to touch him—to pull him into my arms—but my radar told me that wouldn't be a good move on my part. "I'm sorry you're stuck here until we can take her home."

"I'm going to have Nate take me to the dorm, and I'll take Kat's car home."

"You're leaving the hospital?" I wondered if I looked as incredulous as I sounded.

"I'm going home."

I might as well have been sitting in the waiting room with a total stranger discussing a change in the weather or the ridiculous price of gasoline. For the first time since I'd met him, I was getting *nothing* from Mark Brennan. No affection, no attraction, no anger. No emotion whatsoever.

That scared the hell out of me.

I rushed to explain. "Kat was going to tell you tomorrow."

My husband turned his head to stare at me, and a frightened shiver raced through me when I met his gaze. All I read in those dark eyes was contempt meant for me.

My stomach tied itself into nervous knots.

"I'll just bet she was," he said, sounding cynical.

"I swear. She was going to tell Nate tonight, and then they were driving home tomorrow to talk to you."

He snorted a disbelieving laugh that pissed me off.

Where was the benefit of the doubt? Mad or not, I thought he owed me at least that much.

"You know, Mark... I remember once upon a time when you swore you had plans to talk to someone who cared about you very much, but she happened to find you before you could say anything. But when you told her you were going to call her, she believed you. She cut you some slack."

"That's not even the same thing." Mark knit his brows in irritation and waved the notion away with the back of his hand.

My protective guards were popping up left and right, and I allowed my anger, hurt, and fatigue to take control of the reins. Unfortunately, Mark seemed to have a knack for pushing my buttons. The old sarcastic and defensive Jackie was coming back with a vengeance.

"Yes, it was," I said, letting my annoyance be plain in my voice. "I guess it's fine when *you* need time, but if Kat needed a couple of days to adjust, you get all pissy."

"She's *my* daughter. She should've come to me."

"But she didn't, did she? She came to me. She needed me. Not *you*. *Me*."

Jackie, what in the hell are you doing?

"That was below the belt," Mark replied. "You know, I really expected better from you." He shook his head. "I expected better from you in a lot of ways I probably shouldn't have."

"What's that supposed to mean?"

"You disappointed me, Jackie. You know, you haven't even apologized."

He was right. I shouldn't have just said it, either. I should have shouted it.

I'm sorry, Mark. I didn't mean to hurt you!

But I wasn't sorry for the reason he thought I should be, and my pride wouldn't let me back down a solitary inch. I'd protected Kat—just like I had promised her I would. It wasn't my fault this whole thing had turned out to be such a nightmare. I couldn't have anticipated any of this.

I was sorry for a lot of things, but not for helping Kat. And I damn well wasn't going to apologize. Not for doing what I thought was best.

"You know," I said. "I *am* sorry."

He cocked his head, obviously thinking he'd won my concession.

I quickly set that notion straight. "I'm sorry Kathy and Nate have to go through all this. I'm sorry we lost our grandchild. But I'm *not* sorry for helping your daughter."

"That's *it?* That's all you have to say to me?"

I nodded my stubborn head and dug in my heels. I knew what he wanted, but I wasn't going to apologize for lying because I hadn't. I just hadn't told him everything.

There's no difference, my thoughts accused. *A lie is a lie, whether it is by omission or otherwise.*

"It's different," I mumbled to myself.

Mark just stared at me with angry brown eyes.

He got to his feet. "Since no one in this family seems to need me, I'm calling a cab and getting Kat's car. Then I'm going home. I need some time to think."

"To think? What exactly do you need time to *think* about, Mark? Hmm?"

"Whether I can trust you anymore."

He might as well have hit me. It would have hurt less.

I should've stopped him. I should've apologized. I should've told him how much I loved him. Instead, I simply watched Mark leave as I stood there with nothing but my pride to keep me company.

It was all suddenly too much. The days of tension waiting for Kat to confess, the fact that I'd lost my first grandchild, and my husband walking out on me were just too much. The weight of it all bore down on me, crippled me, and threatened to drive me to my knees.

I got to my feet and ran to the closest ladies room.

Away from prying eyes, I began to cry in long, ragged sobs. I allowed myself the luxury of weeping for several minutes, entirely grateful no one else came into the restroom to see me making a spectacle of myself. When the tears were spent, I stood there and hiccoughed while I splashed my face with cold water. Then I stared at myself in the mirror.

"What a fucking mess."

My husband had just walked out on me. I pictured him going home, packing my bags, and setting them on the porch. He would most likely want me out of *his* house. At least we hadn't closed on my old house yet. I could go there if Mark really wanted me gone.

He doesn't want you to leave. He just needs a little time alone to adjust to all this.

How could I face the world on my own? How could I survive without Mark in my life? How could I survive knowing he had discarded me?

He didn't discard you, you silly fool.

I stared at my reflection. I looked tired. I looked sad. I looked like I needed a good, stiff drink.

"Get it together, Jackie." I splashed some more cold water on my face as I searched deep down for some calm and some courage. I could do this. I *had* to do this.

From somewhere inside me, I found enough strength to soldier on. I would be an Army brat to the bitter end. Kathy and Nate needed me. I would be there for them.

I just prayed the rest of our problems would work themselves out in time.

CHAPTER EIGHTEEN

I finally got Kat tucked away in her bedroom before I slipped into my own.

Mark's unmarked sedan was gone when we got home, replaced in the garage by Kathy's beat-up Chevy. I would have figured he was called to work, but there had been no text message, and he hadn't left a note. Mark was gone. Where, I didn't know. For how long, I had no idea.

I'd really blown it this time. Not because I'd helped my stepdaughter. I was still sure I'd done right by Kat, and in a way, helping her through all this had helped me lay many of my own ghosts to rest. It was the aftermath, the revelation of her pregnancy and miscarriage that I hadn't handled very well.

Very well?

I'd screwed the pooch on this one.

I should've swallowed my stubborn pride and apologized to my husband. I just hadn't been able to force myself to do so. My inability stemmed from thinking everything that had ever gone wrong in my first forty-two years had been my fault. I'd already said, "I'm sorry," more times than any other woman on the face of the planet. I'd said it to my mother. I'd said it to David.

The irony of the whole situation was that I really *was* sorry. I was sorry that I'd hurt Mark, even if I'd done what I thought was best for everyone involved.

Why couldn't I tell him that?

When I should have been soothing him, I couldn't put aside my stupid, obstinate pride.

"I'm an idiot." I flopped down on the bed, entirely exhausted.

My cell phone vibrated for a second, signaling a text message. I fished it out of my pocket, hoping it was a note from Mark telling me he was at a crime scene. I retrieved the message.

Cop stuff. Back later.

I wanted to cry again when I read the cold words, desperately wishing there had been some mention of love. I stretched out on the bed, grabbed Mark's pillow, and held it to my chest. Burying my nose in his scent, I tried not to lose hope.

He'd promised. On the day we were married, he'd promised to stick around no matter how rough it got.

Well, the waters were definitely getting choppy—but until today, I'd never feared that he would leave. We had weathered our share of arguments, but I had never been afraid I would lose him. Not once.

I was afraid now. I was *petrified.*

"Mark promised," I reminded myself over and over. It didn't help much. I could feel sleep dulling my thoughts, and I gave in, desperately needing some rest.

The last notion that floated through my mind was that my husband always kept his promises.

I'd just have to trust him.

***

"Is there anything else I can get you?" I asked as I picked up the tray of empty dishes from Kathy's dresser.

"No thanks, Jackie. I'm just really tired." She leaned back against the stack of pillows.

"Do you need anything else for pain?"

"Nah. It's not bad now. I'm just a little crampy. Nothing I can't deal with."

I nodded, happy she was making a wise choice. "It's better not to take the strong stuff unless you really need it." I inclined my head at the tray full of dishes. "I'm taking this stuff to the kitchen. Just holler if you need me." She closed her eyes, and I left the room, shutting the bedroom door behind me.

Putting the tray on the kitchen island, I tried to squelch an enormous, wide-mouthed yawn. My nap hadn't done much to revive me. I was exhausted, I was frightened, and I was nursing a growing annoyance with Mark.

He hadn't called, nor had he sent another text. He knew I hated it when he was out of touch, and I wondered if he was staying quiet just to get to me. That seemed out of character. It was more like something *I* would resort to.

As I put the dirty dishes in the sink, the phone rang. I hoped it was my husband. Grabbing the dishtowel, I dried my hands and picked up the handset. The ID read the police station.

About time he checked in.

"Long time, no hear, Detective Brennan," I said. Then I tried to rein in my annoyance and be a bit more conciliatory. After all, I loved the guy. "I was hoping we could make up over a nap. But, here I was, all alone in our big bed, waiting for you to come home and get naked."

"Mrs. Brennan?"

I have a really, really big mouth.

"Yes, this is Mrs. Brennan. I'm sorry, I thought you were my husband."

"This is Lieutenant Barrows. I need to tell you something."

Time stopped. Just *stopped*—right along with the beating of my heart.

I knew what was coming. I *knew*, and I wanted to scream in anguish.

Moments like this changed lives forever—just simple seconds of time that we should be able to stop and hold in place to keep disaster from striking. It's like the precious seconds before a car crashes into yours—those seconds that seem to last an eternity as you see the car coming right for you and realize there isn't enough time for you to be able to do a fucking thing about it.

Why couldn't we suspend the laws of the universe and stop that moment and just... *fix it?*

The fear thrumming through me made me want to go bury my head under a pillow and scream.

No. No. No.

I wasn't ready. Whatever it was, I wasn't ready.

"Detective Brennan was shot."

I sat down hard on the floor. Mark was dead. I could hear it in the lieutenant's voice. I could feel it in every muscle, every nerve, and every bone. Mark was dead.

"Mrs. Brennan? Are you still there?"

I stupidly nodded my head. I wanted to talk to the guy, to get some more information. I really did. But I couldn't. I just couldn't.

The phone slipped from my fingers and clattered on the tile.

Mark. My Mark.

He was dead.

I tried to grab the handset sitting on the floor next to me. My hand trembled, and for the briefest of seconds, I stared at it as if it wasn't my own. Then I groped to pick up the phone.

"Where is he?"

"Methodist Hospital. Do you have a way to get there?"

I nodded.

God damn it, Jackie, stop nodding!

"Mark's dead. Just say it. He's dead."

"He's *not* dead, Mrs. Brennan. He's at Methodist. They're taking him to surgery. Do you need a squad car to come get you?"

I'd already grabbed my purse and was running to tell Kathy where I was going.

***

I didn't even remember the trip to the hospital.

I'd been on the cell phone most of the time. Kat was next to hysterical when I told her, but she'd calmed down enough to call Carly at Faith's. She decided to wait at the house until Carly was able to make it home and Nate came to get them. I don't think she was ready to face the hospital again, and she wasn't physically strong yet. I had faith that Nate would help her through this.

Patrick told me he was heading directly to Methodist, and I was afraid he was driving too fast—as usual. At least this time he had a good excuse.

My heart was breaking from fear and guilt—guilt that Mark might leave this life hating me because he thought I'd lied to him. I couldn't bear it. But I had to—I couldn't fix this now.

I wiped away the tears that were flowing freely down my cheeks and tried to concentrate on getting to the hospital in one piece.

I strode into the Emergency Room, feeling so cold it was as if there weren't a drop of blood circulating in my body. I almost retched at the smell and my overpowering dread, but I forced the bile back down my throat with a hard swallow. I didn't even stop at the reception desk. Instead I went right through the enormous doors leading to the treatment area and walked toward my future—a future I was positive would no longer include the love of my life.

I bit back a grieving sob by chewing on the inside of my cheek. It wouldn't do Mark any good to have me standing there bawling like an infant when I saw him. I was a cop's wife—a *detective's* wife. I needed to pull myself together and damn well start acting like one.

"Strong, Jackie," I whispered in an empty affirmation. "Be strong for Mark."

But Mark's dead.

"Then do him proud."

"Are you Mrs. Brennan?" a nurse in pink scrubs asked when I stopped at the busy nurses' station.

She had to know who I was by the absolute panic that had to be smeared all over my face. I wasn't sure I was ready to see some nurse pull back a white sheet to show me my deceased husband. I would *never* be ready to face that.

But it was clear I had no choice.

"Yes, I'm Jackie Brennan. Where is he?"

"He's waiting for you."

"He's alive?" My heart pounded so hard and fast I was sure everyone else could hear it.

He's alive! Mark is alive!

She nodded. "He's stable. He wouldn't go into surgery until he talked to you. The surgeon's scrubbing up. We really need to get him to the O.R. soon."

He's alive! Mark's still alive!

I took a couple of shuddering breaths and tried to find some kind of control over my tumbling thoughts. "I understand. Just give me a minute with him." I had no idea why he would want to wait. I was tempted to tear him a new one for being so damned obstinate.

I followed the nurse to a small treatment area. When she pulled the curtain aside and I saw Mark lying there on that gurney, my legs almost gave out as the world spun around me.

Get it together, Jackie.

He looked like a macabre science project. The left side of his chest was covered in big gauze bandages that had already bled through. Small tubes were coming out of both his arms and a bigger one poked into his left side. One of those goofy nasal oxygen cannulas was stuffed in his nose. His right index finger had an enormous clip on it that glowed red next to his skin. All around him, bags of fluid hung on machines that beeped and whirred and turned my blood to ice water.

"Sweet Jackie," he rasped and held out a hand to me.

I rushed to his side and grabbed his hand, giving the back of it a gentle kiss, wanting to crawl into the bed with him and wrap my body around him like a cocoon. "I hear you're being stubborn as usual."

He actually smiled. Then he coughed and winced. "I needed to see you first. If I'm not going to make it—"

"No! Don't you *dare* say it!" Tears started streaming down each of my cheeks. "You're going to be fine, Mark. Just fine."

"You'll have to take care of things. I got all the paperwork done after we got married. All the life insurance will go to you."

"There won't be any life insurance money. You're not going to—"

He held up his hand. I figured he would be wagging his index finger at me if it wasn't entirely encased it that stupid clip. "Don't argue with me. Please." He chuckled and coughed. "For once."

I nodded, sniffing back more tears.

"I know you'll take care of my girls—especially after what you did for Kat."

I squeezed his hand. "You know I will. I love them like my own."

"That's why I put everything in your name. I didn't want them to fight over anything if I... if I..."

"Please, Mark," I squeaked, trying not to wail my anguish and despair, trying to be strong. I clutched his hand, wanting to draw strength from his warmth. "Please don't say it."

"I couldn't go into surgery without talking to you, without saying I'm sorry."

"I'm sorry too. I didn't mean—"

"Don't, babe. You don't need to apologize. I know why you didn't tell me. As soon as I calmed down, I understood. You were trying to help Kat."

I nodded, not trusting myself to talk without weeping. I thought I should say something meaningful, but nothing came to mind except, "You can't die. I need you."

He smiled, the warmth of it thawing me. "You need me. That was harder for you to say than 'I love you.' Wasn't it?"

It was a hell of a lot harder than he would ever know. I just nodded.

"I need you too."

Two orderlies in teal scrubs came into the room and started to pack things up to take Mark away. "Sir, we need to get you to the O.R.," the tallest one said before he nodded at me. "You'll need to go to the surgery waiting room. Take the main elevators to the third floor and turn right. It's just down the hall."

"I love you, Jackie," Mark whispered, refusing to release his grip on my hand. "I love you so much."

I kissed the back of his hand again as one of the orderlies covered him with another blanket. "I love you too, Mark. More than I ever thought possible."

"You're everything to me."

"Don't you dare die on me, Mark Brennan. Don't you fucking well die on me. You hear me?"

My husband gave me a weak smile. "I'll sure try my best to stick around. I want to grow old with you."

"I'm already old—and you've aged me another twenty years in the last hour."

I savored that final, weak chuckle, fearing it would have to last me a lifetime. I brushed a kiss over his lips before they wheeled him down the hallway and out of sight.

"God go with you," I whispered at the closing doors, fearing I would never see my husband alive again.

I just stood there feeling the panic and grief bearing down on me, crushing my will to live. If Mark died, he would take my heart and soul with him.

How easy it must have been for women in the past... If things got too intense—too real—they could just faint. They could simply slip away and not deal with reality. I wanted to swoon. I wanted to drop into dark oblivion where I didn't have to think. I wanted to drink myself into a blessed stupor. I wanted to scream. I wanted to run away pulling at my hair like some crazed lunatic.

But I didn't do any of those things. Instead, I sucked it up and headed out to find out if any of our children had made it to the hospital yet. If they hadn't, they would be here soon.

Our children. Not his. Not mine. *Ours.*

I wasn't going to fall apart. Not now. They needed me. I'd allow myself the luxury of going entirely to pieces at some other less critical time.

With courage I didn't really feel, I marched back to the waiting room. I saw a couple of uniformed officers and instantly found my lightning rods. I needed some answers, and I needed them *now*. They looked like the best place to start.

I shoved my way through the doors. "What in the hell happened?" My shout drew stares from the poor souls waiting to be seen in the E.R. "He's a detective, not a patrol officer! How in the hell did he get shot?" I was being horribly rude, downright hostile, but I couldn't seem to get a grip on the emotions roiling through me.

Both officers calmly took off their hats and tucked them neatly under their arms. While my world was falling apart, their utter composure pissed me off.

"Detective Brennan answered a call for a silent alarm at a convenience store over on Pleasant Street," one of the uniforms replied. "He was first on the scene and caught two men fleeing after an armed robbery. When he identified himself as an officer, they shot first. He brought one down, but the other caught him in the chest. Uniforms just nabbed the second guy. When he found out he'd hit a cop, he pissed himself."

Give me five minutes alone with a Louisville slugger and that asshole, and I'll save you the trouble of adjudicating this case.

"Is the first one dead?" I asked.

"Perfect shot through the heart. Detective Brennan never misses. I've seen him at the shooting range. Bull's-eye every damn time," the second officer said with a note of macho pride that I really didn't care to hear.

Patrick came running through the entrance, straining to look through the increasing throng of blue uniforms that were suddenly appearing in the waiting area. "Mom!" He jogged over to me and hugged me so tight I couldn't draw a breath until he turned me loose again. "What happened?" he asked as he held my shoulders and stared down at me. "Nate said Mark got shot."

I nodded, resisting the urge to throw myself back into my oldest son's arms and wail my despair. "Come on. We're going up to surgery."

CHAPTER NINETEEN

Hell no longer frightens me.

After sitting in that waiting room, I knew exactly what Hell would be. It would be living in limbo. It would be watching the people I love feeling helpless and confused and frightened. It would be not getting a damn word about how the person you love more than life itself is doing while his chest is laid wide open on some operating table and a guy you don't know touches your lover's beating heart.

How much worse could Hell possibly be than this?

Kathy, Nate, and Carly had arrived not long after Patrick, and I'd set up shop in the surgery waiting room. Carly seemed to be taking it the worst. It had taken her a good, long thirty minutes to stop crying in my arms.

Now, she sat next to Patrick, who'd slung an arm around her shoulders like a good older brother. He fetched everyone drinks and snacks, and he offered Carly a shoulder to lean on all evening. Once she'd spent her fear, she'd stoically waited. She was definitely fifteen going on forty.

My breaking heart swelled with pride for both of them, and that notion comforted me like a warm hug.

Patrick would be graduating come May. He'd been looking for jobs anywhere—except Indiana. I couldn't blame him. He would be moving on to start his own life somewhere far away. I didn't even want to think about how sad I would be when he left.

Would I go through empty nest syndrome all over again?

At least I would still have Carly at home for a few more years. That girl had an incredible future waiting for her. She was a triple threat—smart, funny, and pretty. She was going to take the world by storm one day, and the world would never be the same.

I glanced over at Kathy and Nate who were sitting next to Carly and Patrick. They held hands and talked quietly. He kissed her forehead more times than I could count. Every time I saw the gesture, it reminded me of Mark and the way he would always calm me in the same, sweet way. I felt a wave of nausea and crippling grief for everything I could lose—for what we could *all* lose.

With a hard swallow, I pushed it aside, channeling Scarlett O'Hara.

Later. I'll think about that later.

The loss of their baby was something Nate and Kathy would never get over, but they'd found enough love between them to come together during this crisis. Perhaps they might have a future together after all.

That which doesn't kill us...

As I glanced around, I realized that everything Mark and I had ever wanted was right here in this waiting room. The kids had finally become a family, pulling together when they needed each other. I only hoped we wouldn't have to pay the ultimate price for finally achieving such lofty goals.

I met more cops than I thought a town our size could possibly employ. They'd come by to offer reassurances. Several told me they'd donated blood because they wanted to help however they could. I did little more than nod at each of them, wondering if they would see my response as rude, but not honestly caring if they did. If I said anything—if I tried to thank them—I would lose what tenuous control I had left. They seemed to understand, giving me nods, compassionate glances, and a few pats on the shoulder.

I paced circles that seemed futile and senseless, but I couldn't make myself sit still. Each lap around the big room, I'd stop and look at the clock.

One hour.

Two hours.

Three hours.

Patrick would stop me often, asking if I wanted a drink or something to eat. I simply shook my head and waved him away, preferring to wallow in my own misery like some wounded, wild animal. He finally forced a cup of coffee and a donut that tasted like ashes on me and stood there until I finished all of it.

Images of Mark played in my brain. I saw snapshots of the best year of my life. We were ice skating on our first date. There was the first time we made love at the cabin. I remembered that look in his eyes when he told me he loved me, and how he'd proposed. Our wedding came to life again, as did the anguish when Kathy lost the baby.

How could I possibly survive a single day without him?

My chest hurt, and I wondered if this was how it felt when your heart shattered into a thousand, tiny pieces. I wanted to go to the chapel, but I was too afraid to go, sure that the doctor would come out of the operating room the moment I left. I had to settle for praying as I paced.

Dear God, I love this man. Save him. Please. I'll start going back to mass. Honest. I'll go every Sunday, and I'll drag Mark with me. I'll follow all the commandments, whether I like them or not. I'll tithe half of my pathetic income. Please don't let him die. Please.

"Take me instead, but save him," I whispered to no one, hoping God would listen and take me up on my offer because I didn't want to live if Mark died.

More pacing. More clock watching.

Four hours.

A fifty-something man in teal scrubs—with one of those goofy caps on his head and booties over his crocs—came sauntering through the doors. "Mrs. Brennan?"

I hurried to him with questioning eyes, hands still locked in prayer, trying to search his face for the most important words I would ever hear.

"Mark's doing fine," he said.

I squealed and threw myself on him like he was a rock star and I was a fanatic admirer.

"Thank you," I wailed against his shoulder as my tears flowed freely.

My chest was so tight I could barely breathe. The poor doctor probably thought I was a lunatic, but I didn't give a shit. The man deserved a hug. I started to kiss his cheeks. He had saved my husband. He'd saved me. "Thank you. Thank you."

He patted my back for a minute and chuckled. "Mrs. Brennan? Are you okay?"

Patrick came and pulled me away, despite the fact I wanted to cling to the surgeon like fly paper. I would have washed his car, cleaned his house, and probably borne his children if he'd just asked.

"How is he, doctor?" my oldest asked as he stood next to me, holding my hand.

"The bullet missed his heart. He's a very lucky man. There were a lot of little bleeders we needed to tie up, and his lung needed some work. We had to repair a rib that shattered with the force of the bullet. He'll be in intensive care for a while, but I expect Mark to make a full recovery. After he clears the recovery room, we'll get him set up in I.C.U."

Carly, Kathy, and Nate had all come to stand around Patrick and me as a united front with nothing but support for Mark. We were, at last, a family.

"Can he have visitors?" Nate asked in a voice so choked with emotion that it almost made me start weeping again.

Dr. Wonderful nodded. "Very short visits. The nurses will let you know when. For tonight, I think it's best if just his wife sees him. The rest of you can visit him tomorrow. We need to keep him quiet."

"That leaves me out," Patrick said. With a laugh, he held his hands up in surrender.

I could hear the relief in his voice. He really didn't hate Mark after all. All Pat's protests were nothing but bluster.

This was a night of pure revelation.

Patrick quit clowning and took my hand again, giving it a reassuring squeeze.

"He'll need lots of time to recover," the surgeon continued. "He can't push himself too hard."

Carly put her arm around my waist and pressed against me. "We'll make sure he doesn't. Won't we, Jackie?"

"You bet we will," I said, leaning my head against hers.

"We *all* will," Kathy said coming to her sister's other side.

Nate completed the family chain.

Thank you, God. I owe you. Big time.

***

Mark looked so pale, so much smaller than the towering presence I'd come to need in my life.

The nurse nodded to the chair that was on the other side of the bed, and I obediently took a seat and reached for his hand. I was sure I would never, ever let it go again. I measured time by the steady beats of his heart on the monitor, still offering prayers of thanksgiving, and constantly kissing his hand. I kept reminding myself I hadn't lost him, but I was still having a hard time believing it.

"How long will he be out?" I asked the nurse who appeared way too young to be running around in an I.C.U.

Why did everyone look so damned young anymore?

Of course, I felt older than Methuselah at that point. Mark was due some major scolding when he was better. No one should have to go through this. How many wives and husbands of cops had stood in my shoes?

I vowed to form a support group for the spouses of the local police officers.

"He's come around once already. He'll be in and out until the anesthesia clears his system, but the morphine will keep him pretty groggy." She adjusted an IV pump and turned to face me. "I just can't say for sure."

"Thanks, anyway." I scooted the chair a little closer to the bed and laid my head against our joined hands. "I love you, Mark. I've never loved anyone as much as I do you, and I never will. You stay strong. You come back to me. I need you. Do you hear me?"

"You're so bossy." His weak, raspy voice was music to my ears.

Raising my head, I looked up at my husband. His face was pale. He was hooked up to God knows how many machines. He was so drugged, he couldn't keep his eyes open.

I had never seen anything so wonderful in my whole life. "Always. Someone's got to keep you in line, mister."

I wasn't sure what else to say. He'd probably already eavesdropped on the thoughts I had spoken aloud, and I figured things had been entirely too serious for far too long.

What does one say at a time like this?

"I'm mad at you, detective."

"Mad at me?"

"You weren't wearing your vest." I squeezed his hand and smoothed a stray hair away from his cheek.

"Detectives don't wear vests."

"Detectives don't go after armed robbers, either," I scolded. "But I'll lay into you for that later."

"Oh? You'll lay me later? I'll need to get some rest then." He chuckled, gave my hand a weak squeeze, and drifted back to sleep.

With that, I kissed his lips knowing—finally—that he would be all right.

***

Men make the worst patients. The entire time he was in the hospital, Mark bitched and complained. He hated the food. He hated the nurses. He wanted to go home.

The first time he'd gotten out of bed, he almost fainted. The next time, he was able to walk to the door. The next time, he made it to the nurses' station. After that, it was my job to help him build his strength by making him walk. We walked down each long corridor and did laps around the nurses' station as I rolled Mark's IV stand alongside us. Unfortunately, the more strength he got, the more bitching he indulged in.

He hated the hospital gown. The television didn't get ESPN. He was tired of seeing the same room and halls every day.

I just listened to it all and smiled. The more ornery my husband was, the more I knew he was getting back to being himself.

After a week and a half, I was able to take him home. Then I got to assume the role of recovery drill sergeant. I had to make sure he did enough without doing too much.

It wasn't an easy job.

Mark was as weak as a newborn kitten, but as stubborn as a mule. The day he came home, he demanded a shower right after we walked in the door, saying he was tired of smelling like the hospital. I helped him take off his clothes and got him in the shower. He hadn't even gotten all of his body wet when he needed me because he'd sapped what little strength he had. I shed my own clothes and got into the shower stall with him. I helped Mark clean up, then got out and stood there dripping wet and naked as I dried him off and got him into a clean t-shirt and boxers. He crawled into our bed and immediately fell asleep while I finally got dried and dressed.

Part of our daily ritual was to continue walking. We started by just going around the house at first. As the spring weather took a turn for the warmer, we took a few laps in the yard. Next, we walked down the block and around the neighborhood. Mark grumbled the whole way. It was too far. It wasn't far enough. He told me I was being mean by forcing him to do all the things the surgeon instructed.

I just smiled sweetly at each thing he bitched about and gave him no quarter. Before too long, he was pushing himself to try a little more each day.

The most frustrating thing for both of us was the lack of a love life. The surgeon hadn't given us any specific instructions about resuming sex—other than we could make love whenever we were "ready." I tried to be patient with my patient, but three days after Mark came home, I literally jumped him. I desperately needed a physical connection, a sign that I hadn't lost him. We had made love fast and furious, me on top so he didn't have to work too hard. He was so exhausted afterward, he'd slept for six hours, and I'd felt horribly selfish.

***

Walking around the block a month after his surgery, Mark moved a little slower than usual. I'd been so used to pushing him harder every day that I immediately thought he was relapsing.

I swallowed the panic rising in my chest. "What's wrong? Am I going too fast?"

He didn't answer as he kept pacing at a slow clip, his eyes focused on the horizon.

"Mark? Are you feeling worse?"

His whole recovery had been three steps forward, one step back, and I reminded myself he might simply be having a bad day. The doctor had dug a bullet out of Mark's chest. My husband was entitled to a few bad days.

When he stopped, I didn't realize it right away, so I was four steps ahead of him before I turned around. "Are you in pain? Having any trouble breathing?"

He shook his head while I returned to his side.

"Then what is it?"

"What if… if… I'm never…*right* again." His gaze caught mine and, for the first time since he was shot, I saw fear.

"Right again? You mean back to work?"

He nodded, but the fear didn't leave his eyes. There was something more bothering him than whether he could be a good detective again.

"You'll go back when you're ready, probably just a couple more weeks. The doctor said—"

"The doctor doesn't know," he snapped. "He can't tell me if I'll be myself again."

I took his hand in mine. Despite the warmth of the day, his fingers were cold. "He said you'll be fine."

"I know I'll be fine. But will I be *right* again?"

I suddenly understood. Mark had resigned himself to his own mortality. He'd never been afraid to die, and that was what made him a great cop. What he was afraid of was showing a chink in his armor and admitting he was human after all.

"You're getting better, Mark."

"I'm getting older," he countered.

"Aren't we all?" I replied with a chuckle.

"I'm going to be forty-nine, Jackie."

"Thirty-nineteen," I corrected. "And old is just a state of mind."

"I'll remind you of that when I have to start taking Viagra," Mark said with a smirk.

"Is that what you're really afraid of? Getting too old?"

His reply was a curt nod.

"I'll still love you when you're ninety-nine. I'll chase you around the house with my walker."

"I'll let you catch me." He stared down into my face, searching my eyes. "I'm not always going to be so…vital. I'll slow down. We'll *both* slow down."

"Of course we will, but it won't change a thing. We can just line our prescription bottles up on the counter and clean each other's dentures."

I put my arms around his waist, pulled him close, and kissed him. Instead of one of our scorching kisses that made us both want to hop into bed, this one was slow and deep and full of all the love and tenderness I could muster.

"I love you, Mark Brennan," I said. "I'll always love you."

"This is forever, isn't it?" He squeezed me hard against him. "Promise me it's forever."

"Forever and ever."

***

Mark went back to work on his forty-ninth birthday—six weeks after being shot.

EPILOGUE

"Happy birthday, Mark." I sat up from where I'd collapsed against my husband after we made love.

I eased our intimate connection and rolled to my side, wrapping my arm around his chest and putting my cheek on his broad shoulder. I played with the patch of dark hair on his chest, loving the feel of it against my fingertips.

"I'm getting too old for this," he said with a chuckle.

"Like I told you before, old is just a state of mind."

"Says the woman who says she's going to be thirty-thirteen instead of forty-three."

God, I'd almost forgotten how close my birthday was. I thought back to my last birthday—to the promises I had made to myself while I was blitzed out of my gourd on white zinfandel and feeling much older than I really was. What was it that I had promised myself?

Ah, yes...

I swore not be a clichéd middle-aged woman.

I gave myself credit for success on that score. I hadn't looked for Botox injections or investigated a face-lift. There'd been no crash diets or fretting about a new gray hair or laugh lines. I'd learned to love myself, to be comfortable in my own forty-something skin.

I swore to be myself despite what chronology was telling me.

I'd held true to that vow, too. I'd been brave enough to date. I had found the courage to get married. I'd enjoyed the best sex of my entire life. I had even embraced myself and stopped apologizing for being who I was. I now thoroughly loved being noisy, stubborn, middle-aged me.

And I'd promised to make this a year of self-discovery and productivity.

Hell, yes!

I sat up, leaned over, and kissed my handsome husband. "Thank you, Mark."

"Thank me? For what?"

"For the greatest year of my life."

The End

Author Biography:
Sandy lives in a quiet suburb of Indianapolis, where she teaches psychology. Published through Forever Yours, Carina Press, and indie-published, she has been an Amazon #1 Bestseller multiple times and has won numerous awards including two HOLT Medallions. Represented by Danielle Egan-Miller, Browne & Miller Literary. Find her at sandyjames.com and as "sandyjamesbooks" on Twitter, Facebook, and Pinterest.

Other Books by Sandy James:

Damaged Heroes Series
Murphy's Law (Book 1)
Free Falling (Book 2)
All the Right Reasons (Book 3)
Faith of the Heart (Book 4)
Twist of Fate (Book 5)

Safe Havens Series
Saving Grace (Book 1)
Runaway (Book 2)
Redeemed (Book 3)
Hideaway (Book 4)
False Pretenses (Book 5 ~ Coming soon!)

Ladies Who Lunch Series
The Bottom Line (Book 1)
Signed, Sealed, Delivered (Book 2)
Sealing the Deal (Book 3)
Fringe Benefits (Book 4)

Alliance of the Amazons
The Reluctant Amazon (Book 1)
The Impetuous Amazon (Book 2)
The Brazen Amazon (Book 3)
The Volatile Amazon (Book 4)

Single Titles
Turning Thirty-Twelve

Rules of the Game
The Seeker

Nashville Dreams Series
Can't Walk Away (Book 1)
Can't Let Her Go (Book 2)
Can't Fight the Feeling (Book 3)

www.ingramcontent.com/pod-product-compliance
Lightning Source LLC
Chambersburg PA
CBHW060814120626
46557CB00001B/220